Home Is Where
The Heart Is

by

Casey Dawes

Mountain Vines Publishing

To Marcia,
Enjoy the wide open spaces!
Casey Dawes

Book cover design by For the Muse Designs
Edited by CEO Editor (ceoeditor.com)
Interior design by Concierge Self-Publishing (www.ConciergeSelfPublishing.com)

Published by Mountain Vines Publishing
Missoula, MT
Contact email: info@ConciergeSelfPublishing.com

To the students, teachers, and staff of Target Range. Thank you for your warmth, support, and hugs throughout the years.

Chapter One

CJ Beck forced herself out of the nightmare of desert heat and blood and opened her eyes.

Moonlight bounced off the snow outside and lit her childhood bedroom with the cold glow of a Montana winter. Even under piles of quilts, she shivered. Thinned by years in the Middle East, her system could no longer handle Rocky Mountain temperatures. Only the dry air was familiar.

She lay still for a few minutes, scanning the walls of the room that reminded her of someone she used to know. Framed photographs threw shadows—photos she'd taken of every animal on the ranch before she'd fled the pain after high school graduation. In the last two decades, she'd schooled herself enough that the hurt no longer made its way past the steel walls of her will.

She threw back the covers. Chamomile tea and a sweet would help her drift back to sleep, maybe even one without dreams. Sliding her feet into fur-lined slippers, she pulled on a heavy flannel robe and left her haven on the upstairs floor. Out of habit she tiptoed past her brothers' rooms, even though they were empty now. Jarod had taken over the guest suite downstairs, leaving the master bedroom bare. Dylan had his own cabin on the ranch, full of canvas and paint. Kaiden yanked oil from the ground somewhere in Wyoming, and Cameron was in the same desert hellhole she'd just left.

She padded into the kitchen. God bless Birdie. The housekeeper had left a full kettle of water on the stove, teabags, cup, and spoon to the side. CJ lifted the cookie jar lid without a sound—an art practiced from the time she was nine.

As the water heated, she lost herself in the moonlit Rocky Mountain Front marching south, snowy peaks etched with granite lines. She used to know them all by heart. Her fingers traced the peaks on the cold glass. If she could bear to pick up her camera again, the moonlight-outlined shapes would make an eerie picture.

But the bag full of lenses and camera bodies that had been permanently attached to her for decades was no longer in her reach. She'd packed it away when she'd returned to the ranch.

She didn't belong here. Not anymore. Jarod had made sure she knew the ranch ran fine without her. Dylan was kind in his vague kind of way. Birdie fussed, but she didn't seem to know what to do with the woman living upstairs.

Other than to leave out tea and cookies at night.

CJ smiled. When all else failed a western woman, she baked.

Why couldn't she wrap herself in the cocoon of Birdie's love like she had when her mother had gotten sick?

Because at thirty-five she was all grown up. What a joke that had turned out to be. But it meant she had to kick her own self in the butt and get on the horse again—no one else was going to help her.

Tomorrow. She'd call the bureau chief tomorrow—get some kind of estimate as to when they'd let her return to work. She hadn't been injured, not physically, anyway. How long could they keep her on bereavement leave?

Her mind returned to the desert, and she barely tasted the bite of ginger in the molasses cookie she dunked into the tea before pushing it into her mouth. She needed to get past her phobia about the camera and get back to work—it was important. People needed to know the demons loose in the world, and she needed to tell them in the only way she knew how—with her pictures. Some said she was cold-blooded, but it wasn't true. It was only the face she showed the world.

The pictures of ordinary life—kids laughing, men dancing, and women doing embroidery work as they gossiped—no one ever saw those. No one ever would. They were her proof that she still had a soul, even though the last thing she'd done before her husband was killed was to tear at his flesh with words.

All that was behind her. She'd learned her lesson—finally. Men couldn't to be trusted. Her father's betrayal hadn't done it. Nor had a broken heart brought on by her high school boyfriend. Nope. It had taken the third affair by her husband of five years for her to finally get the message.

But she was strong. She'd survived all that crap. If she had to walk alone, so be it.

She placed the cup in the sink gently, so not to wake Birdie, who slept in the spacious set of rooms behind the kitchen. Then she slipped back upstairs.

# # #

The sun was well up when CJ rose the next morning. She sighed with relief. No more dreams had haunted her through the night.

The aroma of fried bacon tickled her nose. Sliding her phone from the nightstand, she checked the time. After nine, which meant it was coming up on noon in New York. May as well get the call done before facing the family. Maybe her brothers would be done eating by then so she didn't have to make conversation. Dylan was okay, but in the week since she'd been here, the amount of words Jarod had spoken to her wouldn't fit in a grain pail.

They'd been close. Once. Even though he was younger, he'd always looked out for her, even breaking off a long friendship with Nick Sturgis after her boyfriend had dumped her for a California beauty queen. But after their mother passed, they'd both retreated into their emotional corners.

Couldn't be helped now. She'd be here a few weeks, get her next assignment, and then head back to her real life.

Max picked up on the third ring.

"Gearheard here."

"It's me. CJ," she said.

"Oh, hi. How are the wilds of Montana? Got snow?"

"Of course we have snow. It's January. Hell, even New York probably has snow."

"Yeah." He went silent.

"So I was wondering … when can I get my next assignment?" She pulled her knees up to her chin and wrapped her arms around them.

Max cleared his throat, and her shoulders tensed.

"About that. You've been in a war zone somewhere for the last ten years or so. That's tough on anyone, especially a woman. You need a break."

"I'm as tough as any man."

"Yeah. And I've seen guys crack, too. It's not pretty."

"I'm fine."

"You saw your husband's head blown apart by a sniper's bullet. You are anything *but* fine."

"It's the life we chose to live," she said. "We knew the risks." Although lately, the risks had increased. Instead of only being accidental victims, journalists were becoming targets in their own right.

Had that been what had happened to Ben? Or was it just a case of wrong place and wrong time to indulge in an after-dinner cigarette? Of course, she'd been the one to drive him to need that smoke.

"I know." Max was quiet again. "But it's still too soon to send you back. You need to take a rest—heal. Then maybe an assignment here in the States. Ease your way into it."

"Here? I'd be bored out of my mind. Nothing's going on."

"There's plenty going on," he said. "Not every bad guy is overseas. We've got homegrown ones right here."

"Please," she said, desperation creeping into her voice. "I can't stay here. I'll die of boredom."

"Look," he said, "the only way I'm sending you anywhere is if you get a clean bill of health from a psychiatrist. And not just any psychiatrist. I want one who understands the trauma of war. You've got an air base near you, don't you?"

"Great Falls. About an hour." Whatever it took. She'd make an appointment, convince the doctor she was fine, and get back to her life. There was no other way. Life was a series of either/or choices and her first one had been to leave Choteau, Montana, as far behind as she could. It was still the right decision.

"Good. Find a psychiatrist in Great Falls. Go see him. Have him send a report to our office on your fitness to go back into a war zone. Then we'll see."

She opened her mouth to protest, but shut it. She'd fight that battle when she had to.

"Yes, sir," she mocked, not quite able to keep her displeasure at bay.

"I know you're not happy about this." He was silent for moment. "Look, CJ, I was worried about you even before this happened. You and Ben were playing too fast and loose with life, as if the bill wasn't ever going to come due. You need some perspective. I went to the Rockies when I was in my twenties. If any place can heal you, that's it. Get to know your family again. Who knows? Maybe you'll like it there. Look. I've got a meeting. Take care of yourself. Talk soon."

With that, he was gone.

5

Someone rapped on her door and cracked it ajar.

Dylan.

"Birdie said if you don't get downstairs, you'll have to eat cold cereal. She's not letting you touch her pans."

"I learned how to cook. I only burned things when I was a teenager."

"Birdie doesn't even let *me* cook, and I'm all grown up with a cabin and my own fridge and everything."

"Then how come you're always over here for breakfast?"

"I'm lazy?" He grinned, his even, white teeth highlighting the winter tan on his face. His black hair fell in an unkempt artistic pattern around his gray eyes. Her brother was a handsome dude.

"How come no one's snatched you up?" she asked.

"Well"—he pushed open the door and perched at the end of the bed like he'd done when they were kids—"it seems no one will have me. My prospects aren't good." Dylan had always phrased things like he lived in the 1800s.

"Not selling any paintings?"

He shook his head. "I sold a passel, but then the economy tanked, some of the rich California wannabe ranchers headed home, and that was that. I'm stuck working here with Jarod while the rest of you gallivant around the world." The words may have sounded bitter, but Dylan said them with a mock seriousness meant to be funny. At least she hoped it was.

"You could do something else," she said.

"I wouldn't know how," he said.

"Yeah. Got it." Ever since she could remember, Dylan had been daubing paint on paper. After Dad died, he'd be gone as often as he could, a makeshift field easel strapped behind the saddle of his favorite horse. She and her second brother had been cut from the same cloth—dreamers who saw the world through different eyes. A total contrast to the other three boys—

hardheaded realists, all of them.

"At some point, someone has to come waltzing through town looking for an unsuccessful painter and part-time ranch hand. I have faith."

She smiled.

"What about Jarod?" she asked. "Think he'll ever find someone?"

"He says he'll start looking when he has the ranch under control."

"Which means never."

"Which means never." He glanced over at her. "I'd hoped when you got married, he'd be able to move on, but ..." He splayed his hands and shrugged his shoulders. "I'm sorry about Ben. How are you doing?" he asked, leaning toward her.

"I don't want to talk about it," she said.

"You coming?" Birdie yelled up the stairs.

"C'mon, sis. Put on a robe and get downstairs or Birdie'll have a cow." He got up, pausing at the door. "It's good to have you home again."

She stared at the open door for a few seconds then swung her legs out. Her feet hit the rough wooden floor.

Cold. Everything about this damn state was cold in winter.

Her feet quickly found the slippers she'd left behind when she'd gone overseas and threw on a quilted robe. The slippers' flattened fleece was still warm, and the extra layer kept out the chill—barely. Even though her dad had redone the upstairs heating several times, it sweltered in the summer and froze in the winter. The walls really needed to be ripped down and insulated.

Jarod probably didn't have the money for that, and since no one had been living upstairs til she'd returned, there was no need. When they were kids, they'd shut the door to the stairway after they'd gotten up, and lived in the spacious ... and warm ... first floor during the winter months.

"About time," Birdie said when she entered the kitchen. She pulled a plate from the oven and placed it on the table: fresh scrambled eggs from the hens out back, bacon no doubt purchased from one of the traveling Hutterite trucks, and homemade biscuits.

"You're going to make me fat," CJ declared.

"You need some weight on those bones," the housekeeper declared. "Now sit down and get out of the way so I can get some baking done. If I don't attend to those boys' sweet tooths, they are grumpy as two-year-olds without naps."

"Thanks," CJ said as she slipped into the chair closest to the wall and picked up the coffee mug Birdie slid toward her. Coffee and a toasted pita, perhaps with a bit of lamb, had been her standard breakfast fare for years, often with the secondhand smoke her husband gave off as he took his version of the morning meal.

Familiar food was a relief. She dug into the yellow eggs—so much richer than the pale-yoked versions they'd served in overseas eating establishments that catered to Americans. She savored the meal as she watched Birdie perform the same routine CJ remembered from her teenage years.

The housekeeper had come to them the year her mother was diagnosed with cancer, a reference from someone who knew someone. It was supposed to be temporary; her mother was going to get better, for sure, but that had never happened and Birdie stayed on, dispensing food and fierce compassion from her lair in the kitchen.

CJ's throat tightened with affection for the housekeeper.

Not good.

Emotions left a woman vulnerable. Better not to show them.

Best not to have them at all.

# # #

"I'm sorry, but late tomorrow morning is all he has," the receptionist told her an hour later. "The day after, he's leaving for Florida or someplace like that, and he won't be back until mid-February."

"I'll take it," CJ said, hoping the weather would hold. Snowstorms were unpredictable in January. She got directions and headed back down to the kitchen. May as well pick up anything Birdie needed while she was in the city. Probably some warmer clothes, too. If the doctor was going to be gone for a month, thirty days from now was going to be the earliest she could get out of here. Unless she could convince him during their first meeting that she was fine.

Which she was. All of this fuss was about nothing.

"I have to go to Great Falls tomorrow," she announced as she came into the kitchen. Rows of cooling oatmeal cookies lay on racks on the counters. She picked one up.

"I saw that," Birdie said as she took another tray out of the oven.

"How could you?"

"Same way I did when you were a kid." She put the tray on the top of the stove and shut the oven door. "Got eyes in the back of my head."

"I believe it," CJ said with a smile. She looked around. "How many are you making? There must be two dozen already."

"Your brothers would inhale those within a few days—even less now that you're home."

CJ sank her teeth into warm, buttery goodness. "Thanks for leaving the tea things out last night."

"Hope you enjoyed the cookie as well."

The housekeeper missed nothing.

"I just hope I get up some morning and it's all still sitting there," Birdie said.

"Why's that?"

"Because then I'd know you were sleeping through the night again."

That miracle was probably never going to occur again in her life. She couldn't remember the last time she'd slept through without waking up in the early hours of the morning. "Need anything in Great Falls?" She took a step toward one of the racks.

"Don't even try." Birdie shifted cookies from the sheet to the rack. "Let me think on that. Go ask Jarod. I know he's been muttering about pipes and fittings. Something froze in the barn and broke a thingamajig."

CJ chuckled.

Birdie shrugged and smiled. "Go. Get out of my kitchen." She grabbed two cookies. "And take these to the boys." She plucked one more and handed it to CJ. "And one for the delivery girl."

Even though they were into their thirties, her brothers would always be "the boys" and she "the girl" to their surrogate mother. The youngest hadn't even made it into his teens when she'd arrived.

"Sure, Birdie." CJ headed to the mudroom off the kitchen. Setting the cookies on the dryer, she began to bundle up for the short trip across to the barn. One of her brother's jackets—probably Kaiden's—kinda fit. Pair that with gloves she'd last worn as a teen that she'd found in a drawer upstairs and she'd be warm enough. Her desert boots worked fine even in the snow.

She crunched across the dirt-churned snow to the classic western barn—its boards weathered and worn, replacement wood standing out in contrast. Working ranches didn't have time for pretty maintenance jobs like the "gentleman" ranchers who'd flocked in from Texas and California and driven up land prices so regular folk had a hard time finding places to live.

Not her problem to solve. There were worse conditions elsewhere—mothers watching their children starve, men killing each other over the best way to interpret a religious text. It was madness.

"Hey, Jarod," she called out as she entered the dim light of the barn. She blinked a few times to help her eyes adjust.

She hadn't been in here since she'd gotten back. Jarod had made her feel like the barn was off limits. It hadn't changed that much. The high roof corner cobwebs had thickened and the floor more stained, but the disassembled machinery looked like it was in the same pieces as when she'd left. A pile of pipes lay at one end of the floor. To the other side, a rubber-covered cement aisle was lined with horse stalls. One of the animals had been a chewer, judging from the top rail of the stall.

"Shut the darn door!" A muffled voice came from somewhere under a tractor.

She pulled the door tight, which the wind had pushed open, and latched it.

"Jarod?" she shouted again. "Birdie said you might need something from Great Falls."

Metal clanged against metal, and a set of blue-jeaned legs morphed into her brother—her *glaring* brother.

"What do you want?" he said.

"Whoa. What crawled up *your* ass?"

Jarod shook his head. "You always did have a potty mouth after you went to school, but I swear it's gotten worse."

"War zone'll pretty much do that to you. Sorry." Church-going Jarod had always disliked any kind of swearing. He was already uncomfortable enough around her; she didn't need to add to his unease.

"So ..." he said, his tone more measured this time. "What do you want?"

"I have to go to Great Falls tomorrow," she said. "I need to see someone—just some hoops I need to jump through before they let me return to work. Birdie said you might need some things—pipes?"

Jarod looked her up and down. "Sure you can handle it?"

"I grew up here. And I've spent the last bunch of years fending for myself in difficult circumstances. I can handle it." She gazed steadily at her brother, a contest of wills like they'd had when they were teens. Even though she was a year his senior, he'd always been messing with her life.

He hadn't talked to her for days after she told him she was leaving for college in Kentucky.

"Okay," he said. "I'll make out a list. You can get it at North 40. They've got pretty much everything." He looked at her hands. "Get some gloves, too. Those are about as worthless a bathing suit in January."

"Uh-huh." She handed him the cookies. "They're from Birdie. She's baking up a storm. It's amazing you guys aren't rolling around the ranch," she added with a smile.

"She's upped her game since you came home. Says you're too skinny."

"So she's mentioned. One of those is for Dylan."

Jarod stared at the cookie in his hand. "Dylan's out feeding cattle. He won't be back for a while." He grinned. "I won't tell if you won't tell."

"Birdie will tell."

"I'll just have to fess up then." He bit into the cookie.

"Just get me the list by tonight," she said. "I want get started early tomorrow." She turned to head back to the house.

"You don't have to leave," he said.

"The barn or the ranch?" She looked at him over her shoulder.

"The ranch. It's your home as much as mine or the rest of us."

She smiled. It was the nicest thing he'd said to her since she'd been back. But the statement was dead wrong. This wasn't her home. Not anymore. No place was home for someone like her.

"Thanks. But, yeah, I do." She opened the door and made sure she latched it behind her before plodding back to the house.

Chapter Two

By the time CJ returned to the kitchen, the flat-screen television that hung on one of the kitchen walls was turned to a talk show CJ didn't recognize.

"Sit with me," Birdie said. "It's good."

CJ stood and watched long enough to get the gist about some dirt on the latest movie favorite. "I've got things I need to take care of. I'll check in with you later."

She walked through the formal dining room filled with antique furniture that had been passed down through the last hundred and fifty years of Beck family occupancy. Solid but dark, it had stood the test of time and small children, although several of the panes of glass in the china cabinet had been replaced after Cameron's errant aim with a baseball.

The living room had been created for comfort, not formality. She sank into one of the soft armchairs and stared out the big picture window toward the Rocky Mountains. The midday sun, low on the southern horizon, lit the foothills rolling toward the granite peaks. By four, the peaks themselves would be aglow, before the sun made its relentless winter trek to the other side of the planet.

Winter nights were too long in this place.

What was she going to do with herself for a month if she couldn't convince the psychiatrist to let her go? When she was a teen, taking pictures of anything and everything had kept her busy, but since she couldn't even look through the lens of a camera without freaking out, that wasn't going to work.

The suede was soft under her hands. Dropping her head back, she sank into the cushions. Sleep hovered at the edge of her consciousness. If she could just drift, all her worries would go away for a while ... unless the desert wind reclaimed her dreams.

She forced herself awake and pulled out her phone.

A few messages checking in to see how she was doing. They'd steadily declined over the weeks after she'd left the Middle East, first to follow her husband's body to the nearest base, then on to London where she and his parents buried him in the family cemetery. There hadn't been much to say to them. They'd been upper middle-class owners of specialty shops who'd never understood their son's obsession with journalism, nor their daughter-in-law's upbringing in what they thought of as the wilds of America.

And so she'd left. Max had demanded her return to New York and then sent her on to Montana for "a few weeks' rest."

Ha. He'd tricked her into coming here, and now he was trying to force her into staying.

Her Instagram feed showed her what she'd been missing: stellar and heart-rending shots from the war—Pulitzer Prize-winning photos. While in her secret heart of hearts she'd hoped to produce something this good, her technique had never been up to par. Her work on the war front was serviceable—journeyman acceptable—but not star material.

That's because she'd never revealed her true self in those pictures. Being vulnerable in a war zone was a bad idea.

Being home was making her melancholy.

She'd do her laundry. It would be a luxury to use a real machine instead of hotel sinks and well water in buckets.

Heaving herself from the chair's comfort, she headed upstairs and collected her pitiful, small pile of dirty clothes. Maybe she should pick up some flannel shirts tomorrow. Her standard olive-green tees weren't practical for anything other than an extra layer of material over her minimal sports-style bra. She'd been grateful for her small breasts in the deep heat of the desert. Some of the more endowed women she'd met complained of chaffing and prickly heat.

She trotted back down the stairs and into the mudroom. Birdie was still watching television but had put out sandwich fixings and was eating her own at the kitchen table. After starting her laundry, CJ returned to the kitchen.

"Have some lunch," Birdie said. "Jarod should be in soon, and if you don't get it now, the pickings will be slim."

"What about Dylan?" she asked as she assembled the luncheon meat, lettuce, mayo, and tomato into a sandwich.

"I made him a sack lunch this morning. He's feeding cattle on the far side of the range. It's tough trying to handle everything between the two of them. You should stay and help for a while."

"They don't need me. I'll just get in the way."

"*You* need *them*. They're family. Everyone needs a family of some kind—even if it's one they make up on their own. You're one of the lucky ones—you got born into one."

"We're siblings, not family. Not anymore. Not since ..." She shrugged. "We're all out there making new ones, like you said. Ben and I were close with the journalists we knew. We understood each other. That's my family."

Birdie sighed. "Someday you're going to need to make peace with what happened. All of you will."

"I'm fine just the way I am," CJ said with a smile. "I've got a career. I travel. I'm making my mark on the world. And the boys are fine without me hanging around, too. They've got their own careers. You can stop worrying about us all."

"And every single darn one of you is alone." Birdie picked up her sandwich and turned back to the television, signaling the end of the conversation.

CJ hesitated for a moment. Damn it. She was tired of eating

alone. Being alone. Even before Ben's death, she'd taken most of her meals isolated in the middle of strangers.

She sat down next to the housekeeper.

"That Matt Conner," Birdie said. "He's a really sharp interviewer. Watch how he does it."

"Uh-huh." CJ looked at the screen to be polite. Birdie had a point. The man's questions were polite but insightful, gently leading the guest down the path to her own execution.

"Don't let her get you hooked," Jarod said as he stomped into the kitchen.

"And don't fill my house up with your mud," Birdie shot back, glaring at his snow-covered boots.

"I'm only going to the sandwich board," he said. "Just a little tiny path."

CJ glanced at the tracks he'd made and raised an eyebrow.

He chuckled and turned to the fixings. With a slight smile, Birdie went back to her show. The housekeeper and her brother had a well-established routine—one in which she had no place.

"Get the tractor fixed?" she asked to ease her awkwardness.

"Nah. Got to order some parts online."

"I *am* going to Great Falls."

"Cheaper online. It's the way of the world now." He turned and leaned against the counter. "I hate taking business from local owners, but with gas to get there and the slightly extra cost to cover their shipping, I've got to go with online. If it were one or the other ..." He shrugged and took a large bite of the sandwich.

"Get a plate," Birdie said without turning around.

"Yes, ma'am." Dishes clattered as he pulled a plate from the cabinet.

"Things that tight?" CJ asked. She hadn't thought about the ranch's finances since she left—ever if she was being truthful with herself.

"It's a Montana ranch," he replied. "Comes with the territory. Ranchers and farmers don't need to go to Vegas. We gamble every day that the weather's going to do what we need, that feed and equipment prices stay down and cattle prices stay high."

"And you still go to Vegas every year," Birdie said.

"That I do. National Rodeo Championships. Wouldn't miss 'em."

"Do you regret giving it up?" CJ asked. Back when they were teens, her brother had participated in calf roping in the junior division of local rodeos. He'd talked about going pro. But then ...

"It is what it is," he said. "Someone has to be here. Other than Dylan, the rest of you took off as soon as you could." An edge of bitterness lined his words.

"What if we sold it?"

Birdie's sandwich dropped back on her plate.

"Sold it? Are you crazy? It's Beck land—part of us—whether you want to admit it or not."

"And it was someone else's land before that, and Native land before that, and home to who knows what else before that. It's just land."

Jarod shook his head. "It's never just land. I woulda thought you'd understand that by now. What do you think they're fighting for over there where you were? The land. Places they can control and live how they want. It's always about the land. Don't you forget it."

"I just thought you could do what you wanted. It's not too late to do rodeo. Then you'd be free."

He shook his head.

"I am doing what I want. That's the part you don't get, CJ. This is my heritage. I'm the steward." He took a deep breath. "This ranch is who I am—I'd just as soon rip out my heart as sell it." He put his plate on the counter. "I was wrong. You should go back to your life as soon as they let you. I pray to God you understand it a lot better than you do mine." He looked at the half-eaten lunch. "I'm not hungry anymore."

He stomped back out of the kitchen.

"How can you walk away from your family when you don't even know them?" Birdie asked as she clicked off the television and stood. After placing her dishes in the sink, she said, "I need some things from town. Can you run up and get them?"

May as well. She wasn't serving any purpose here.

"Sure. I'll get my things."

# # #

The highway north to town was clear of snow, a good thing. The ranch pickup on which CJ had learned to drive was awkward under her hands now. She hadn't driven much in decades, and then only tiny cars on European city streets.

The truck was high and big, reminding her of the military Humvees in the desert. She'd gone out on some patrols, but she'd had to fight each time to be included. Women soldiers may have become slightly more normal, but female war photojournalists were not.

The prairie stretched to the east, undulating to the horizon line. To the west, the foothills raised snowy lumps to the stretch of gray peaks of the Front. Ragged and enormous, the land dwarfed human activity.

It wasn't any more familiar than the desert.

Did she even have a home anymore? With Ben gone, their dreams of owning a small cottage in the Lake District had disappeared. Nothing tied her to England anymore. His parents were strangers.

She should feel more emotion about his passing, but all she

felt was dullness. Like her mother. She'd heard her mother cry only once—not when her father died, but earlier, on one of the nights he hadn't come home on time for dinner.

CJ had learned something was up when she'd gone to see her father about some harebrained scheme or another. When she was thirteen, her father's halo was beginning to tarnish, but the sun still rose and set on the man—at least until that day. She'd hesitated when she'd heard him on the phone in the ranch office.

After listening for a while, she'd turned and walked away, securing her heart in its first layer of armor.

No one in the house ever mentioned it. No screaming matches like she'd indulged in with Ben right before he'd been killed. Instead, her mother buried it away until it turned into the cancer that ate through her the last five years of her life.

God, she was being maudlin. Ancient history. She had to stop letting the past control her and head to the future, whatever *that* meant. Getting out of this place as rapidly as she could would be a good start.

The road led into the south part of town, past the medical center that had expanded while she'd been gone. A few houses where she'd attended birthday parties until they all started hitting their teens and separating into different cliques. The main drag. There was the Roxy movie theater, amazingly still running after all these years. Shiny new stores interlaced with those that hadn't cleaned their windows in decades. Some new offices filled the upstairs. As she paused at a stop sign, she read the glittering gold letters on one: Cassandra Sanders, Esq., Attorney-at-Law. A female lawyer. Interesting. Must be giving the old boys' club an apoplexy. A stereotype of a rural, small town, but true.

She pulled into the grocery store, list in hand. Mainly fresh vegetables—Birdie hated having them laying around for long. A few canned goods and a bag of flour. She should be able to get in and out of the store before running into someone she knew.

"CJ?"

She turned to the sound of the voice. Stan Sturgis. A nice man but not one she'd hoped to run into on her first trip to town.

"It *is* you," Stan said, taking a few steps before enveloping her in a brief bear hug. Leaving his hands on her arms, he looked her over for a second before stepping back. "It's good you're back. Looks like you need a little pampering. I heard about your husband. I'm sorry."

Damn small towns.

"Thank you," she choked out.

"I'll have to let Nick know you're home. He'll be happy to hear that."

I bet.

"I'm only going to be here for a short while. Just til I get clearance to go back. Tell Nick I said hi ... and Emma, too." Both of Nick's parents had always made her feel like part of the family. Thankfully, Nick and his wife, Grace, had moved to Great Falls before CJ had left the States. No chance of running into them.

"I'm sorry to hear that. But I guess you've got to do what you were born to do. Just stop by the store. Emma will be happy to see you. The first cup of coffee's on me." He held up the bag of beans he had in his hand.

"Thanks. I will. See you around."

"S'long."

She felt his stare on her back as she headed to the produce section. She needed to get away before running into anyone else from her former life.

# # #

Nick Sturgis took a ticket as he entered the windblown

airport parking lot in Great Falls. Set high above the town on a mesa, the place was known for some of the highest airport winds in the country, far exceeding Chicago's O'Hare. If a pilot could take off and land in Great Falls, they could handle wind anywhere.

He pulled his aging Ford pickup into one of the wider slots in the lot, closed the creaking driver's door behind him, and held onto his hat as he walked to the terminal, the strong air currents buffeting him about.

It was how Trevor must feel, tossed about by things out of his control. He barely knew his son anymore, and now his ex had decided he was responsible for raising the thirteen-year-old since she couldn't handle him anymore.

"He's out of control, Nick," Grace had complained from her fancy house in Seattle. "Never listens. Hangs out with kids we don't like. And always taking pictures with that camera of his. It's creepy. You need to see what you can do with him. My dad put money away for him to go to USC like he did, but unless he gets his grades up and straightens out his attitude, I don't know what's going to happen."

Then she'd given him a date, time, and flight number and told him to pick up his son.

Poor kid.

Nick checked the board and headed toward the gate. As he did, he thought he recognized a stocky figure a few gates over. Someone he'd never hoped to see again. Nah. He must be mistaken. There were coincidences, but this wasn't one of them.

The man turned his face in his direction. Nick tensed and turned away. It was too early in the morning to have a confrontation with Ronan Smith.

He headed for a coffee kiosk before grabbing a seat outside security. The acrid aroma cleared his brain, lulled by an early morning drive across the plains.

If Trevor brought his camera, he'd be able to show him some amazing places to photograph. He'd be able to see the flash of mallard green as drakes swam through patches of open water surrounded by frozen cattails. The mad noise of snow geese landing on Freezeout Lake. The harsh granite of the Rockies softened by late afternoon sunset.

It would be good to have his son around full time again. All he had to do was figure out how to be a full-time dad. It should be easy. His own father was a great dad—still was. They'd have to stop by the store on the way home. His parents would be happy to see their grandson.

Yeah. Going to be fine. As long as he could ignore the very real fear churning in his belly.

The sound system squawked out an arrival notice. Trevor's flight.

Nick stood and stared at the gate for disembarking passengers, slipping the rim of his cowboy hat round and round in his fingers. He shouldn't have worn it. His city son would think he was playacting, not understanding the very real need for a good hat with the work he did.

Oh, god, his son was going to think his old man was lame.

There he was. He'd gotten taller—almost his height, and five eleven wasn't short. His hair was a combination—brown from Nick, blond from Grace. Dark eyes.

Good-looking kid.

Nick grinned and raised his hand in greeting.

Trevor nodded but didn't smile back, just lumbered toward him in that awkward way teens had when they hadn't quite gotten used to the size of their bodies.

Nick walked toward him and pulled him into a bear hug.

Trevor's arms flailed around him but never quite made contact.

"Good to have you here, kid," Nick said as he released him.

"Yeah."

"Let me take that." Nick grabbed the handle of the rolling suitcase. "That all you brought?"

"Yeah."

Nick gave his son a once-over. "Any warmer clothes? Boots?"

"Nope."

"We're going to need to get you some then. It's cold at home. Then we can grab a burger and head back. Sound good?"

"Okay." The word was accompanied by a shrug.

Maybe it would get better once the kid settled in.

"Truck's out this way." Nick pulled the handle and took a few steps before he glanced over his shoulder to make sure Trevor was still with him. Silently, they made their way out the sliding glass doors and over the frozen pavement to his rusty red truck.

"You haven't gotten rid of this thing?" Trevor asked. "It's a heap of junk."

"Engine runs good and it's got a strong bed for the stuff I need to carry. No need for a new one."

"Whatever."

It was going to be a long road with this kid, and he didn't know the first place to begin. He placed the suitcase behind the passenger seat and motioned to Trevor to get in before sending the passenger door home with a resounding thump.

He climbed into the driver's side, put the truck in gear, and began the descent from the airport, across the Missouri, and onto the city's main drag—a horror that connected truck routes coming in from the east-west highways to the interstate that linked the northern and southern parts of the state. The road was also home to numbers of big box stores and stand-alone malls, both indoor and out.

After navigating several blocks of traffic without a drop of conversation, he pulled into the lot and parked. He turned to face his son.

"Look," he said. "I don't know what happened back in Seattle. If you want to tell me, fine. If not, fine. You're here now and here's where we'll begin. It's going to be way different from your life in the city."

"Duh."

Nick tamped down his temper. "Yeah, duh. But it means you're going to have to adapt. And if I remember correctly, change isn't something teenagers handle real well."

Trevor gave him a look that questioned the possibility his father had ever gone through the teen years.

"You're going to have chores—physical, hard chores, not taking out the trash or walking the dog."

"We don't have pets. Mom thinks they're too messy."

That'd be Grace.

"I've got two dogs, six horses, three mules, and I don't know how many barn cats. They keep breeding."

There was a hint of a smile on Trevor's mouth.

"They all need to be taken care of one way or another, except the cats. They fend for themselves, thank goodness. Keep the mice at bay." He checked out his son. Looked like the first smile was all he was going to get. "C'mon, let's get you some ranch wear. I got a few other things I got to pick up."

He slid out of the truck and waited.

Trevor gave another shrug and opened his door.

They headed toward the store.

Chapter Three

"Tell me about your family." The psychiatrist's voice was calm and steady.

It made CJ want to throw up.

"Father and mother deceased, two brothers on the ranch, one in combat, and one in the oil fields of Wyoming." She ticked off her siblings on her fingers.

"Go on," Dr. Wikowski said.

"What do you mean? That's all there are. Unless you want to count my mother's brother and his family in Nebraska. We never see them. My dad was an only child, and all the grandparents went years ago."

The psychiatrist made a few notes on his yellow pad. He was a short man, his slim body a match to his stature. Rounded shoulders attested to hours spent hunched over books. Glasses and a receding hairline gave him a scholarly look.

"That's the kind of information that would be in an outline of a family tree. I want to know about the relationships. How do you feel about your brothers? Your parents?"

"I don't have relationships with my brothers. I'm barely here. My parents are dead. So no relationships there either." As soon as the words were out of her mouth, she knew they were a mistake. She sounded cold and uncaring. Wounded.

"And your husband was killed a few months ago."

"Yes." She looked away. There should be tears in her eyes, but there weren't. Her mother had schooled her well. Showing emotion to a man just wasn't done. They had something on you then.

"You know why you're here, right?"

"So you can give me a piece of paper that will let me get back to my real life," she said, drawing her gaze back to him.

"Not quite," he said with a smile. "You have to be ready to get back to your 'real life.'" He air-quoted the last two words. "From what I understand, your work requires you to be in danger. Not only that, but poor decisions on your part can put others in danger."

"I'd never do that!"

"Not intentionally," he said, raising his index finger in a gesture to pause. "But inadvertently, your attention might be distracted at a critical moment, or you may say something that another person misinterprets and put them at risk."

"That could happen to anyone," she said. He was being ridiculous.

"Yes."

"Then I'm ready."

"No."

"Why the hell not?" She sat up straight, or as erect as she could while seated in a soft couch.

"That's what we're going to find out."

"That makes no sense at all." She shook her head in frustration. "You're benching me, but you don't really know why."

"Well, I don't have an official diagnosis, but based simply on how you answer questions about people close to you and your hair-trigger frustration, I'd say there's some trauma in your background somewhere."

You think?

"But that's in the past," CJ said. "It's over. I've moved on."

"Have you?"

The icy blue sky of winter shown through a square window on the upper wall. She'd forced herself to stop thinking about home when she left for college in Kentucky. One of the reasons she'd decided on a place so far away was the total change of culture. She'd thrown herself into classes, parties, and mint juleps but caught herself before she'd gone too far. Still, there were things she wished she hadn't done.

But she no longer dwelled on them, any more than her father's affair or her mother's retreat into the dark bedroom. Her father had moved into the guestroom. There was no grand screaming match, just cool politeness and lack of affection until the night her father had spun out of control on an icy Montana road.

Her breath hitched. She'd hung the moon and the stars on her daddy. Little had she known he was the beginning of a very bad string of men. Too bad she didn't learn the lesson the first time.

She swallowed and returned her gaze to the doctor. He gazed steadily at her, his eyes seeming to plumb the depths of her pain.

It would be so easy to give in, to indulge in a fantasy that someone could actually make that black knot of tar disappear from the pit of her stomach. But that wasn't reality. Reality meant suck it up and take it. Other people depended on her to be steady and straight.

She shuttered her soul.

"I'm fine."

"If that's how you want to play it," he said.

"That's how it is."

He looked at his notes for a long moment as the silence lengthened. She kept herself quiet.

Leaning forward, he placed his forearms on the clipboard. "We can help you make it better," he said. "You don't have to live with it—whatever it is—forever. One of the things we've learned after a decade and a half of this forever war is that burying feelings doesn't work—not ultimately."

"Uh-huh." She didn't have PTSD, and wasn't that what people had who went crazy and shot up people?

"The biggest problem psychiatry has, even after all these years, is that people think there's a stigma, that there's something wrong with them." He chuckled. "There's something wrong with *all* of us. We all have times in our lives when we could use a little help. The trick is to learn to accept it."

"Aren't you leaving on vacation?"

"Yes, but it's impractical to have you come into Great Falls on a weekly basis anyway. I've started working with therapists in small towns across the state, sort of a satellite system. There's a good therapist in Choteau ..." He consulted his notes. "Geraldine Morgan."

Did he expect her to *see* this woman?

"They've got therapists closer to my work," she said.

"Ready to leave Montana so soon?" he asked.

"I'm ready to get back to my job. I told you that. I keep telling everyone that. No one seems to be hearing me."

"Look, I'll consider that, but ... tell me about leaving home the first time."

"I went to college, same as everyone else." Being defensive wasn't helping her cause. "I did lots of research. I knew I wanted to be a photojournalist. I'd hoped to go to Missoula or, at worst, Billings, but none of them had good programs." Spin it like she was an idealistic high school kid eager to change the world.

"Why did Kentucky seem right?"

"Good program and a chance to see someplace totally different from Montana." She leaned forward, not feigning eagerness. "I wanted ... still want ... to make a difference when I take a picture. To get people to feel something, but also to do something to change what I'm showing ... or if it's a good thing, to continue it.

"But first I needed to learn to work with people who were different from me. They couldn't see me as an outsider. They had to *trust* me." She stopped, remembering the women who'd let her into their circle, sharing their joys, sorrows, and fears. Showing their pride in their children and in their art. She'd sent a few of the photos she took of them back to Max in the early years, but he wasn't interested unless it showed combat.

No one cared about women's lives.

"So why didn't you come back to Montana?" he asked.

Because she thought she'd been in love, he'd left her for someone else, and she couldn't bear to watch them together. Small towns were a blessing and a curse. Better the anonymity of the international stage.

She shrugged. "I applied for an internship and things just happened from there."

"I see."

The damn man saw far too much.

"So?" she asked.

"So ... then what? Tell me about your husband."

Oh, she so didn't want to go there.

"We'd seen each other around. Journalists—especially those of us with cameras—are a small group. We've got each other's backs. If someone drinks too much, someone takes them home instead of trying to rape them. If there's danger, we let each other know stuff the briefing staff didn't tell us. The only time we go into competitive overdrive is when we're going for the same story."

She looked up at him.

He waited.

She took a deep breath. "Ben was part of that circle. We were ... uh ... attracted to each other. We scratched that itch. It didn't mean anything. Then one of our colleagues died and we ended up married."

She looked at Dr. Wikowski expectantly. He *had* to be satisfied with that explanation.

He waited a few seconds then scribbled some notes.

"That's it?" he asked.

"Well, Ben died a month ago, but you already know that. He was having a smoke ..." God, how she'd hated his habit. "The cigarette must have alerted the sniper, and ... then ... he was gone." Gone. Right after one of the worst arguments they'd ever had. She took a deep breath. "Max—he's my bureau chief, but you know that, too—he pulled me out. Sent me to London—that's where Ben was from—and I buried him. But his parents don't like me. There was no place else for me to go. So I came here."

They were both quiet for a few moments then the scratching of his pen on paper broke the silence.

Her sentence. No way after that performance was he giving her a pass. She hoped Geraldine Morgan was an easier foe.

"Here's what I'm going to need to see," Dr. Wikowski began.

# # #

CJ flinched when she entered the florescent-lit warehouse-sized store a half hour later. Too bright, like the burst of an explosion. She almost turned around to walk out, but she'd promised Jarod, and she needed warmer clothes.

Dozens of Carhartt shirts hung on spinning racks. So many choices. She'd forgotten a world beyond khaki and olive drab. A few of the garments were designed for dressy occasions, but most were flannel. She touched the shirts, her toughened fingers unused to the soft, warm fabric, the kind a Montana woman would wear to prove she was still a different gender, no matter that she could sit a horse as well as the next man.

She was going to be here for at least another month. Pulling out three shirts—neutral colors—in different sizes, she made her way toward the jeans, pausing to admire a pair of cowboy boots with elaborate etched stitching. Her hand stroked the polished leather. If she were staying ...

A familiar figure caught her eye. It couldn't be—not with a kid that big walking with him. Even under the winter coat, she recognized broad shoulders and a narrow waist and hips, echoed by what must be his son matching his stride beside him.

She turned back to the jeans, the almost twenty-year-old scar on her heart threatening to crack.

Nick Sturgis. Had to be. Next to taking photographs at Jarod's rodeo events, he'd been the most important thing in her sixteen-year-old life ... until Grace Bender had sashayed into high school.

All water under the proverbial bridge. She'd built her portfolio for her career and left her home behind in the dust.

Her fingers trembled as she selected a few jeans of different sizes then slipped into the changing room to try things on. As she slid the shirt up her arms, she trembled. Could she make it out of the store without running into Nick?

Who cared? That was over a long time ago ... except she still remembered everything about him. How good it felt when he held her tight and soothed her. His lips on hers.

Ugh. She really needed to get over this man thing.

She buttoned up the shirt and slid on the jeans, the stiff fabric unfamiliar on her legs. Too loose. Off with the clothes. Another set. Still didn't fit. The smallest size came close. Relieved, she went back to the racks, picked up a few more of the same, and tossed them in her basket.

Mentally, she ran through her list. The old jacket she'd found would do for a month; no need to spend money she didn't have. Her desert boots worked fine on the ranch and would also handle a stirrup if she had a chance to saddle up a horse again. Gloves. Jarod had been right about that. Nothing the boys wore would fit her hands, and it was too cold to do without.

She snatched up a pair on her way toward the "ranch" part of the ranch store. Pulling her brother's list from her pocket, she started to hunt through the various sizes and shapes of fittings and pipes he needed her to bring back.

"CJ?"

Her breath caught and she turned unwillingly.

"I thought that was you," Nick's voice said.

Damn him.

# # #

CJ Beck. As if his life couldn't turn more upside down.

Nick plastered a smile on his face and held out his hand. "Nick Sturgis. We dated each other in high school." Lame and awkward as hell.

"I remember." Her hands stayed wrapped around the overflowing plastic basket she carried.

He swung the outstretched hand toward his son, pretending he'd meant to do that all along. "This is my son, Trevor."

The two eyed each other like they were alien species.

She was thinner than he remembered. Her strong Scandinavian face had a deep tan, but underneath was a pallor that said she'd been through trauma of some kind. Straight, dirty-blond hair was pulled back from her face. The khaki pants she wore were shapeless but full of pockets, and an olive-green T-shirt peaked out from a jacket two sizes too big.

"Are you in the military?" Trevor asked.

"I'm a photojournalist. I was taking pictures of the war ..." CJ's eyes darted to the right and then her gaze returned to

33

Trevor's face. "Something happened and I needed to come home."

"I'm sorry." Trevor hesitated. "But that's a really cool job. I used to take pictures at home."

Those were nicer words than Nick had heard his son string together since he'd picked him up at the airport.

"Where's that?" she asked.

"Seattle."

"He's come to stay with me now," Nick said, smiling hopefully at his son. Maybe seeing CJ would be the right lever to begin to pry open the wall the kid had erected between them.

Trevor looked away from him.

Or not.

"I hope you enjoy Great Falls," CJ said, shifting her stance as if preparing to move off.

"I don't live here," Nick said, his attention drawn back to her. Her voice held a tinge of sadness and fatigue. What had happened to her during the time they were apart?

"Oh?" She finally looked at him fully, her gray eyes wary.

"We moved back to Choteau after Trevor was born—Grace and I."

"Where is she?" CJ searched the metal parts as if his ex might be hiding in a bin somewhere.

"We split when Trevor was nine." He touched his son's shoulder, but Trevor stepped away again. "Grace moved to Seattle. She's remarried."

"Oh, I see. Well, it was nice meeting you again." She hesitated and looked around before landing her attention back on him. "I need to get this paid for and loaded and head back. See you around." She started toward the checkout lanes before turning back. "Trevor?"

"Yeah?"

"If you have your camera, I'd be happy to take a look at your work, give you some pointers."

"I don't have it."

"Oh, sorry. See you." She gave a little wave then turned back to the front of the store.

"Why don't you have your camera?" Nick asked his son. "I thought you never went anywhere without it."

"That's kid stuff." Trevor shrugged. "Can we get outta here? It's boring."

"Yeah. Sure." Nick took one more look in the direction she'd gone. Seventeen years had brought huge changes to them both. They weren't the same people they'd been in high school; the only thing they had in common was the past.

Then why did long-dead emotions stir at the sight of her?

# # #

When she got to the register, CJ looked back over her shoulder. Nick and the boy were no longer in sight. She took a slow, steadying breath. *Damn.* She thought she'd gotten over him a long time ago. The tremor of her pounding heart told her differently.

One more reason to get out of Montana as quickly as she could.

Ridiculous. Her reaction didn't make any sense. They'd broken up a long time ago. Seeing him again must have triggered the more recent emotions from Ben's death. Not romance at all. Pure anger.

Anger at being dumped. Anger at Ben's repeated promises that he'd be faithful to her, or at least conduct his affairs a little more discretely so she wasn't embarrassed by overheard gossip. The last had been the worst. He'd screwed her rival for a prime magazine spot. And then his lover had gone on to get the

35

assignment.

Nothing like kicking someone when they were down.

CJ pulled out Jarod's list and double-checked it against the number of parts in her basket. She'd missed two. Going back without them wasn't an option. She was trying to prove she cared to Jarod, and the man was all about details.

She took a different route back to the plumbing section. Fortunately, Nick and his son were no longer there. Now, which bits of pipe and fittings did she miss? Painstakingly, she pulled them all out from her basket, found where she'd gotten them from, and rechecked the list. After she found each one, she put it back in the basket.

A laugh brought her attention up abruptly from the pile of metal in front of her.

"Do you need help?" Nick asked.

"I got this."

"Sure?" he asked with a grin.

"Very." She pinned him with a gaze developed in the desert warzone: the observer, unemotionally attached.

The grin faded. "Okay then. See you around." He turned and walked away.

Not if she could help it.

Finally satisfied that she had everything, she picked up the basket and headed for the checkout. Fifteen minutes later, she drove out of the parking lot, the bags piled next to her in the seat. She flicked on the radio then hit the disk player when the farm reports started droning. Old country ... Patsy Kline and Hank Williams. Should have figured as much. Jarod was hopelessly stuck in the past.

And if she didn't decide what to do, she was going to be stuck with her own past as her only accomplishment. In spite of her resistance to Dr. Wikowski, he knew what he was talking about.

She'd seen it happen in the field. Too much alcohol, drugs, or risky behavior. After a while, the beginnings of the downward spiral were obvious, at least in other people.

The Rockies loomed in front of her, their sheer surfaces rising perpendicularly from the snow-covered plains. Some of the most impenetrable areas of the country lay within its bounds, secret caches of animals, like wolverines, rarely seen by the humans who lived relatively close by. The grizzlies were starting to return to their original hunting grounds east of the mountains, and the wolf population was growing, both providing conflict between nature and what humans defined as progress.

Could there be life without conflict?

Too grandiose an idea. What she needed was a personal life without strife, no matter what was going on around her. The only way she could survive doing the work she wanted—exposing slices of the world to the rest of it—was if she had a strong core of security and peace.

For the last eighteen years she'd been faking it. She knew it, but how else was she supposed to survive?

Maybe she *should* see the therapist.

But what if the woman wasn't any good? Then what? Would CJ still be able to check off the marks on Dr. Wikowski's list so she could return to doing her job? Or should she just forget about all of it and search for a job with a different agency?

Or abandon overseas work all together. Max was right about one thing. There were plenty of problems within the border of the United States.

She stared out at the cattle lined up along a path of brown. Jarod wasn't the only one feeding livestock during the winter. Across most of Montana, cattle didn't survive without daily truckloads of forage. Ranching was a day in, day out, rain, shine, or ice storm kind of job. She admired Jarod for doing it, but it wasn't her.

The two-lane road threaded through small towns that were there and gone before most people had time to register that they were actual places. Dilapidated buildings followed by pristinely kept homes. Like most of the state, it was a jumble of old barbed wire and tumbleweeds binding people's lives together.

No one really left Montana. Oh, yeah, someone could physically cross a state line and never come back, but somewhere in their heart, the big sky called to them for the rest of their lives.

And she was one of them. Except all the state had ever brought her was pain far worse than leaving her home and family behind.

Somehow, she needed to reassemble her suit of armor, present herself to the local therapist as a totally rational, sane human being, and move forward. Maybe if she played her cards right, she could finally get a big assignment at a major magazine.

Chapter Four

"C'mon, let's see your grandparents before we head up to home," Nick said to Trevor as he pulled into a parking spot front of the red-painted general store in downtown Choteau.

"I guess."

"They'll be happy to see you. They've missed you."

The kid skipped the "whatever," but a slight shrug of his shoulders sent the same message.

It was going to be a long winter.

Nick held open the door as the cheery bell rang a greeting. No one was at the register, but that wasn't uncommon. His mother and father ran the place with a few part-timers. They were forever giving jobs to high school kids, returning soldiers, and folks down on their luck. People who didn't stay long but always got a good reference when they moved on.

A door swung open from the back and his dad, ever-present cup of coffee in hand, came toward them, a broad smile quickly forming on his face.

"Trevor!" Dad said. "Let me see you."

Quickly, Nick's son was enveloped in a bear hug, whether he'd been willing or not.

"Hi, Gramps," Trevor said after he'd been released. The smile on his face was genuine.

"Emma, get out here," his dad bellowed toward the back. "Our grandson's here."

"Just what we've been waiting for," Mom said as she, too, emerged from the back. Instead of coffee though, she carried a pile of towels in one hand. "I was just about to hang these up," she said, looking at them. "Ah, but they can wait." She tossed them on the counter. "Let me see you. Oh, my. You've gotten so big. And you look just like your dad at that age."

Trevor flicked him a glance as if to say it wasn't a comparison he appreciated as Mom slipped her arms around him and gave him a gentle squeeze.

"So what do you need?" she asked.

"We're good," Nick said. "We stopped at North 40 before we came home."

"Oh?" His father raised an eyebrow. "What did you need there?"

"Trevor needed some winter gear. Seems like Seattle doesn't really have weather."

"It *rains*," Trevor said. "That's weather."

Dad laughed. "Miserable weather, but weather." He looked at Nick. "What about gym clothes for school? They don't have Choteau gear there."

"Well, no."

"Then we'll get you fixed up. Trevor, come with me." Just like he had when Nick was a child, his dad walked to the section of the store that contained everything a team-spirited Bulldog needed.

"Coffee?" his mother asked.

"That'd be nice." God, he was tired. Not so much from the driving—that was bad enough—but from the tension between him and Trevor. Much as he'd tried, nothing he said elicited more than a few grunts from his son.

"C'mon back," she said.

He followed her down the uneven wooden floor, the thin boards worn from decades of footsteps. They went through the kitchen section of mugs, Lodge cast iron cookware, and a small selection of canning supplies gathering dust until the following season's harvest.

"It can be tough," she said as she handed him a mug. "That

age isn't easy with boys no matter what. Both you and your brother were terrors."

"Henry was worse than me."

His mother looked down her nose at him in a way that always had made him toe the line. "I beg to differ."

She was probably right. His older brother had always been a do-gooder. Still was. He and his wife owned a small spread up by Valier where they were raising three tow-headed sons.

Intact marriage, kids doing well in school, farm in the black. Totally opposite from Nick's lifestyle as a single father and outfitter.

"Yeah," he said. "Okay."

"It doesn't make you wrong in your life," she said. "You've just chosen a more difficult path."

"I'm not sure I did the choosing."

Again the look down the nose. If she'd had glasses, it would have been perfect.

"Every choice we make, no matter how small, leads us to a next choice."

"I chose Grace over CJ and that made all the difference."

"You said it," his mother said. She studied him. "She's back in town."

"Yeah, I know. We ran into her at the store. Gotta love Montana."

"Small towns, long roads," she said, reiterating a common statement of Montanans who dealt with living in the fourth largest state with a population that had only recently hit a million people. There were more cows per acre than people.

"So what are you going to do?" she asked.

"Nothing. She was pretty clear that whatever wall she put up years ago is still quite solid."

"Is it?"

"What do you mean?" he asked.

"Rumor is, she just buried her husband in London. It could be ..."

"It could be what?"

"I don't know. Fate?"

Not happening. He shook his head.

"I did enough damage back then. She doesn't need a repeat dose. Plus, it didn't sound like she is staying very long."

"You and she were only kids. And ... well, neither of you were aware of much other than your lives. But most people in town knew about her father. Daniel always had a roving eye. He was a good-looking man and he knew it. His wife was ... well ... more prudish. Sometimes I wonder how they ever got those five kids."

"The usual way, I imagine," he said, uncomfortable with the discussion. He shifted his weight on his feet."

She shrugged.

"Besides, that was their issue," he continued. "What's that got to do with CJ now? It's all in the past. Best left that way."

She sighed.

"CJ is hurting. And just like her mom, CJ is burying her feelings."

"What does that have to do with me?"

"Because you let her down when she needed you most."

"I was a kid. Besides, there's nothing I can do about that now. It's all water under the bridge." He shook his head. "Right now I've got a son who's hurting. His mom doesn't want him anymore. How do you think *he* feels?"

"Terrible. You're right. He's your priority. But ..."

"No buts. CJ and I—" He couldn't believe he was saying the two names in one sentence. "CJ and I are ancient history. We've already had lives involving other people. Some things just don't get a do-over." He glared at his mother, something he didn't do very often. But he'd lived with the guilt of seeing his former girlfriend fall apart for most of his adult life. He didn't need a reminder. The sooner she went back to wherever she'd been for the last seventeen years, the better.

His mom nodded. "Okay. How can we help you get Trevor settled?"

"The first thing is to get this kid into school and legalize whatever Grace has in mind."

"You don't trust her," his mother said.

"Not on your life."

"Good thinking."

# # #

CJ parked the truck near the barn.

"Where do you want the parts?" she asked Jarod when she found him outside staring at a horse as it paced the corral.

"Barn. I'll get 'em in a sec. Thanks for picking them up. Saved me a trip."

"Can't get them online?" she tweaked him.

"They're heavy. Shipping's a bear. It's always a balancing act, this ranch business." His gaze never left the horse as it tore toward one end of the corral and came to a skidding stop before it eyed the barrier, his breath crystalizing in the cold air. Then it repeated the actions in the opposite direction. It was a bunch of coiled energy against the background of snow and sky.

"Beautiful, isn't he?" Jarod asked.

"Sure is. What are you going to do with him?"

"Not sure yet. He's a rescue. Some gentleman rancher bought him for his daughter, but he was more than she could handle. He was going to dump him for dog food, but I offered him fifty more than the butchers and he took it."

"Lucky horse."

"Yeah." A slow smile drifted across her brother's face before he turned away. "Let's get those parts."

She walked in step with him back to the truck to help him unload. They didn't speak, but the tension between them had dispersed like seed on the wind. There could be peace in steady work.

Once the piping was unloaded, she headed up to the house with the rest of her things. Out of habit she stopped in the kitchen. Birdie was peeling meat from chicken bones while a pot of root vegetables simmered on the stove. Sweet and savory aromas of thyme and rosemary filled the kitchen.

"How'd it go?" Birdie asked.

"As well as could be expected," CJ answered.

"They going to let you go back?"

"Not at the moment," CJ said. "They want me to see a therapist in town"—she clicked her phone to bring up the note— "Geraldine Morgan."

"She must be new. I don't know her."

"Anyway, if I see her for a month, I get to go back to see the psychiatrist when he returns from Florida."

"Doesn't seem like much time." Birdie gave the liquid in the pot a stir then added the bowl of chicken she'd salvaged from the bones.

"It'll be enough time to convince her I'm fine."

Birdie shot her a look, the same one she'd used on CJ when she'd been less than truthful about something that happened at school. She had no idea how the housekeeper knew things that had happened ten miles away, but she seemed to have a sixth sense about the reality of school life.

"I *am* fine," CJ stated.

The cover went back on the pot.

"I've got to hang up my new clothes. Do you need any help?"

"What are you going to do with yourself while you wait?" Birdie asked.

"What do you mean?"

"Therapy takes only a few hours a week. What are you going to do the rest of the time?"

CJ sank into a nearby chair. She hadn't thought about it. Weeks stretching ahead with nothing to do, no story to chase ... just the perpetual sameness of small-town Montana life in the dead of winter.

"Got any ideas?" she asked. If she kept busy, the time would go faster. Hell, even mucking out stalls or trucking feed into the far pastures would be better than staring at the television or fanning the spark of jealousy as she watched Ben's last lover make her mark in the news world.

"Your mother's office needs cleaning out."

"She's been gone a long time. You mean no one's been in there since then?"

"Nope. Jarod does the books in your father's old office off the guestroom. After she passed, we just boxed up the papers and stuck them in there. Figured if we needed something, we'd just hunt for it. Once the taxes were done for that year, didn't seem like anything else was needed. But who knows. There could be something important."

Great. Going through her mom's old stuff while she was already an emotional wreck. What a swell idea that was.

"I'll think about it."

"If you cleaned it up, you could use it as your own office. Work on your pictures. Did you take any that weren't of the war when you were there?"

"A few." CJ struggled from her seat and grabbed a mug from the rack on the wall. After filling it with coffee, she leaned against the counter and sipped.

The sunsets had been amazing in the desert—heavenly created sand paintings of pinks, turquoises, and ochres. Then there were the more intimate ones of families and kids. The ones Max had dismissed. Her heart had been in those, but the world wasn't interested in her heart.

It was like Jarod and his horse or Dylan and his paintings. The Beck family had a number of soft spots. Where had they come from? Dad had barely worked the ranch, spending much of his time being the head of some organization or another—Rotary, ranchers, cattlemen. She'd never seen him do anything artistic. It was all business—and affairs.

Mom had done the normal winter crafts: needlepoint, knitting, scrapbooking with a few friends. But it had never felt like she had any passion for anything. It was more like it was expected of her, like much else in her life.

"What do you love?" she asked Birdie.

"You all, of course." The housekeeper loaded the chicken remains in a plastic bag and thrust it in the freezer compartment. "And cooking and baking." She turned to CJ. "Somehow feeding people always seems like loving them in the most basic way."

"That was true in the Middle East, too," CJ said. "Celebrations, even victories, always had a feast. A goat or lamb was killed with a lot of ceremony and roasted for days. Then it was served with grains flavored with cumin, mint, saffron, spices we don't usually see out here. Good food."

Saliva ran freely in her mouth as she mentally tasted the mint and lamb dishes that were common fare. Her relationships with many of the women had given her more access than many of her peers.

If only the work that resulted from those relationships had meant anything.

Even if she had no intention of delving deep into her psyche with Geraldine Morgan, she needed to be able to take pictures again without going into a panic attack. Maybe the studio would be a start.

Then there was Nick's son.

Their encounter had been brief, but she had seen the pain in the boy's eyes. The only time he'd sparked any interest was when they'd talked about her career. Except she wouldn't want any kid following her footsteps. But still ... he was a kid who was hurting. She just had no idea how to help him or even if she should.

"Do you miss it?" Birdie asked, back on her feet once again, this time pulling flour and honey from the cabinet.

"Yes and no. I certainly don't miss the bloodshed and horror of what people are capable of doing to each other. But the culture? The people I got to know? Yeah, some." She poured a bit more of coffee and sat down again. Pulling her new gloves from the plastic bag, she tore at the tag that held them together.

A drawer opened and Birdie held out a pair of scissors. "Some things need to be cut apart," she said.

CJ snipped at the plastic link between the gloves.

"Anyway," Birdie said, a sense of efficiency in her words, "if you don't want to clean out musty old offices—and I can't blame you—you can see what Jarod needs. Or I'm sure the school could use some volunteers. They're always looking. Or there's clubs— 4H, that kind of thing."

All of a sudden, the solitude of the office seemed like a fine idea. Especially if she could make it hers.

"Thanks, Birdie." She stuffed her gloves back in the bag, rose, and kissed the housekeeper on the cheek. "Anything I can do for dinner?"

"Nope. Got it in hand. Go figure out what you're doing with your life."

CJ gathered up her bags and trudged up to her room. The chamber had been small but efficient. The walls were of a hue reminiscent of the sky. Her childhood photographs, lovingly framed by Dylan, hung on the walls. The quilts on the iron bedstead had been put together by grandmothers and passed down. Her mother's crafts hadn't extended to quilting.

But best of all, it had been all hers. No boys allowed.

She grinned. Now she had the whole floor to herself, including the bathroom. Sharing *that* with four brothers had sucked.

She had her whole life to herself.

Sinking to the mattress, she stared at the ceiling. If she stopped running, if she called a time-out, where could she be in a year's time? The line of Dr. Seuss's book swam into her mind. "Oh, the places you'll go!"

Yeah. Right.

Still. What had the last seventeen years of running away done for her? Maybe it was time to do something different.

Maybe.

But the time away had worked out okay. She'd been to many of the great spots of the world—Louisville during the Derby, London, Paris, Cairo, Istanbul—as well as some of the armpits like the New Jersey Turnpike, coal mines of West Virginia, the hellhole of the last years in Syria. But on the whole, the balance had been positive.

Shit.

Life should come with instructions. Which path should she take now? The dilemma of all humans—what actually happened on the road not taken? But she was stuck with only one choice. A human could only live one path at a time, even though it was a piss-poor plan. If she ever got to meet God after the pearly gates, she'd let him know just what she thought of it.

But that was then.

Now what?

She pulled out her phone, searched for Geraldine Morgan's number, and hit enter. After a few rings, it went to voicemail.

Of course. No therapist ever answered their phone directly.

She left a message.

Deed done, there was only one thing left to do. She headed down to her mother's office.

# # #

Nick opened the door to his home, seeing it from his son's eyes. Yeah, entering a house through a mudroom was classy.

"You can dump your shoes and coats," he said. "Got slippers?"

"Nope." Trevor pointed to the suitcase sitting on the stone floor. "Everything I have is in there."

Okay. Nick scanned his memory for some spare slippers and came up empty. "Heavy socks?" he asked.

Trevor shook his head.

"Well, the floors are heated. If you leave your boots here, you should still be fine."

"Whatever."

Nick was rapidly beginning to hate that word.

"Okay. Follow me and I'll show you your room."

"I remember."

Of course he did. He'd lived here for the first four years of his life. Until Grace had scooped up her son and dragged him, along with the man who'd replaced Nick, to Seattle. Trevor would have more opportunities, a future, she'd claimed.

And so, he'd let his son go.

"Okay." Nick hung his coat on the thick wooden peg on the

49

rough-hewn wall, toed off his boots, and opened to the door to the main living quarters. He and Grace, back in the days when they could still agree on anything, had gone for a plan that included a great room of polished logs rather than separate kitchen, dining, and living areas. A huge plate glass window looked out over the foothills leading to the gray wall of the Rockies. A porch lined that side of the house, easily accessed by the kitchen for family dinners spent close to nature.

A corridor led off the great room where his office, the main bathroom, Trevor's room, and the master bedroom lay. It was simple and spacious, but its simple practicality grated on his ex within a few months of moving in. Grace had been destined for glitzy dinner parties, elegant jewels, and the movers and shakers of the world. Nick no longer blamed her, like he didn't blame the wolf for being a wolf.

But that didn't mean he trusted her.

Trevor headed down the corridor, dragging his suitcase behind him, *clunkity clunk* on the concrete floor.

Nick stared down the empty hallway. Now what? After the hustle and bustle of the airport, the store, his folks, and the ride home, he sagged with exhaustion. It had been an emotion-laced day, with CJ's appearance an added dollop of sadness.

She'd looked like crap—haunted by things she had seen and probably done. It wasn't supposed to be that way. He looked down the corridor. Hell, none of it was supposed to turn out the way it did. Their high school dreams had included a cabin in the woods, jobs that involved long hours out in the wilderness they both loved, and a family of rowdy kids someday.

He padded over to the kitchen and pulled out the spaghetti sauce he'd planned for dinner. He set the pot on the high-end gas stove he'd purchased for Grace one year, a last-ditch bribe to get her to stay. Pulling out a second pot, he set water on to boil, and turned on the oven. He'd pulled together a loaf of garlic bread and wrapped it in foil before he'd left for the airport.

"I left you clean towels in the main bathroom if you want to take a shower," he hollered down the corridor.

"I'm good." Trevor came out into the main room.

"Grab the salad from the fridge and pick which dressing you want."

Bottles clinked and thudded on the table.

Nick glanced over where Trevor was slumped into the couch cushions poking at his phone. "Don't you have cell service?" he asked.

"Not here. I've set up a wireless router, though. We're Aerie House." He gave his son the password.

"Got it."

Nick grabbed himself a beer when dinner was ready. "Coke?" he asked.

"Yeah."

They sat and Nick bent his head and said a quick thank you for the food before them. He wasn't a big churchgoer, but he'd been raised in a tradition to be grateful for what he had. His father had sworn it was the true secret to lifelong happiness. He looked up to see Trevor staring at him.

"I take it Mom doesn't say grace."

Trevor snorted.

"Dig in," Nick said, picking up his own fork. After the first few bites, he realized he was hungrier than he'd thought. Trevor was head down, forking in food.

Good.

"Help me wash up," he told Trevor when they finished.

The kid looked around. "No dishwasher?"

"You're looking at him." Nick tossed the kid a towel. "You're the dryer."

Trevor shook his head but took up his place next to Nick. They worked steadily but silently, the still dark air outside the kitchen window. The new moon made the pinprick of stars all the brighter. Maybe having his son would turn out okay. Yeah, Trevor was moody, but he didn't know any teenagers that weren't. His brother's kids, both in their teens, certainly weren't known for their calm demeanor.

"I've got to feed the horses," Nick said when the last plate was stowed. "Probably need to head to bed soon. We've got to get up early tomorrow to register for school."

"I'm not going to that dumpy school," Trevor said. "You don't have a job. You can homeschool me til I talk Mom into letting me come home again."

Fatigue ramped up his anger rapidly. "I most certainly do have a job. And so do you. Yours is to go to school and learn. I don't have the training to educate you. This is not open for debate."

"You can't make me go." Trevor stood toe to toe with him.

"I most certainly can." His kid was almost his height, but he didn't have the muscles that came from working day in and out at physical labor.

"Then I'll just run away. I'm going back to Seattle. And the sooner you and Mom figure out how, the better." He stormed off down the corridor.

The slam of his door echoed through the house.

It was going to be a long winter.

Chapter Five

By Sunday, CJ had barely made a dent in the office. There were many boxes of papers that made no sense to her. She'd need to check with a tax accountant to find what she needed to keep. Official-looking government documents were piled underneath receipts from her childhood. Surely, she didn't need to keep a receipt for the first dress her mother had ever gotten her—a Christmas present the year she turned thirteen.

God, she'd been disappointed. She'd pouted like only a young girl could. Half the girls at school were changing—dressing up and getting their feelings all twisted up with boys. She belonged to the other half, the girls who tried to hang onto their freedom to act just like the male half of their small world. With four brothers, CJ'd been the worst.

She'd refused to wear the dress. What had happened to it? Probably packed up and given to Goodwill along with other things she'd outgrown, including stacks of her favorite jeans and T-shirts.

A pang of remorse hit her. Her mother had only been trying to help, and she'd treated her poorly.

"Sorry, Mom," she whispered as she glanced heavenward, closed up the box, and stood. Arching back, she stretched out her cramped muscles. Probably enough for a Sunday. Jarod and Birdie should be back from church soon. Dylan was holed up in his cabin, but he'd told her they'd be getting a call from Cameron in the late afternoon.

"Then I'll patch in Kaiden." Apparently, he was in charge of all things electronic in the house, especially if it had to do with the internet.

She paused at the light switch, her gaze caught by two whimsical plates a great aunt had dragged back from Amish country somewhere in the Midwest.

"We grow too soon oldt and too late schmardt," declared one.

"May your house be warm, your friends many, and your sausages long," stated the second. It was as good a blessing as any, and it always made her grin.

She shook her head. This room was going to take forever. One more box before she left?

A small one, older than the others, was tucked up on a high shelf. Using the tips of her fingers, she maneuvered it, and a whole lot of dust, to the edge of the shelf before tilting it over so she could guide it down.

Heavy.

She placed it on top of a nearby stack and peeled the tape that kept it shut. The brittle yellow plastic shattered under her fingers. How many years had this been put away?

A stack of faded cloth books filled the box.

She pulled out the first one and carefully opened it.

"Property of Catherine Anna Miller" was penned in neat script in the center of the first page with "1942" written below it.

Catherine—that had to be her paternal grandmother. One of the two she'd been named after. Josephine had been her mother's mother's name.

The two flowery, old-fashioned names had been shrunk to CJ as soon as she refused to answer to anything else.

Probably nothing more than courtship and getting ready for marriage. It's what women did back then.

Although, 1942. The war was on.

She turned the page.

"It's not fair!" the first entry declaimed.

CJ continued to read.

"Why do the men get to fight the Nazis and we have to stay home and 'tend the fires'? Dang! I want to help out, and I'm going to do it by hook or by crook!"

CJ smiled. Her grandmother wasn't the quiet woman reading by the fire she vaguely remembered. She'd been a spitfire when she was younger.

Leaning against the doorjamb, she closed the slim volume in her hand. For the first time in her life she felt a connection to someone else in her family—a lifeline she hadn't known with her father or mother.

"CJ!" Dylan bellowed from the other side of the house. "It's almost time for Cameron to call."

She flicked off the light and closed the door before rushing to the living room. It had been too long since she'd seen Cameron.

Jarod was sitting in his favorite armchair, looking detached from the whole event. The only way she knew he was with them was the tracking movement of his eyes as he watched Dylan fiddle with wires and turn knobs.

"Used to be," he muttered to CJ, "you picked up the phone, dialed a number, and got someone."

"Oh, you're soooo old," she teased. "Bet you used to talk to the operator, too, to connect you."

Dylan laughed, and even Jarod cracked a smile.

"Got me," he said.

Birdie bustled in, wiping her hands on her apron. "Is it time? Do you have him?"

"Almost. He's due in five, four, three—"

The screen on the far wall clicked a few times and pixilated itself to life.

And there was Cameron. She covered her mouth with awe. Even though she'd never taken advantage of the any of the online video services to call her family while she was overseas, it seemed like a miracle.

By the look on the faces around her and the one on the screen, it looked like she'd missed out on something big. Why hadn't she ever called?

Because she didn't think anyone really cared.

Her heart twisted.

"CJ," Cameron said. "It's good to see you."

"You, too, little brother."

"She loves rubbing that in, have you noticed?" Dylan asked.

"Yeah, but it's good to hear her say it after all these years." Cameron's eyes—his big, strong soldier eyes—misted.

How long had it been since she'd seen him? Five years? Ten? Somewhere in between. He was no longer a boy.

"Let me get Kaiden," Dylan said and clicked a few more keys on the keyboard in front of him. Soon a split screen showing both her brothers appeared before her.

Her youngest brother, now twenty-eight, had the rough look of a man who worked outdoors. There was a cut over his left eyebrow and black grease on his cheek. "Hey, sis," he said as if it was no big deal they hadn't seen each other since she'd brought Ben home for a brief visit after they were married. Ah, well, she and Kaiden had never been close. He was always too eager to pull stuff from the earth to take the time to see what was on top of it.

Her family. What was left of it. But it was all she had.

She looked over at Birdie, who was looking at her. When the housekeeper saw her, she nodded, a smug smile on her face.

"So how are things going for you, Cameron?" Jarod asked, sounding too much like the patriarch of their little clan. "Any chance of getting stateside?"

"Not in the near future," he replied. "There's a lot of activity, none of which I can talk about, of course."

"Of course," she said. "How about you stop re-upping and come home for good?"

"I could ask you the same thing."

Yeah.

"Sorry to hear about Ben," Cameron said.

"Me, too," Kaiden added.

"Thank you," she said.

"What are your plans now?" Cameron asked.

Not the question she'd hoped to field.

"Just a rest while I wait for my next assignment."

Birdie cleared her throat, and Dylan gave the housekeeper a sharp glance before turning his attention to CJ. "Why do I think there's more going on that that?" he asked. "After all, you did take a trip to Great Falls, and I'm sure it wasn't just to pick up pipe supplies for Jarod."

Much as she'd always loved Dylan, he was a curious pain in the ass. If her room looked like someone had been in it when she was a teen, she could pretty much be sure he'd been the one to violate her privacy.

"They just want to make sure I'm okay to go back," she said. "You know, for insurance and all that."

This time Birdie rolled her eyes.

Kaiden must have spotted it because he grinned, his bright white teeth shining in his darkly tanned face.

They were a good-looking lot, her brothers. And yet they were all as single as the day they were born. So was she. Not a good testimony for her parents' marriage.

"If that's your story ..." Dylan said.

She glared at him.

"Have you seen Nick?" Cameron asked.

"Once."

"She doesn't need to see Nick," Jarod interjected. "He hurt

her once, and she's smart enough to know better than to get involved again."

"I'm right here," she said. "Isn't there something else we can talk about besides my life? Kaiden, how's the oil flowing?"

"Good enough we should be able to bring our boys back from the desert and let them all take care of their own affairs."

"That's not the reason we're over here," Cameron said.

"It's the reason you all went in the first place," Kaiden shot back.

"Boys," Birdie warned. "No politics."

"Yes, ma'am," Cameron said. Kaiden echoed the words.

"That's why it's easier to stick with *your* affairs," Dylan said focusing back on CJ. "We can all agree on what you should do."

"And that is?"

"Stay home, find someone, and get married. Maybe have some kids."

"Too late for that," she said. She and Ben hadn't wanted to bring kids into their crazy lives. At thirty-five, she hadn't liked the odds. On one of their trips back to London to see Ben's folks, she'd had her tubes tied. So that was that.

"Never say never," Dylan said.

"In this case, never is the right word." Her voice must have conveyed the finality.

Everyone grew quiet.

Just a nice family discussion … no wonder she'd never come home.

Jarod cleared his throat. "All we need to do is make it through the next two months. Then the weather should start to break. They're predicting an early spring."

"That'll be nice," Birdie said. "I never did feel it came last year. And summer was barely enough to ripen anything."

"Yeah. It was a tough year for feed last year. We didn't make as much as we normally do. I kept the herd a little smaller this year. If it's a good spring, I'll keep more of the calves than normal to make up for it."

Both Kaiden and Cameron nodded. They all had a stake in the ranch, although Jarod and Dylan received salaries for the work they did.

Would any of them every return? Or should they consider a transfer of ownership to her oldest brother? He was the most passionate. And as soon as she'd jumped through the requisite hoops, she'd be gone again. Kaiden's life was in the drilling fields. And Cameron? Who knew?

Before she left, she'd talk to a real estate person and get their thoughts.

"And Jarod's got a new horse," Dylan said.

"Really?" Cameron's eyes lit up. Next to Jarod, he was the most horse-crazy of the bunch.

"It's a rescue," Jarod said, shifting in his chair. "Someone bought him who wasn't ready to take care of him."

"What are you going to do with him?" Cameron asked.

"Not sure yet. Got to get him gentled first, then see what he can do."

"Looking forward to seeing him."

"And when's that going to be?" Birdie asked.

"Soon, I hope. I've just got a few more missions and then I should be up for some leave." Cameron's voice was gentler with her than it had been with anyone else.

"That'd be good," CJ said. In spite of the wrangling and underlying disagreements, it would be satisfying to have them all together again. "Maybe we could have a reunion this summer. All five of us in the same place."

Her brothers stared at her.

"What? Don't you think it's a good idea?" she asked.

"Yes," Kaiden said. His eyes darted about as if he were waiting for someone else to say what was on his mind. Finally, he shrugged. "We're just surprised you're the one to suggest it, since you've been away from home the longest, sis."

Tears stung her eyes as she looked around. It was like a huge hole had opened up in her chest, a longing for something she didn't even know she was missing.

"Then we should do it," she said, fighting to keep control of the shake in her voice.

"Yep," Jarod said.

"Without a doubt," said Cameron. "I'll find out when I can get there and we can plan on that." He looked off screen for a second and then nodded. "But now, I have to go. Talk with you in a few weeks." His half of the screen blinked.

Dylan hit the keyboard again and Kaiden's face filled the whole screen. "Just let me know when to call in again, Dylan, okay?"

"Got it."

"And good to see you again, CJ." He waved and then he, too, was gone.

She looked around the room for a few seconds then couldn't bear to be there anymore. "I've got some things to do in my room," she said and fled to her sanctuary.

# # #

From Catherine's diary, October 1942:

"They called up Stephen today. He's happy about it. I'm not. I told him he better get over there, knock down all our enemies, and come home to me. Daddy thinks I'm too young to get married, but what else am I supposed to do? It's not like there's

any jobs for girls in this stupid town."

CJ smiled as she looked up from the diary page the following morning. She and her grandmother had been kindred spirits, for sure. Choteau was a lot bigger than it had been in her grandmother's day, but opportunities were still limited in the conservative town. It was probably just as well she and Nick hadn't made it. He'd been attached to staying here, cuddled up to the Bob Marshall Wilderness, but what would she have done? Taken pictures of cute baby deer?

She shrugged as she shut the blue book with a thud. She wasn't planning on doing anything at all with Nick Sturgis, other than staying as far away from him as possible.

She glanced at the old camera she'd found when she'd gone through the drawers to make room for her clothes. Nick's son might be able to use it.

Maybe later. Now she had to get up and get going. Today was the day she had to make her first appearance at the therapist's office since scheduling the appointment last week. She had to dress carefully, prove she had her act together and was comfortable in her own skin. That was how she was going to play it. Cool and collected. No need to go digging in the murk of her dysfunctional relationship with Ben, her parents, her brothers, or the state of Montana.

Jarod and Dylan were finishing up their stacks of pancakes when she walked into the kitchen and headed for the coffeepot. The salty aroma of bacon had her glancing hungrily at the grill stretched across a few burners. She sidled toward the stove. Her hand was almost to the closest strip when a silicon flipper smacked it.

"Ouch!" she yelped. "Damn, that hurt! What was that for?"

Dylan chuckled.

"Manners, young lady. You're not with the troops. You'll eat off a breakfast plate like a civilized person. And while you're at it, you can watch your language." Birdie emphasized each point with the flipper in her hand.

"Yes, ma'am," CJ said, still rubbing her hand.

"Sit," the housekeeper said.

She picked up the coffee and took her place at the kitchen table. Dylan smirked at her and she stuck her tongue out.

Jarod shook his head, picked up his plate, and put it in the sink. "Thanks, Birdie," he said as he slid on his Bulldogs cap and headed out to the mudroom.

The housekeeper slid the plate in front of her, along with the butter dish and syrup.

CJ sat there for a few moments, breathing in the aroma of hot breakfast served on a plate, guaranteed not gritty with ever-present sand. Then she slathered the pancakes with butter and syrup and dug in.

"Oh my god," she said after the first few swallows. "This is amazing."

Birdie placed a white envelope in front of her, its back covered with the housekeeper's scrawl.

"What's that?" she asked.

"You're going into town, aren't you?" she asked.

"Yes."

"Then you're going to the store. That's what I need."

"Got it."

Dylan rose from the table and placed his plate in the sink as well. He pulled a couple of envelopes from his back packet. "Can you stick these in the mailbox on the way out?"

"Okay."

She could see what was happening. Slowly but surely, they were pulling her into their web. It was just temporary. Hopefully, they understood that.

After depositing the envelopes and flipping up the flag on the mailbox, she turned north on the highway. Good thing she was leaving. Otherwise, she'd have to invest in a car of her own. Dylan had a small pickup he used, but the ranch truck was Jarod's only transportation. And it was a gas-eating horror.

She let her gaze roam between the rolling hills to her left and the grasslands stretching to the east on her right. This scenery felt right in a way the desert never had. The sandy expanse had always felt too expansive without the inspiration of the mountains reaching toward that big, blue sky.

Pulling into town, she drove toward the residential section in the western part. Geraldine Morgan apparently ran her office from her house.

CJ parked in front of a pastel green house with dark green trim. As instructed, she went to the back of the house and up a set of three cement steps to a small landing. The door in front of her had a shellacked wooden sign that invited her to come in without knocking.

She entered a tiny anteroom with a rack for her coat, a round table with a few magazines, and two armchairs in some modern design.

Shedding her coat, she took the top magazine and perched in one of the chairs. She idly gazed at the fashion magazine, unable to relate to anything she saw. Did women really pay attention to all this stuff? Even though she'd eventually been willing to wear a dress, she'd never fully landed in the girly girl camp.

The inner office door opened and a smiling redhead peered out. Green eyes appraised CJ.

Was she found lacking?

"CJ Beck?" the woman asked.

"That would be me," she said.

"Geraldine Morgan." The redhead held out her hand. "You can call me Gerry."

CJ rose and shook it. Cool but firm grip.

"This way," Geraldine said, walking back into the office. "If you'd close the door behind you ..."

CJ tossed the magazine back on the table and did as she was asked.

She settled into one end of a brown suede couch. A cream candle on a nearby table scented the air with vanilla, in spite of the fact it was unlit. Pleasant landscapes hung on the paneled walls.

Gerry settled herself into a matching armchair in front of her, a clipboard stacked with papers and a yellow legal pad on her lap. She leaned forward.

"I've got forms for you to fill out, but I don't want to waste our session on that. You can take them home and bring them back with you next time."

"Sure." Be cooperative.

"Dr. Wikowski sent me your records," she said. "Sounds like it was pretty rough where you were."

"No different than any other war zone. It goes with the territory."

"I see." Gerry scanned the papers again. "So, I have the bare bones of your family life, but I suspect there's a whole lot more to it than who was born and died when."

"Why is that relevant?" CJ asked. "It all happened a long time ago. I left Montana when I was eighteen, and other than holidays and vacations, I haven't been back much since."

"Why did you leave?"

She should have expected that question, but it still took her by surprise.

"I went to college."

Gerry consulted her notes again. "In Kentucky. Seems like a long way to go for an education."

"They have a really good program in photojournalism. Plus, like I told Dr. Wikowski, it was different. I wanted to explore. What eighteen-year-old doesn't? I'd been living in this town my whole life. The only question my parents ever asked was if I wanted to go to college in Missoula or Bozeman. They really expected me to become a teacher or something."

"And that wasn't what you wanted?"

"Nope. I'd been taking pictures since I was a kid. That's what I wanted to do. Once I understood there was actually a career to do that—other than the same old wildlife every other Montana photographer does—I was hooked." She leaned forward to indicate her passion.

"And now?"

"What do you mean?"

"Are you taking pictures now?" Gerry gestured to the papers in front of her. "You were sent home on bereavement leave. From what you've just told me, photography is extremely important to you. I want to know if you've taken pictures recently."

"Sure," CJ lied. Her chest was beginning to hurt from this cat-and-mouse game Gerry was insisting on playing. Why couldn't everyone just accept that she was fine—or would be once she got back to work?

"What of?"

"Huh?"

"What are you taking pictures of?"

"Just stuff. Snow and mountains. You know. The usual."

"Nice. I'd love to see them the next time you come."

"No problem." CJ leaned back on the couch to show she was perfectly relaxed about bringing in pictures that didn't exist.

Chapter Six

"So your older brother ... Jarod, He takes care of the ranch?" Gerry asked.

This woman must have been an investigative reporter in another lifetime. She was as relentless as the rest of them. The lowball question would no doubt be followed by one with a laser focus. CJ readjusted herself physically to handle the onslaught.

"Yes."

"And Dylan works with him."

"When he's not painting."

"Oh, so there are two of you with an artistic bent. Were either of your parents artistic?"

CJ looked down at her hands. They were back to her parents. Exactly what she didn't want to talk about. "I don't know," she mumbled, not looking up.

Gerry was silent.

As it lingered, CJ became aware of the hiss of the radiator against a far wall. It dominated her thoughts, becoming louder and louder in her imagination. Almost like a bomb about to go off.

Her heart began to race. How long to get to the door? What if it were locked? The window. Would the office chair be heavy enough to smash through it? What would happen if she misjudged and hit an artery with a shard of glass?

"Are you okay?" Gerry asked.

Who was she? CJ stared at the stranger.

Breathe. It's a panic attack. Just breathe. In and out. Using the technique she'd learned from one of the other embedded journalists, she calmed herself down. Safe. She was safe. Just an office far from the front.

"You just had a panic attack, didn't you?" Gerry asked softly.

CJ nodded and took another deep breath. "But I got myself out of it. It happens to all of us once in a while. Why wouldn't it? Shit happens out there. But it's all part of the job. A job I am perfectly capable of handling." She shifted. Why wasn't this couch comfortable?

Gerry looked at her steadily until she was forced to look away.

"Dylan also works at the ranch, right?" the therapist asked.

CJ nodded.

"There are two more ..."

Sigh. May as well give the woman what she wanted. "Cameron's in the army and Kaiden's in the oil fields."

"Thank you." The scratch of pen on paper as Gerry made notes.

CJ scanned the ceiling. Not even a cobweb in the corners. High attention to detail.

She shifted again. "Look," she said. "My dad had affairs. His last was in Lincoln. He died on the way home from seeing her. Icy roads. My mother died of cancer a year after that." She stared at Gerry. That should satisfy her.

"I'm sorry. How old were you then?"

"Fifteen when my father ... um ... died. Sixteen when we lost my mother." She pushed against the emotion that threatened to rise from the pitch-black pit where she relegated her painful past.

"The others were younger?"

CJ nodded.

Gerry waited.

She was so over this. And there were four more sessions?

"Birdie came into our lives when I was fourteen. That's when my mother first got sick. She just kind of took over and never left."

"A second mother."

"Yes." CJ smiled. As much scolding as she'd received from the housekeeper, she'd received twice as much love. So different from her real mother, who was stingy with both hugs and words of rebuke. In fact, her mother had never made a stand about anything, no matter how minor. She couldn't even decide which vegetable she wanted to serve with dinner. After she was gone, it was almost as if she'd never existed.

CJ looked up briefly at Gerry but didn't say anything. She wasn't sure what all of it meant. At thirty-five, she pretty much was who she was.

After a few more moments of silence, Gerry asked, "How are your relationships with your brothers now?"

Truthfully. Non-existent. But that wasn't going to help her case.

"Fine. We haven't seen much of each other, but we did all have a nice chat yesterday. Dylan is a whiz with videoconferencing."

Gerry nodded.

"What do they care about?" she asked.

What kind of question was that? "Jarod cares for the ranch, Dylan painting, Kaiden oil, and Cameron serving his country."

"That's what they do. What do they care about?"

"I don't know."

"Then that's the first assignment. You need to discover what they care about."

"How am I supposed to do that?"

"Ask them." Gerry made a few more notes on her pad. "Also, I'm looking forward to seeing your new photos." She glanced at her watch. "I'm afraid our time is almost up. Do you have any questions?"

CJ leaned forward, debating her answer. She didn't want to reveal too much, but she didn't want to be in limbo any longer than she had to. She cleared her throat a few times and finally took the plunge. "What do I have to do to get back in the field—so you give Dr. Wikowski the okay?"

"That depends on how you want to play this."

"What do you mean?"

"Even after one session, I can tell you're very resistant to this whole process, although Dr. Wikowski had warned me that was the case. Therapy is work. It means digging through the icky parts of your past and making peace with them. From what I can tell, you are really good at burying your emotions and pretending you are fine."

"I *am* fine. That's what I keep telling you."

Gerry shook her head. "Unexamined feelings are like unexploded mines. One wrong move and they explode. Panic attacks like the one you had a few minutes ago can occur and immobilize you. Your future relationships will suffer if you don't deal with the ones you've had in the past or present."

"I'm done with men, so not a problem." CJ forced a smile.

Gerry laughed. "That's what most women say when the men they've been with have hurt them. Give it time. Speaking of which ..." She stood and grabbed an envelope from her desk. "Here are the papers I need filled out. Same time next week?"

"I guess."

"Good. Have a good day. Drive safe." Gerry opened the door.

"Bye." CJ left the office and walked back to the truck, halfway in a daze.

# # #

Birdie's list was going to have to wait. CJ needed a cup of coffee. Almost by rote, she slid her car into the angled parking in front of Bridges Coffee Shop and slipped into the café.

"Hello, Mae," she called out. Like a small-town cliché, the

woman had been behind the coffee counter since CJ could remember. At sixteen, she used to do her homework at one of the tables while she waited for one of her brothers to finish up some sport or another before driving them both home.

The décor hadn't changed much. Rough wooden panels in a dark brown surrounded the dozen 1950s metal tables and chairs. Booths with red vinyl lined one side of the small space. The same imitation Charles Russell cowboy art hung on the walls, interspersed with cheerful 1940s placards of smiling waitresses holding steaming pots of coffee and menus.

Decades of brewing coffee and hot grease added a familiar aroma to the air.

"CJ? Is that you?" Mae asked, turning around with a fresh pot of coffee in her hand. She set it on the counter. "Look at you, girl, all grown up. How long's it been since you've been back?"

"About five years." She'd brought Ben here after they'd gotten married to introduce him to the family.

"Back for good?" Mae held up the pot and CJ nodded.

"Not for good," she replied. "Just a little R and R before my next assignment."

"You sure are talented. And brave. Great Falls was always adventure enough for me. One time I went all the way to Seattle and, my word, I never thought I'd get home again. Cream and sugar are in the stand." Mae pointed at the coffee fixings snugged next to the salt and pepper, ketchup, and napkin dispenser.

"Thanks. I've learned to drink it black." Milk in the desert had been too unreliable and sugar was an alien concept.

Cold air seeped in as a new arrival came in through the door. Four highway workers, florescent vests over brown snowsuits, clomped through the café and surrounded a table at the back.

"Be right with you, boys," Mae yelled out. "Catch up with you later."

The door opened again. Mid-morning must be a busy time for coffee.

"Coming through," a woman called. Only the blue pompom on the top of her hat was visible behind the stack of boxes she carried.

"Just in time!" one of the highwaymen called out from the back. "Pie's here!"

"Hang on," Mae called out.

CJ hopped off her stool. "Here, let me help." She grabbed the topmost boxes and carefully removed them from the stack. The face peering out from the rest of the hat looked familiar.

"CJ?" the woman asked.

"Yes. I'm sorry, but who—?"

"Trish Small. We went to high school together."

"Oh, yes!" Trish had been one of the few cool kids who'd actually been nice to her.

"Here, let me get those," Mae said, taking the boxes from CJ. "Coffee?" she asked Trish.

"To go," Trish said as she followed Mae back to the kitchen behind the counter. "Sam forgot his lunch and I need to drop it off. I swear he does it at least once a week."

Trish came back out. She was an older version of the pixie blond cheerleader she'd been. Her smile still reached all the way to her eyes, except now those eyes had small lines at the edges.

"C'me're you," she said, enfolding CJ into a big bear hug. "It's good to see you. Where have you been?"

"Middle East."

"Amazing. Who would have thought when we were kids you'd be so famous?"

"I'm not famous." She grinned at Trish. "Just another working journalist."

"Still," Trish said. "It's a long way from baking pies. And

running after two teenagers."

Trish had teenagers? Envy stabbed CJ's gut. She hadn't wanted motherhood, but for the first time she felt the emptiness of it.

"Must keep you busy."

"Here you go." Mae handed Trish a to-go cup.

"Yeah, it does. In fact, I have to run now. But let's catch up. Here's my card. Call me."

"Okay."

"Promise?" Trish put her hand on CJ's arm and looked up into her eyes.

"Yeah, promise." CJ took the card and watched her old friend dash back out the door.

CJ settled onto her stool and cradled her mug of coffee. She hadn't been able to snowball Gerry into giving her a quick pass. If anything, the woman was going to be more of a hard-ass than the doctor in Great Falls.

What did her brothers care about? She'd never really thought about it. At least it would give them something to talk about. She'd tackle Dylan first—he'd be the easiest to open up. Of course, he would ask her what was important to her. That was something she really didn't want to discuss because she had no idea what the answer was. The only thing that had seemed important for most of her life was getting as far from Montana as she could.

Then there was the camera. She'd picked it up any number of times after she'd come home, but her hands trembled every time she tried to take a picture. Why even try to get back to the Middle East? Did she really think some magic was going to happen and she'd be able to take prize-winning pictures in the midst of explosions?

She sipped the acrid brew. Better than she'd gotten in the desert but not as good as Birdie's.

Maybe it was time to stop running and give this therapy thing a chance. She'd known for a long time that she'd never really dealt with the deaths of her parents, and now the nasty final argument and watching her husband's head explode were layered on top.

Okay, Ms. Geraldine Morgan, let's give it your best shot.

# # #

Nick parked his truck on the snowy street. A cup of coffee was what he needed before he headed back up the hill to get a few hours of work done before he had to pick up Trevor again. The kid had never had bad tantrums when he was two. Why did he have to wait until thirteen to start stomping his big feet and flailing his arms?

He plucked his cell phone from its holder on the dash. May as well try Grace one more time while he was in town and had service. He'd been trying every day to talk to her, but she was either "too busy" or didn't answer.

But he had questions that needed answering and a niggling feeling that an adjustment to their custody agreement might be in order to keep everything on the up and up.

No answer.

He slammed the truck door with a little more force than necessary, causing the rooftop snow to cascade over his arms. Good going. He brushed it off and stomped his way to the entrance of Bridges.

"Sit anywhere you can find," Mae sang out as he walked in.

All the tables were occupied and most of the booths. He turned to the counter.

CJ.

"Mind if I sit here?" he asked, sliding onto a stool, leaving one between them where he perched his cowboy hat.

"It's a free country," she said and looked up at him. Her gray eyes took his measure. "I do have to ask if you're stalking me, though." A smile played at the corners of her mouth.

"Hazards of small-town living," he said. "It's almost impossible to avoid someone." He grinned. "It's always good to see you."

Her skin tightened slightly and her eyes widened.

Any conversation with this woman was going to be an emotional minefield. But he had to try. Besides working on a relationship with his son, he'd always needed to make amends for breaking it off with CJ right when she'd needed him most. Her return to town after all this time was the first chance he'd had to fix the past.

Not that anyone could ever change what had already happened. All he could do was forge new bridges.

"Here you go," Mae said, sliding a mug of coffee across the counter to him. "Anything else?"

"Trish bring in pies yet?"

"Fresh out of the oven."

"I'll take a slice of whatever you've cut into—and get one for CJ, too."

"I don't need—"

"Sure you do. Trish bakes the best pies in the entire state. Put it on my tab," he added to Mae.

"Thanks."

He nodded and took a sip of the coffee.

"Are you back for good?" he asked, giving her a sidewise glance.

She was staring at the wall in front of her. "Nope."

"How long are you back for then?"

"As long as it takes."

He shook his head. Prickly pears were more informative.

"Flathead cherry pie. The last two slices," Mae said, placing the plates in front of them. "The guys from the highway crew just about wiped me out."

"Thanks, Mae. Looks great."

"Thanks," CJ mumbled.

"What brings you into town?" Mae asked as she slammed two pieces of whole wheat bread into the beat-up toaster on the counter behind her. "I thought you'd be hunkered down for the winter in that cabin of yours."

"I had to get my kid to school."

"Trevor?" Mae placed her hands wide on the counter and leaned toward him. "He's living with you now?"

"For the moment."

"He must be ... geez, how old is he now?"

"Thirteen going on two."

Mae laughed, a big belly laugh that asked for no apology.

"Most of them are like that. He'll get over it. You did."

"Oh, c'mon, I was an angel."

Next to him, CJ snorted.

At least he got a reaction from her.

"Yeah, imagine that," Mae said.

"Mae!" one of the men in the back yelled out. "Can we get some more coffee here?"

"Hold your horses," she hollered back. "Can I get you two anything else?" she asked.

"I'm good," he said.

"Me, too," CJ said, smiling fully at Mae.

And she still knew how to smile. He was glad he hadn't robbed her of that forever.

"I take it there's no school bus where you live," CJ said.

"What? Oh. Well, that's only part of the problem. Trevor isn't really happy he's here. He's gotten used to city living and a stepfather with an open wallet."

"You must have missed him, though."

"Grace and I split when he was nine. He loved it here then, but she insisted my schedule wouldn't allow me to be a good single dad and convinced the court she was right."

"What do you do?"

Had it really been that long since he'd seen her? He took a bite of pie, savoring the tart fruit tamed with sweetness, before sipping his coffee.

"I'm an outfitter." Kiss of death to most women. Grace had pretended to be okay with it, but then he found his absences were only a convenience so she could hook up with anyone who struck her fancy. Not the most faithful sort, his ex. But he supposed he deserved what he'd gotten.

"Never pictured you as the type to haul men out in the woods to shoot poor defenseless animals."

He gave her a sharp glance, but she was grinning.

"I don't take them unless they have a plan for the meat. They can either get it butchered here and shipped home or donate it to those who need the food. If all they want is a head and a rack, they can find someone else."

"It must keep you away from home a lot in the fall."

"And spring. And summer. I take folks fishing, as well. That's the most peaceful. Whole families come to experience the outdoors. Trevor used to come with me when he could on those. He's actually a pretty good horseman."

"But not Grace."

"No."

The sound of conversation and laughter sprinkled over them as people visited between tables and kidded Mae, who gave it right back to them with gusto. Chairs scraped as a group got up. A meaty hand landed on his shoulder and he turned.

"Hey, Jim," he said, nodding at the sheriff.

"Hey, Nick. I just thought I should let you know. Ronan Smith's back in town. He's got a cabin up north of town, edge of the Bob."

"He still trapping?"

"Yep. Came in and made sure I knew all his permits were in order."

"I wish he'd picked somewhere else to go."

"You and me both. Maybe he'll just stick to himself and forget all about you."

"Yeah. Thanks, Jim. I'll keep an eye out."

Jim gave him another tap on the shoulder, nodded at CJ, and left the coffee shop.

"What was that all about?" CJ asked.

Nick turned back to his pie and dug into another piece. Somehow it had lost its flavor, tasting more like sawdust. Nonetheless, he chewed slowly, trying to think of the best way to explain.

"Ronan's a trapper."

"So I gathered." She shifted on the stool, leaning back against the wall behind her to give him her full attention. Somehow during his exchange with Jim, she'd polished off her slice of pie.

"Liked it?" he asked, nodding at the clean plate.

"Yeah." Her smile was like the sunrise on the eastern plains. "Who knew my old friend Trish would grow up to be such a fabulous baker?"

"Baker, mover and shaker," Mae interjected as she topped off their coffees. "If there's volunteering to be done, she's always first in line. You may remember her husband, Brad Small."

"He played a mean game of basketball, I think," Nick said. "Well over six foot. Totally wrong name." He chuckled.

"He's an accountant, does Rotary, coaches basketball, all the rest of it. Nice guy." Mae whisked off as a new group came in and headed toward one of the open booths.

"So the trapper ..." CJ said.

Even in high school she'd been persistent.

"He was trapping out of season in places he shouldn't have been. I reported him to FWP. He was pissed and threatened to get even."

"Nice guy."

"Yeah. As long as he obeys the law and stays away from me, we'll be just fine." He gulped his coffee halfway down. It was time to get a move on if he wanted to get anything done before he had to pick up his son.

"You know," she said softly. "I have an old camera I'd be willing to let Trevor use while he's here. It might make him feel more at home."

He put down the mug and looked at her. "You'd do that?"

"Sure. I can bring it to your place and show him how to use it."

"That'd be really nice. Thank you." He dug out his cell phone. "What's your number? I'll text you directions. Will Saturday work for you? About one?"

"Yes." She gave him the number. "See you then." Her voice was soft, almost as if she still cared.

"Yeah. Thanks again." He threw some bills on the counter. "See you, Mae!" he yelled toward the back.

Chapter Seven

From Catherine's diary, April 1942:

"We're going to war. Every boy in our senior class has already talked to a recruiter and will leave for basic training after graduation. I tried talking to Mom and Dad about joining the Women's Army Auxiliary Corps, but they won't even give me the time of day. Mom keeps saying my place is here, preparing for when Stephen comes back after the war is over.

"That could be years! I can't just sit here and wait. I'll die!"

# # #

CJ had finally hit on a system of doing a first pass of office organization. With the help of a few extra boxes, she sorted papers into years. Once she had a little more of a handle on what was available, she'd call Trish to see if she could get an appointment with her husband to figure out what she had to keep and what she could safely shred.

"Any idea where Dylan is?" she asked Birdie when she'd finished her breakfast and rinsed her utensils.

"It's Jarod's turn to feed the cattle, so I imagine he's down in the barn, doing whatever chores his brother gave him. He usually finishes them as fast as he can so he can spend the afternoon painting."

"Thanks."

CJ bundled up against the weather. The January days had turned cloudy again, precursor to the minus-zero temperatures that usually hit at the beginning of February. She shivered as she made her way to the barn. Flannel shirts helped some but not enough against the raw humidity of approaching snow.

The barn door creaked as she opened it. Probably another thing on Jarod's to-do list. She should help them out—she could certainly oil a door. The odors of horses kept too long indoors and aging hay tickled her nose, bringing on a sneeze.

"Who's there?" Dylan called from the back of the barn.

"CJ." She made her way back to where he was tallying calving supplies. The mothers would start dropping the end of February, and calves would need to be found and tagged soon afterward. They'd also help along any who were struggling.

She'd forgotten all about calving season. For her first seventeen years, it had been part of the ritual of the year, giving it structure, like the first and last days of school. Now it was as unfamiliar as the sight of Humvees and tanks had been when she first dropped into a war zone.

"How's it going?" Dylan asked. "Come to help?" He gestured at the supplies with his clipboard.

Why not?

"Sure. What do you need?"

"You can either count or write."

She took the clipboard.

He flipped through bins, calling out names and amounts as he rapidly tallied the items they'd need. She was quiet as he worked; he didn't need her interrupting his rhythm.

"Thanks, sis," he said when he'd reached the bin at the end of the row. "That saved a bunch of time."

A warm glow infused her. It was good to feel useful.

"Coffee?" he asked.

"Sure." That would give her the opening she needed.

He led the way to the small space Jarod had set up as the barn office—a beat-up wooden desk, chair with one leg shorter than the rest, and, most importantly, a small fridge and coffeepot. Straw bales provided seating for guests.

She perched on one, pulled up her knees, and leaned against the rough wall. He filled a mug and handed it to her. She let the warmth seep into her chilled hands for a few minutes before taking a sip.

She almost spit it out.

Dylan was grinning at her. "It's an acquired taste," he said. "Jarod likes it strong."

"That's one word to describe it." She grinned.

It felt a little more like home.

"We've missed you," Dylan said. "It feels like we're complete again."

"But Cameron and Kaiden are gone."

"Yeah, but Cameron's only got a year left and Kaiden pops back a few times a year. You left and never came back."

His voice was tinged with pain.

"I thought you were fine without me," she said.

"We weren't." Dylan sipped his coffee without wincing. "You were ... are ... our older sister. It was funny. We all looked up to you but wanted to protect you at the same time. After you went to college, we couldn't do either. It's the natural way of things, but ..."

He let the unfinished sentence hang in the air.

"I'm sorry," she said. "I never realized."

"Yeah. I get it."

She stared at the opposite wall. She'd been important to her brothers. Her leaving hadn't been as easy for them as she'd thought it was. She could see it now: a jigsaw puzzle with a few key pieces missing—her parents and the oldest sibling. No matter what she did in the future, she was going to have to take that into consideration.

"What do you care about?" she asked.

"What do you mean?" He shifted on his bale of hay. Even when he wasn't around, it was clear that the desk chair was Jarod's.

"I have to go to a therapist because of Ben's death. Now I have to do this assignment that makes no sense to me. I'm not sure what you guys—I mean, I love you and all that—but I have to ask each of you what you care about."

"Oh."

God, that sounded awful. She was only asking them what they felt because of a therapist.

"That didn't come out right. I mean ... I'm interested in how you feel, but it never occurred to me to ask."

She was pathetically terrible at this.

Dylan smiled. "It's okay. None of us are very good at this. I'm not sure Mom and Dad ever had an in-depth, honest conversation in their lives. I certainly never heard one. And with what Dad was doing ... well ..." He shrugged.

He was really kind, her brother.

"So what do I really care about?" He took another sip of bad coffee and then set it down. Leaning forward, he said, "I care about our family. Yes, I think that most of all."

"But what about your painting? Your art?"

"Of course I care about that. And it will come. But if it were a choice between giving up a paintbrush or giving up any member of my family, it's easy for me. If anything happened ..." His voice choked. "I'm not sure I'd be able to paint again anyway. My family, our home, it is my heart."

He stopped talking.

Stunned by his passion, she couldn't move. How had she never seen this much depth in Dylan? She'd always thought of him as a bit flakey with his paints and long jaunts into nature.

How well did she even know any of them?

"Listen, CJ, I'm not trying to put you down. You asked me how *I* feel, and I'm telling you."

"Do you think the others feel the same way?" Her insides felt really, really small.

"Honestly, I can't tell you. Like I said ..." He gave a wry smile. "None of us know how to have a real, honest conversation with each other. Maybe not anyone."

The last comment hit her like a fist in her gut. Had she and Ben ever had a real conversation? Or had she been so afraid of losing him that she'd told him what she thought he wanted to hear?

She beat back the tears in her eyes. How much had she missed out on by staying away for seventeen years?

"Anyway," he said, standing and sticking his cup on the tray next to the pot. "Thanks for your help. It's a gift. I can get to my painting an hour early." He leaned forward and kissed her cheek. "Love you, sis."

"You, too." She stayed on the bale as he left, unable to move. Apparently Geraldine Morgan was more insightful than she'd given her credit for. Would things have been different in her marriage if she'd been able to speak the truth not only to Ben but to herself? Would they even have gotten married?

The only time her truth came out was when Ben had shredded every last bit of dignity she had. She'd seen the way other journalists slid their eyes her way when she walked in on conversations not meant for her ears. The first time he'd strayed,

83

she'd answered tit for tat, figuring that had been her mother's mistake. She had to make him feel *exactly* what she had. The depth of the betrayal.

She'd picked up on an older reporter's flirt. She'd felt dirty every second she spent in his bed, so she'd ended it after the first night. But still, every time she'd seen him afterward, he'd greeted her with a smirk. It took two weeks before Ben had discovered her affair and their fight had been loud and explosive.

Who had she become?

Not the big sister Dylan remembered.

She rested her head on her knees and let herself cry for the young girl she'd been.

# # #

"Don't forget, CJ's coming at one," Nick said to his son. "Your English homework needs to be done before she arrives."

Trevor rolled his eyes. "Can't you believe I'll get it done? I always get it done."

"Just like you did all week?"

"I got it done. Not when the teacher wanted, but ..."

"Not good enough."

"Mom never cared."

"I do."

"So you say." Trevor pushed himself away from the table and stood.

"What's that supposed to mean?"

"Nothing." Trevor stalked down the hallway.

Nick shook his head and removed the plates from the table and gave them a quick wash. Would CJ be any better at talking to his son than he was? It wouldn't take much. But he needed some kind of breakthrough. After a week of battling his son to get to school, often late, his respect for his parents had grown substantially.

Had he been this bad?

If he had, how had they done it? He was going to need to spend a lot more time picking his parents' brains. And his brother's. Henry was a lot closer to the world kids lived in today. How would Trevor react to a trip to Valier to see his uncle?

Probably not well. Close to an hour travel through the same small towns he had passed from the airport. But still, Henry was family. And Trevor needed to become part of it.

The boy was his son. But could he be a good enough father?

"Hello?" CJ's voice called from the half-open door from the mudroom.

Was she expecting to find a naked man in his living room?

"C'mon in," he called back as he walked to the hallway. "Trevor," he called down. "CJ's here."

"Already?" Trevor's door popped open. "I'm not done with my homework."

"We'll wait," he said.

"I could finish it tomorrow," Trevor tried.

"Nope. That's not the deal."

"Homework?" CJ said as she walked into the living room on stocking feet.

"Yep."

"You drive a hard bargain."

"I was a teenager once. I remember." He grinned at her.

She grinned back. Then she wiggled her toes. "Nice floor."

"It's thermal heated."

"I like it." She came farther into the living room. "Wow," she said, looking around. "It's just like we imagined when we had ...

um ... plans for the future."

Her comment shocked him into giving his home a second look. She was right. As teens, they'd spent hours planning their adult life, including the kind of house they'd build. He gestured toward the large window overlooking the valley before it rose again to climb to the mountains.

"Wow," she said as she came up next to him.

Shit. He thought he'd created a home for Grace, but he'd made the one he and CJ had dreamed about instead. No wonder his ex had accused him of still carrying a torch.

He glanced over at CJ.

Close. She was too close. All he wanted to do was reach his son, not rekindle an old love affair. In fact, if he wanted anything, it was to have CJ forgive him for his long-ago transgression. But it wouldn't be fair to her to even bring it up.

And what was the point? It was ancient history—an event that still gnawed at his sense of self-worth.

"I'm done!" Trevor pounded down the hallway.

"Hi." CJ stepped away from Nick and smiled. "How are you doing?"

"Okay." Trevor gave a quick glance at Nick, then returned his gaze to CJ.

She held up a camera.

"I found this when I was clearing out drawers in my bedroom. I used it when I was your age."

"Is it digital?"

She laughed, a light musical sound that woke something inside him. "Nope."

"Oh." His face fell.

"They didn't make good digital cameras back then. There are still some journalists who swear by film."

"But where would you get it developed?" Trevor asked.

"There are specialized shops that do good work. Of course, it's not useful for news, the turnaround is too slow, but for fine prints and artwork, nothing beats film. And if you can shoot in black and white, you'll understand the basics of composition."

"I shoot in black and white ... with my digital camera back home."

"Ah," she said. "Good for you. Now, let's see what you can do."

"Where are we going?" he asked.

"Outside."

"There's nothing out there."

"There's light and shadow. And we'll bring your father along as a subject for study."

Trevor shot him a look as if doubting he were worthy enough for his observance.

Nick struck a pose.

Yep, this was going to be a very strange afternoon. He just hoped it worked.

The three of them trudged out into the bright end of January sun. For the first time Nick looked, really looked, at the crisp shadow thrown by the barn on the glistening snow, how the sun shown on the boards, creating small crevices of darkness along some of the warped boards.

There'd be work in the spring, but he could see what CJ was getting at. Who knew shadows could have so many grades of black?

"Okay," she said. "Where is the sun?" she asked Trevor.

"In the sky," he replied with a smirk.

"Ha. Ha. Where in the sky, smarty?"

He looked up and pointed to the southwest.

"Yep. This far north, the winter sun is always going to be a little south of us, so a photographer has to account for that. The light is low on the horizon. The shadows are going to be harsher and hit a person's face in a way that can distort their features. Sometimes we can intentionally use that."

"Okay." Trevor sounded dubious.

"We're going to use every shot in this roll of film. But you're only going to change one thing at a time. Nick, if you could come sit over here." She pointed to the stump he used to split wood. "Face the south directly."

He complied.

She handed the camera to Trevor and pulled out a notebook and pencil. "The film speed is 400." She made a note. "Do you know how to find the f-stop and the shutter speed?"

"No. I'm not really sure what those are."

Nick stared out at the horizon as CJ explained the workings of the camera to his son. She was a good teacher, patient and listening. She would have been a good mother, too. So many missed opportunities. Was there a way to make them up now? Could he give back to her what he'd taken away? Would she even give herself a chance to trust him again?

Did he want a second chance for her, or for himself? He'd tried with Grace. He really had. But he was small-town Montana and she was big-city glamor. He'd never had the desire for money and status that had driven her soul. He'd thought he could give her enough, but it was only after several years of trying that he realized there would never be enough in Grace's life.

And what about the boy, his son? If he got too close to CJ, would Trevor suffer when she left, which she inevitably would? He had to be realistic. Second chances existed only in mythology and on the Hallmark Channel. By their mid-thirties, both he and CJ were firmly set on their paths in life. Not that they couldn't change but that they probably wouldn't.

So she would leave.

"Okay." CJ's voice intruded on his thoughts. "Stop scowling, Nick. You look like that Midwestern farmer with a pitchfork."

He turned the edges of his lips up.

"Marginally better," she said, turning to Trevor. "Now, get his face in the viewfinder. Just his face—that's where you're going to get the best shadows and light. He's got wonderfully sharp features."

She made him feel like a scarecrow—Ray Bolger in the *Wizard of Oz*. He suppressed the urge to get up and do a song and dance number, but his lips stretched further into a smile. He'd forgotten how much CJ used to bring out his silly side.

She wasn't the only one who'd lost because of his boneheaded move.

"Now, take the picture. Good. I should have brought a tripod. It would have made this easier. Oh well. Now you're going to change one thing at a time and take another picture. Tell me what you're changing and I'll write it down."

"You mean like f-stop or speed?"

"Yep."

Trevor gave her the new f-stop and began to crank away at the pictures. As he went, he was more and more at ease with the camera and language. His shoulders began to relax and there was a hint of happiness.

Nick's heart warmed.

"I think I got to the end of the film," he said. "Can you check?" He held out the camera to CJ.

She took it and looked through the viewfinder, automatically putting her finger on the shutter. After a second, her hand shook and she thrust the camera back at Trevor. "You're right. We'll take it back inside to unload it. It's too bright out here." She turned away, her face wan underneath her deep tan.

What the hell had just happened?

Chapter Eight

Blood. So much blood. Ben's lifeless body crumpling in front of her.

No! Not now. She was home.

Open your eyes. Look. Mountains. Sky. Snow.

Breathe. In. Out. In. Out.

Montana air. Crisp, clean, and a little on the thin side.

She was safe. The past was done. It wasn't happening again.

"You okay?" The touch on her arm made her jerk away.

She refocused her eyes.

Nick.

Another face from a long time ago. A time she'd tried to forget.

God. So much in her life to forget.

"Yeah. Fine. I'm fine." She took another deep breath. "Just—" She waved her hand in the air. "—stuff."

"Cup of coffee?" he asked.

"That'd be nice. Thanks."

"Hey, Trevor, we're going inside for a bit. Coming?"

"In a moment." Trevor handed the camera to his father before going toward the corral. A buckskin horse stood at the railing, eyeing the boy. Tentatively, Trevor held out his gloved hand. Dusty sniffed it then whickered.

"Dusty remembers me!" Trevor shouted to them, looking like the young boy he must have been before teenage angst took hold.

"Yeah," Nick shouted back with a smile.

She took them both in. If only she could use a camera again, she'd want to capture this moment—the pure joy on the boy's face and the deep love on his father's. This is what she'd tried to create in her village scenes in the desert: the common love parents and children have for each other, no matter where they may call home.

They'd been her best work. She'd known it in her bones.

"He'll come in when he's ready. It's good to see him interested. That's the best I've seen him all week. Thank you."

"I enjoyed it," she said as they entered the mudroom.

"You're good at it." He opened the main door and walked across to the kitchen section, putting the camera on the dining table on the way. Grabbing a fresh mug from the rack on the wall, he poured coffee and handed the mug to her before refilling his own.

Still a gentleman. The mug announced, "Save the Bob!"

"Do you spend much time in the Bob Marshall Wilderness?" she asked.

"As much as I can. The fishing there is better than anywhere else, and the silence is supreme."

"They've managed to keep out anything motorized then?"

"It's touch-and-go all the time." He shook his head. "The battle is never quite over. Every five years or so, someone decides the possibility of oil is worth more than the certainty of what it will do to the land. And we've got precious little of it left."

"Ah, progress. You never were a big fan."

"Nope. Although, I do have to admit, I *am* fond of a nice, warm shower." His smile was slow and easy.

"I can't disagree with you on that one."

"Showers were hard to come by in the desert?" He gestured to the couch.

She sat herself on the far end, taking up as little room as possible.

He took the other end.

"Yes," she said. "Sponge baths were the norm unless we made it back to a city with a strong business population. And those were few and far between." She'd spent the last decade dirtier than she cared to think about most of the time.

"Listen, CJ, before Trevor comes in, I want to get something off my chest."

Oh god. He was going to apologize. Then she'd have to forgive him.

She wasn't sure she had it in her.

Nope. Definitely not ready to forgive him—or anyone else for that matter. Not her father for betraying her mother, not her mother for being so weak she just hid away and died, and definitely not Ben for cheating on her over and over.

Last but not least, she wasn't ready to forgive herself for not having the courage to face the past and move on. Instead, she'd let it control her.

"Let's not talk about this," she said.

"We need to," he insisted.

"No. *You* need to. As far as I'm concerned, the past is the past. Water under the bridge and all that. Today is a new day. We can start from now." She pasted a bright smile on her face.

He shook his head.

"I don't buy that for a minute," he said.

"Well, it's all I'm selling," she said.

He stared at her for a few moments.

"Look," she said when the silence began to scratch at her skin, "maybe I should just go."

"No," he said, pinning her with his dark brown eyes. "Forget I said anything, okay? You're right. It happened a long time ago. We should—"

"Dad!" Trevor burst through the door. "When can I ride

Dusty?"

"How about we saddle them up tomorrow and take them down to that trail south of here that should be pretty snow free?"

"Cool!" Trevor looked at CJ. "Want to come? You can teach me more about photography."

He was so earnest, so young. So close to the age she'd been when she realized adults weren't anywhere close to perfect.

That knowledge could wait a little longer for Trevor.

"Sure. It's been a while since I've been on a horse, but it can't be that different from a camel, right?"

"You rode a camel?"

"Once or twice." It was an experience she opted to avoid as much as she could. Camels were nasty, spiteful creatures that'd as soon take a head off than give a ride.

"Cool," Trevor repeated. He picked up the camera from the table. "Did you take the film out yet?"

"No."

He held it out to her. "Can you show me how?"

She eyed it as if it were a baby viper. If she didn't look through the viewfinder, maybe she could stay present instead of tripping back to one of the worst nights of her life. She took it and flipped to the back, her hands automatically performing the rituals of winding the film back into the cartridge and popping the back. All the while, she explained to Trevor what she was doing as he hung over her shoulder. His nearness seemed to make it okay—as if his youth were a magic amulet to protect her.

"I'll send it in to the Great Falls processing company on Monday," she said.

"You don't have to do that," Nick said. "I'll take care of it."

"No." She smiled at him. "This has been a good afternoon, maybe the best one I've had in a while. It's my way of saying thank you. Besides, you're stuck with a rookie on a horse tomorrow, remember?"

"I doubt you've forgotten how to ride."

"We'll see," she said, a tease in her voice. As long as they didn't talk about serious stuff or stuff in the past, it would be fun.

Just like settling into a dentist's chair for a nice, long, root canal.

# # #

CJ met Nick and Trevor at the designated trailhead the next morning around ten. Jarod had frowned when she'd told him she wasn't going to church but at least this time he didn't try to convince her to change her mind.

The sun was bright, a high-pressure system keeping the next band of winter storms and cold hunkered down on the far side of the Rockies. It was the kind of day when she used to insist she didn't need to wear a jacket as a kid, but now she was too willing to bundle up. With her luck, she'd be ready to deal with Montana chill about the time Max decided she was well enough to send back to the desert.

"Hi," Trevor said, notably less enthusiastic about the ride than he'd been the day before.

"Who bit you in the ass?" she said without thinking.

"CJ!" Nick said, leading a dark bay with thick hair toward her.

"Oops," she said, trying to grin to cover her embarrassment. "Forgot where I was."

"It's cool," Trevor said. "I hear stuff like that all the time."

"You do?" Nick asked. "Does your mother talk like that?"

"Huh? Mom? Have you met her? No, just kids I know." Trevor scowled and shuffled toward where Dusty was hitched.

Nick looked at her and raised an eyebrow.

"Don't look at me. I'm not used to being around kids."

"Never wanted to have any of your own?"

"Nope," she said, spinning it with an end-of-discussion tone. That particular dream had gone to pieces when he'd chosen the ice queen, but she'd never let him know that.

Never.

"So where are we going?" she asked.

"Southwest. There's a nice stretch of the foothills in the sun enough that if the snow has a chance to melt, it does." He glanced at Trevor, who was staring at the horse as if trying to determine how to get on. "I better go help."

"Yeah." She watched him walk away. *Damn.* He'd always had a fine ass, and aging hadn't diminished that one bit.

"Well, horse," she said to the bay, "it's you and me to figure this out again."

The mare turned her head to examine CJ, then dismissed whatever she saw and went back to staring straight ahead.

"Yeah, right." She looped the reins over its neck and twisted the stirrup to face her. Jabbing her toe into the stiff leather hole, she swung up and threw her leg over the saddle. Mercifully, she'd given herself the right spin and didn't fall to the other side.

The cold leather creaked as she adjusted her body to the unfamiliar saddle. What ever happened to hers? Probably sitting dusty in the tack room. She'd loved that saddle. Her brothers had chipped in to get it for her one Christmas, choosing one with tooled design, a real girly saddle.

She smiled in remembrance. As much as she fought for her right to be one of the guys back then, she'd begun to realize there were advantages to being a woman, especially if she could bring out a look of adoration from a teenage boy. Her gaze flicked to

Nick. Mercifully, the pang of lost love didn't stab her in the chest.

Being around him was going to be okay, like building scar tissue over an old wound.

She walked the horse over to Nick and Trevor.

"What's her name?" she asked.

"Huh?" Nick turned, his brow in a frown.

"Whoa," she said, causing the horse to come to an abrupt halt. "I didn't mean you," she added to the horse. "I meant him."

The horse nickered.

She could become real fond of this animal.

"The horse," she said. "What's her name?"

"Oh. Star."

"Star? She doesn't have any white patches."

The horse shook her head.

"Yeah. She likes to be the star of the show." The grin on Nick's face erased all the shadow from his scowl.

It returned when he looked back at his son. "Are you getting on that horse or what?"

Trevor's eyes flicked back and forth between his father and Dusty. In that moment, CJ knew what the problem was.

"Hey, Nick," she said, sliding off Star. "Why don't you get ready to take the trail? Trevor and I will join you in a moment."

He hesitated, but she held his gaze steady.

"Okay," he said and stalked off.

"Been a while?" she asked Trevor.

"Yeah."

"It'll come back. It's been years for me, too. As soon as you're in the saddle, the muscle memory will go to work." She gestured to the clear, sunny sky. "It's a beautiful day for a ride—almost perfect. Between the heat the horse gives off and the sun, you'll be toasty warm. We're just going to walk the horses—I'm not ready

97

to do anything more than that. Got your phone with you?"

"Yeah. But there's no reception here. I already checked."

"No, but there *is* a camera in it. You can still work on composition, even if there aren't any fancy settings."

Trevor smiled for the first time that morning.

"Let's go over to that rock. It'll be easier to get on that way." Without waiting for an answer, she led Dusty to the perch. "I'll hold him. Hop up."

He climbed on the rock, stared at the horse one more time, his fingers trembling a little as he reached for the horn on the saddle. Then he hoisted himself up. The movements lacked grace but got the job done.

She handed him the reins and remounted Star.

"Let's go." She clicked her tongue and squeezed her legs and Star ambled toward where Nick was mounted on a tall, black gelding, Trevor and Dusty following.

"I suppose that horse's name is Black," she said with a grin.

"Almost. Blackie."

She laughed. "Glad you didn't use up all your imagination on your horses' names," she said.

"You always were a"—Nick glanced at Trevor—" a pain."

She laughed again, a little bubble of joy bursting from a hidden cache deep inside her. "You gonna take us somewhere, trail boss, or are we going to stand around jawing all day?"

A strangled noise made her look at Trevor. The grin on his face said he was enjoying her takedown of his father. She smiled at him.

Score one for the good guys.

Nick turned Blackie and headed down the trail. CJ gestured for Trevor to follow while she brought up the rear.

The click of the horses' shoes against hidden rocks dominated the still air as they moved south single file down the short trail that led to an old forest service road. Every so often, a raven or magpie swept through the branches of the aspens that surrounded them, its ebony wings glistening black blue in the sunlight. The sway of the mare lulled CJ almost to a point of peaceful lassitude, a point where her hypervigilance softened and almost disappeared. Her eyelids drifted down.

Pushing all memories and futures aside, she surrendered to the present—the warmth of the sun on her shoulders, the rhythm of the saddle, the clinks and clanks of riding gear. In a far-off tree, a woodpecker pounded for beetles, and a snippet of breeze brushed her cheek.

She sighed and shook herself awake as Nick turned onto the broader road the forest service had carved in the wilderness. He paused and gestured for them to come forward.

"How you dudes doing?" he asked with a grin. "Wouldn't want to bring you back all saddle sore. Bad for my reputation."

"It's dudette to you, mister," she said in mock seriousness. "And compared to a camel saddle, this is a piece of cake."

"I'm okay," Trevor said as he shifted on Dusty. There was a healthy flush to his cheeks that hadn't been there when they started, but his enthusiasm had waned again.

"Maybe a half hour more and we turn back?" Nick asked.

"Sounds good," she said.

"Okay," Trevor mumbled.

He was trying; she'd give him that.

"So what'd you do in Seattle?" she asked him as they rode abreast down the road.

"Went to school, played video games. You know, the usual."

"I never got into the video game thing. Two of my brothers dabbled, and the youngest had to be pried away from them for

99

supper."

"How many brothers do you have?" Trevor asked.

"Four. But I'm the oldest. I got to boss them around."

Nick chuckled. "They let her think that."

"Wow," Trevor said. "That's a lot." He looked at Nick. "And you just have Uncle Henry."

"Right. Grandma and Grandpa stopped with me. They knew when they were licked."

"That's for sure," she muttered.

"Hey. I heard that."

"Nice to know you're not deaf."

He groaned.

"So'd you see bad stuff? In the war, I mean." Trevor's voice was respectful.

"Sometimes. But other times, it was nice. The desert has its own beauty. And the people? When they aren't shooting at us, they're just like us, trying to feed their families and have a little fun along the way."

"Doesn't sound like they're like us if they're trying to kill us."

"Yeah ... I get that." How did one explain the entangled mess of the world to a thirteen-year-old? Hell, adults didn't really understand it.

"Whoa," Nick said and pointed to the road ahead.

A big bull elk stood stiff-legged, eying them from beneath a six-point rack that made her head hurt looking at it. His coat was dark and full but marred with a number of dark patches where he'd been wounded during rutting season.

"Tough year, huh, buddy?" Nick said softly.

Dusty danced a little bit.

"Try to stay still," Nick said to Trevor.

"I am."

"Is your phone handy?" CJ asked him.

"Yes, but ..." Trevor lifted the reins in his hands.

"Wrap them around the horn," Nick said. "Dusty'll stay."

Trevor did as he was told, then slowly pulled the phone from his jacket pocket.

Amazingly, the elk stayed where he was. It would have been an amazing shot, but her camera was packed away in her room and she hadn't yet tried taking pictures with her phone. If she did and got spooked again, it would ruin Trevor's shot.

Best to let things be.

She glanced at Nick, and he smiled at her, a full, deep smile of a contented man. Whatever he'd been through to get here, it was obvious he'd landed where he was meant to be.

Maybe someday she could say the same.

# # #

Nick's former girlfriend was just what his son needed to ease the pain of being yanked from his home. It was as about as perfect a Montana day as it got. Spending time in the outdoors, away from the problems of the world, a magnificent animal posing for them. Damn. It was good to be alive.

The only thing that would make the day better would be if he could erase the haunted sadness in CJ's eyes.

"Got it," Trevor said. "No one in Seattle is going to believe this." His thumbs flew over the surface of his phone then abruptly stopped. "Crap. No service."

"Language," Nick said dutifully, although he wasn't really upset. From what he'd heard on the trail, he knew the norms.

"Sorry," Trevor said automatically.

Suddenly, the elk lifted his head and sniffed the air. Ears

101

twitched in different directions and then he took off down the mountain at a rapid trot. The muscles rippled under the tight skin. Amazing that a creature with such crazy proportions could move with so much grace.

"Turn back?" he asked.

"Sounds good," CJ said.

They were silent on the way back down the trail. He wasn't really thinking, just feeling the satisfaction of a morning well lived. It was the kind of thing he'd hoped he could instill in his son. Maybe he still had that chance, although his conversation with Grace hadn't been hopeful.

"He can stay with you until summer," she'd told him. "Maybe you can knock some sense into him. Then I'll take him back for a trial period, see if you've done anything good."

"He's not a car you can try out then return to the dealership," he'd told her, barely holding his temper in check. "He's our son."

"Exactly. That means he needs to behave like my son, not running god knows where all over the city, taking pictures that ... well, they're depressing. All black and white and gloomy. Why can't he be normal and take pictures of girls, for god's sake? Shit. He takes pictures of guys. Do you think he's gay?"

The horror in her voice told him it was not going to be acceptable if their son had an alternative sexuality. And it would no doubt be his fault that Trevor was defective in her eyes.

How had he ever thought she was right for him?

It was going to take a powerful amount of love to make up for whatever self-esteem busting tactics his ex had employed on their child.

He glanced over to CJ. She was similarly wounded. Maybe that's why she could break through to Trevor. Could he enlist her support without getting emotionally entangled with the woman he'd once loved?

"Say," he said to her as he led Star to the trailer. The mare insisted on being in the nose of the vehicle. Standing behind any other horse simply wasn't in her wheelhouse. "I wanted to thank you for helping out with Trevor." He glanced at his son, who was dancing around, waving his arm in the air, trying to get a signal.

"No problem," she said. "He's a good kid. He's just thirteen."

"Yeah. I know." They shared a look that expressed more than words could.

"It was fun," she said. "Probably good for me, too. Got me away from Jarod's disapproving looks for a morning."

"He that hard?"

She shrugged. "I think part of him is stuck in the 1800s. You know, when families stayed together and women weren't out risking their lives in war zones."

He chuckled. "I don't think you've been easy on any of your brothers."

"Probably not."

He searched for the right words then decided to simply ask. "The snow geese should be coming back to Freezeout Lake soon. I'd like to take Trevor so he could see it, maybe take pictures. It'd be nice if you could come. Maybe you could get some good shots, too."

She stiffened.

Shit.

"I'd be happy to help Trevor—I can bring the camera. But as for taking pictures myself ..." She looked off to the west, as if seeking the answer she needed in the rugged peaks. "It depends on ... well ... it just depends."

The agony in her voice almost broke his heart.

Chapter Nine

From Catherine's diary, March 1943:

"I have to do something. Stephen's at the front, fighting the enemy. He can't tell me where he is, but many battles are being fought in Africa. Africa! I hope he stays safe. I will pray every day for that.

"Mom and Dad are being unreasonable. I told them I wanted to go to Seattle to help in the war. Holy cow! Dad launched into his 'no daughter of mine' speech. Mom didn't say much. Maybe I have an ally there. Don't they understand I can't sit by and not do anything to help? This is our country's war. Everyone has to pitch in.

"Janice told me she's working on her parents to let her go to Great Falls and work in the copper plant. If she goes, maybe I can convince them our boys need copper more than I need to help out at the library."

# # #

Monday morning CJ arrived at Gerry's office for her appointment. She was a week closer to getting back to work. She had to be.

"Here you are," she said as she handed the therapist the papers she'd filled out—mostly insurance forms. The bureau had offered all of them the ability to buy into a group plan, much cheaper than individual insurance would have been. Good thing. Therapy didn't come cheap.

"Thank you." Gerry gestured to the couch and CJ took her perch.

"Have you thought about what we discussed last time?"

"I talked to Dylan about what he cares about," CJ said, smiling. One ticky mark on her report card.

"And?"

"And? Oh. He cares about family."

"I see. And how does that make you feel?"

Feel?

"Fine. Family's great."

"It's just not your top priority," Gerry pressed.

"Well, I wouldn't put it like that."

"How would you put it then?"

Wow, this nice, pleasant-looking woman sure knew how to go for the jugular. What was family anyway? The people you sent Christmas presents to every year? The people who had to take you in?

She looked up at Gerry. The therapist waited with her hands folded over her legal pad.

Didn't these people know when to move on?

No other words came from Gerry's lips.

Guess not.

"They're my brothers and I love them. If they need me, I'll be there. It's as simple as that," she finally said.

"Do you think that's what Dylan meant?"

He'd always hoped to spend much of his time at the nation's parks and monuments, as a sort of artist-in-residence. Instead, he'd stayed in rural Montana to help out on the family ranch.

"Probably not. He stayed. I left."

"And Jarod?"

Jarod had been a top-notch cattle roper with dreams of

winning at the national rodeo. Now he was a rancher ... and still single. Given how the girls had hung on him in high school, it was odd he wasn't married.

"He stayed, too. We have an arrangement—all of us. The ranch is incorporated, and we're all owners. Dylan and Jarod get salaries on top of profits. We also pay Birdie and any other ranch costs. If and when Jarod gets married, he gets the ranch house for his family."

"Very businesslike."

"Yes. It was my idea," she said with pride. "I *do* care about my family," she added.

"Mm-hmm." Gerry made a few notes.

What in hell was she writing? Weren't the answers correct?

She kept quiet. Two could play this game, and she'd been in journalism long enough to know when to stop talking.

"So what does Jarod care about?"

"I ... um, haven't gotten around to asking."

"Don't you see him?"

"Every day." Her interactions with her closest sibling in age were polite, but he didn't ask anything of her and she didn't offer. It was as if there were an international border wall between them and neither of them had any idea how to get around it.

"So what are you doing with yourself? Helping out at the ranch? Taking pictures? Do you have any I can look at?"

"Actually, I've been helping out an old friend with his son."

"Oh? Tell me more."

CJ outlined how she'd run into Nick a few times and he'd confided his son had been abruptly dumped in his lap. "I connected with Trevor somehow and showed him how to use some advanced photography techniques." She omitted the panic attack. It was temporary. She'd get over it somehow. Sheer willpower, if nothing else. Her mother had always told her she brought stubbornness to a new level. "We went riding, and he was lucky enough to get some great shots of a bull elk." She laughed when she remembered how excited he'd been with the reactions from his Seattle friends.

"Sounds like you had a good time," Gerry said.

"I did." *See*, she wanted to add, *I'm capable of doing perfectly normal activities.*

"And did you take pictures?"

"I didn't bring my camera."

"Why not?"

"Because I wanted to concentrate on Trevor's experience." Good thing she'd planned out that answer ahead of time.

"That was nice of you." A few more notes. "So how do you know Nick?"

"We went to high school together."

"Friends?"

It was a small town. Someone could easily mention her past status with Nick.

"We dated for a while. Then a new girl came to town and they got together." She forced a shrug. "It was just a high school thing. They never last, you know."

"Yes, it's hard to keep a relationship going when young people separate. So what happened to Nick? Who did he marry?"

"Uh, Grace."

"The girl he met in high school after you."

"Yeah." Why did it still hurt? Seventeen years had gone by. They'd been kids. Things happened. She should be over it by now.

She'd be fine as soon as she left town and repaired all the cracks she was developing in her emotional wall.

"And how does that make you feel?"

What was it with this woman and feeling?

"How does *what* make me feel?" CJ hardened her voice.

"Seeing Nick."

CJ shrugged again. "It doesn't make me feel anything. That was a long time ago. No big deal."

"Hmm."

"What?" The therapist was beginning to irritate her.

"I think, given your reactions, you feel *something*."

CJ went on the offensive. "Yes, I feel this is a waste of my time. I should be out there doing things to make the world a better place, not nursing a non-existent wound from my teenage years."

"Is that how you'd describe your father's death? Or your mother's?"

"I ... well, no ... but I've gotten past that, too. The past is just that—the past. I've got work to do. People are dying."

"So instead of internal peace, you've decided to tackle world peace."

It seemed like the easier problem of the two.

"I talked to plenty of therapists after my parents died. We all agreed it was sad, but life went on. Everyone's parents die."

"Oh, CJ, they do, but usually not at such a young age. Care to tell me exactly what happened?"

No.

Gerry waited.

CJ took the throw pillow from the edge of the couch, put it in her lap, and began to knead it.

"Dad had an accident out where 200 connects with 287. He was coming back from Lincoln. He spun out and hit a bridge. They said ..." She swallowed. "They said he didn't suffer.

"Mom already had cancer. They thought they'd caught it, but they didn't. She died a year later."

There. Satisfied?

"Was that before or after you broke up with Nick?"

"We broke up two days before my father died."

"Did he reach out to you?"

"I didn't want to see him."

"So you were alone."

"I have four brothers." She glared at Gerry. "And Birdie. I was a lot of things, but alone wasn't one of them."

"So being back home again, after an absence of almost two decades, isn't a problem."

"Nope."

"Then why haven't you picked up a camera?"

"There've been other things to do. I'm taking a little break, that's all." CJ put the pillow back where it had been, straightened her spine, and brushed off her jeans.

A chime dinged in the background.

"Well, that's the end for today. I'd like you to think about what we talked about today and get back to your other brothers on that question—what do they care about?"

"Sure." CJ stood and Gerry followed suit.

"And I'm still interested in some recent pictures. Maybe you could take some on one of your outings with Trevor."

"Yeah. See you next week."

The chill from the arctic air hit her as she closed the therapist's door behind her. She'd forgotten to zip up her coat, and frozen bits of cold sliced through her chest. She pulled the jacket closed and half-ran to the truck. Once she got there, she turned on the motor and let it run for a bit.

Had she helped or hurt her chances to get out of Choteau?

\# \# \#

CJ dumped another box on the floor. Sorting papers was not going to keep her occupied for the next three weeks. Three days of it had already gotten under her skin. She was used to being active, climbing in and out of vehicles, walking the town to talk to people or get candid shots.

On her way to the kitchen, she glanced outside. Jarod was working that horse, the one he'd gotten as a rescue. He had him on a halter and a lead and was patiently running him in circles, stopping and getting him to turn back in the other direction. The animal still tossed its head now and again but seemed to be settling down again.

"I'm going outside for a bit," she said to Birdie as she passed through the kitchen.

"Good. You're inside too much."

"It's cold outside."

"It's winter. You never used to complain."

No, she hadn't. When she was little, her parents could barely keep her inside. Life had been so easy then, but she hadn't had a clue.

She threw on her winter gear then stomped through the cold, crisp air. Nothing could beat the blue of a Montana winter sky. The low angle of the sun deepened the color as it reflected from the snow-covered prairies.

When she got to the corral, she leaned against the railing to watch her brother work. A flick of his eyes let her know he'd spotted her, but he continued doing what he'd been doing. A fountain of patience—at least when it came to animals.

And the horse was beautiful—muscles rippling under a deep bay coat that Jarod had brushed until it gleamed. Every action designed to familiarize the animal to Jarod's touch and smell, and associate that with care and love. Herd animals, horses needed companionship almost as much as humans.

Finally, he unhooked the lead. The horse stood quietly and waited. With a smile, Jarod pulled a plastic bag from his pocket and placed the contents on the palm of his hand. The horse scarfed down the apple pieces. Jarod patted his nose and whispered something she couldn't hear. The horse nickered and took off, racing like a greyhound chasing a rabbit on Florida's defunct dog tracks.

Jarod ambled over to the fence and ducked through to her side.

"Have you given him a name?"

"He came with one." Jarod wrinkled his nose in distaste. "Prince."

"Bit pretentious."

"Came from a pretentious home."

"What are you going to do with ... Prince?"

"Depends on how he works out." Jarod pulled the Bulldogs cap from his head, slapped it against his thigh, then slammed it back down, a gesture he'd been doing for as long as she could remember.

"He looks like he could be a good roping horse," she said softly.

Jarod looked at her sharply. "I thought that, too. He can certainly stop on a dime."

"Or barrel racing."

"Do I look like I'm likely to take up barrel racing any time soon?" He laughed, a very rusty sound.

She added her own chuckle. They stood together and watched the horse— Prince—perform his racing from one end to the other performance. And it was a performance. He tossed his head and pranced, all the while checking out that they were still watching.

A slow smile grew over Jarod's face. He almost looked content. Then he shook his head. "Got chores to do." He headed to the barn and she fell in step beside him, their boots crunching on the frozen mud.

"Any idea how much longer you're going to be here?" he asked.

"Still trying to get rid of me?"

"Nah. This is your home, CJ." The door squealed as he opened it. "Got to get some oil on these hinges."

"I'll take care of it for you."

"Bored?"

"A little," she confessed, leaning against one of the walls and letting the mix of aromas—oil, aging hay, manure, and age—wash over her. She'd loved coming in here as a child, finding the latest batch of kittens and playing with them before they became too feral to touch. Like the ranch house kitchen, it had been updated over the past century, but the bones of the original structure were in its walls.

"There is something you can help me with," Jarod said as he headed to the pile of pipes and fittings on the floor.

"Plumbing isn't in my skill set," she said.

"No, but tracking things down is," he said.

"What'd you lose?" Maybe she'd be sent on horseback to find a stray calf. That would be fun—as long as she bundled up. She could drag Nick and Trevor along with her.

"Tax receipt."

Paper. She was so sick of paper.

"The county should have a record. We can get them to print up another receipt."

"That's the problem. They don't. They're telling me we're

behind and adding fees."

"Cancelled check?"

"Nope." He shook his head ruefully. "I'd made a cattle sale and paid them in cash."

"Oh, Jarod, we talked about this when you took over the ranch. Never pay anything in cash."

"It just seemed easier than going through the bank and all that. I wrote it all down in the ledger—how much I got for the sale, how much the taxes were, and how much I put into petty cash."

"So we have a date."

"Yep."

"Well, I guess I can start there." She gestured to the corner room where he kept a desk and filing cabinet. "I guess you checked in there."

"Tore it apart three times."

"And your pockets."

"Yep. And you know Birdie double-checks everyone's clothes before she washes them."

"Birdie's still washing your clothes?" She'd done a load of her own laundry just a few days before.

"We've tried, but she insists we mess it up."

CJ chuckled. Birdie was as old-fashioned in her ways as Jarod was in his.

"Would you have thrown it in Mom's old office?"

"Nope. I've looked everywhere. I think we have to accept it's gone."

"Then I can't track it down."

"Guess not."

Her brother stared at the jumble of metal at his feet, looking the same as he had one Christmas day when a cheap toy someone had given him at school fell apart in his hands.

"It'll be a big dent in the ranch funds if we have to pay it again," he said. "It's been a long winter and it's not even calving season yet."

If the receipt was well and truly lost and the county had no record, it was going to be a tough sell to convince them otherwise. But she had to try.

"Okay, I'll look into it," she said.

"Thanks, sis." He crouched down and picked through the pieces before selecting two pipes and a fitting.

"What are you trying to do?" she asked.

"Make a watering system out to the corral and pasture in the back. The Ranchers Association had a guy from a conservancy group come in last fall to talk about keeping livestock, particularly cows, from the stream banks. Seems they cave in the banking, adding silt and making the rivers too warm for trout." He grinned, taking five years from his face. "And you know I like a good trout for dinner."

"Yeah."

"They gave us some money to fence it off and develop other ways of watering the animals. So that's what I'm trying to do here."

"Interesting."

He laid the pieces on a worktable next to a pump. "We dug wells last fall and put in piping, but it got cold before we could put in the pumps. I want to get these assembled so as soon as we get a thaw, we can start staging them out. Once that's working, we'll fence off the streams."

"Big project."

"Yeah."

She should probably ask him before she lost his attention to tubing and gadgets.

"What matters to you most?" she asked.

"What do you mean?" He looked up.

"What do you care about? What are you passionate about?"

He slipped off his hat as he considered. Once it had landed back on his head, he answered, "This." He waved his arm in a way that encompassed the whole ranch. "Our legacy. The land. We have to steward it and pass it along to the next generation."

"Why haven't you gotten married?"

"My, you're just full of tough questions today, aren't you?"

"Therapy," she muttered.

He leaned against the bench. "Not to slam you, but after you left, I felt I had to man up and take over. Birdie was great with the house, but there was a lot more than that. Mom had a ranch manager and he stayed on, but someone from the family needed to be in charge. So time, and dreams, slipped away." His gaze was steady on her.

A small bit of shame sent heat throughout her body.

"All the girls I knew went away or got married and started having babies." He shrugged. "It's a small town. Not many people move in. And fewer still have my conservative values. Like I've said, I'm an old-fashioned, churchgoing kind of guy. Women who want that lifestyle are few and far between."

"I'm sorry."

"It is what it is." Another shrug. "I say a prayer every week. Maybe someday it'll be answered." He gestured at the pile of pipe and tubing on the bench. "Meanwhile, I got work to do."

Translation: conversation closed.

"Yeah. Thanks. I'll get to work on those taxes."

"Okay." His back was already to her.

The door squeaked again as she left.

Chapter Ten

Friday morning, CJ got an email from the therapist explaining she would have to move the Monday appointment to the following Thursday.

Good thing she didn't have anything else to do.

"Sure," she wrote back. "I'll see you then." Maybe by that time she'd have one more answer, if Kaiden ever got around to replying to the email she'd sent him. She'd saved Cameron for last. It seemed too trivial a thing to ask while he was so far away from home, especially since the answer seemed to be obvious—he cared about his country.

Not that she didn't believe Jarod, but she gave her mother's old office a quick look to see if any recent papers had landed there. She also checked with Birdie, but the housekeeper hadn't pulled any receipts she hadn't already returned to Dylan or Jarod.

"Shouldn't they be doing their own laundry now?" CJ asked. "They're grown men."

"Exactly. They're too big to have underfoot. I like doing it. It helps give me purpose."

"I'll still do mine," she said.

"Of course."

CJ chuckled, grabbed a fresh cup of coffee, and headed back to the office. She'd make a little more headway, have a sandwich, then head into town to the courthouse. Somebody must have a record of that damned receipt.

She had just rinsed off her lunch plate a few hours later when the back door opened. Heavy boots clopped on the mudroom floor.

"Mail," Dylan sang out. "On the washer." Then the door thudded closed again.

Birdie brought it in. "A couple of things for you." She tossed two fat envelopes on the table and settled into a kitchen chair with the rest. Using one of the kitchen knives, she rapidly ripped through the envelopes, sorting as she went.

"Most of it's junk," the housekeeper remarked. "Don't get any good mail since that Al Gore invented the internet."

"Al Gore didn't invent the internet."

"I know. I just like to say that to get under your skin." Birdie flashed her a smile.

Somewhere, there was an evil bone in that woman's body. She didn't do it often, but she was an expert at needling someone in the right spot to get a reaction. Every time.

CJ rolled her eyes and stared at the envelopes. Clearly, one was full of Trevor's pictures. The other was an official-looking envelope with a foreign stamp and the return address of a London solicitor.

The pictures were safer.

She opened them.

They were good. Not professional good, but the kid had an eye and knew how to frame a picture. Ironically, that was the most important skill other than focus. Everything else could be fixed by computer.

"What do you have?" Birdie asked. "Your pictures?" Her voice was hopeful.

"No, Trevor's. Nick's son."

"Let me see."

CJ passed the photos over and picked up her phone.

CJ: Nick, I got Trevor's photos. How can I get them to

you?
Nick: I'll be in town to pick him up after school. Okay if I
drop by to pick them up?
CJ: I'm planning on going to town later. Text me when
you're there and I'll meet you.
Nick: OK

"Nice," Birdie said and passed back the bundle. "When are you going to start?"

"I'll get there."

"Uh-huh." The housekeeper pushed herself away from the table and opened the door to the cellar pantry. "I'm thinking meat loaf and mashed potatoes for dinner."

"Sounds good." CJ stared at her phone. Maybe if she used a different medium …

She flicked to the camera and focused on the rooster salt and pepper shakers that had been at the kitchen table since her mother was alive.

Her thumb hovered over the button.

In her mind's eye the ceramics exploded, dripping blood all over the worn oak table.

She dropped the phone.

The fat, white envelope would be an enemy, too.

Leaving both on the table, she went to the living room, picked up the latest diary she'd been reading, and settled into her favorite armchair.

From Catherine's diary, June 1943:

"They are allowing me to go. Finally! We all made the trek into Great Falls on Saturday, my father grumbling all the way

there and back about the condition of the roads and the noise of the city. What would he ever do in the great cities of the world like Chicago? (I'm going to go there some day.)

Dad approved the boardinghouse where Janice lives. He had to explore every inch and ask lots of questions before he did. The lady who runs the house, Mrs. Johnson, was very patient. Once Dad learned she knew his cousin George from up on the High Line, things went better. (I can't wait to get out of this state. It's like one big small town. Everyone knows everybody!)

That hadn't changed. She could sympathize with her grandmother. Everybody in Montana always seemed to be in each other's business. Great when someone needed help, annoying the rest of the time.

He also had to spend a half hour talking to the ˙plant supervisor. Holy cow! I didn't think I'd ever get the job. I start next week. I'm packing crates to ship off to the ports on the East Coast. I'm going to make 25 cents an hour. My own money! Dad says I'll need to learn to handle my own expenses, too. But I'll have enough for a lipstick or a movie now and then.

I wish they'd hurry up and defeat Germany so my Stephen can come home.

# # #

"What do you mean I can't have the truck?" CJ asked Jarod.

"Dylan needs it to truck hay to the south acreage," he replied.

"I thought you had the Ranger to do that," she said.

"It needs a part. It'll be here Wednesday." Jarod leaned against the driver's door of the vehicle in dispute. "You know, if you're going to be here much longer, you should probably think about getting something for yourself. Something the ranch doesn't depend on."

He shifted forward, yanked open the door of the truck, hopped in, and backed it to the stacks of hay huddled under a tin roof.

Great.

She stomped back to the house. How much longer was she going to be here? If she couldn't pick up a camera, she couldn't do her job, so what was the use fighting for it? She really should think about a vehicle of some kind—especially one with better gas mileage than the ranch truck.

Tossing the Carhartt jacket on its peg, she walked back through the kitchen. Birdie was sitting at the table, peeling potatoes, glued to another one of her talk shows. She grunted a hello and went on peeling.

CJ picked up her phone and the letter she'd left on the table and retreated to the living room.

CJ: Bad news. Truck's not available. I'm stuck here.

Nick: No problem. I'll swing by after I pick up Trevor. About an hour.

CJ: OK

She stared at the envelope then clicked to Craigslist. There had to be something cheap in town. She'd go to Great Falls if she had to, but that meant getting someone to go with her.

There weren't many listings, and most of them were for trucks or worn-out beaters on which the owner had finally given up. Then she spotted an ad that had gone up in the last twenty-four hours. A white Jeep Wrangler Sport only a few years old.

She called.

"Hello? I'm calling about the car."

"Well, that was fast. My son said it would be, but I've never done this before."

"So, is it still available?"

"Why, yes."

"I'd like to see it." Maybe Nick would give her a lift into town.

"Well, I'm home now. I will be tomorrow afternoon. After I do my shopping. I've been doing my shopping Saturday mornings for all my life, and I don't want to stop now."

Oversharing. Montanans developed it like a lost art.

"Of course. I'll try to make it to your house this afternoon. If not, tomorrow."

"That would be good. What is your name now?"

"CJ. CJ Beck."

"Ah, yes, I knew your mother. Sweet woman. Too bad she had to go like that. The cancer. It's a terrible thing."

"Yes."

"Okay. I'll see you when you get here, CJ. Is that like letters? Odd name for a girl. Of course, my girl, she liked to be called Bobbie. You must be a tomboy like her. So what does CJ mean?"

"It stands for Catherine Josephine—my grandmother's names."

"Oh. That's sweet. But I can understand. Too old-fashioned for today. What?" she muttered in the background. "Oh, okay. My son says I'm talking too long. I hope to see you later. You sound like a nice girl."

The call disconnected.

The white envelope mocked her.

All right.

She picked it up and went into her mother's office. She'd seen an elegant letter opener that seemed perfect for the occasion. Holding the hilt covered with carved hearts, she slit open the envelope. The edge must have been dull, because it hung up on the heavy paper. With an angry gasp, she tore the last bit open with her fingers and yanked out the sheaf of documents.

After scanning the letter on the top, she sank into the office chair and read more slowly. It sounded like she was suddenly very rich. The papers underneath were directives she had to fill out and sign—preferably after seeing a financial advisor and estate attorney—to indicate where the money should go.

She'd never known Ben was that rich.

And she'd never felt guiltier in her life. She hadn't been a good wife to the man she'd sworn to love for the rest of their lives, even in the short time they'd been together. Instead of confronting him about his first affair, she'd had revenge sex. She'd made sure word got back to Ben. Once it did, they had their first screaming match, loud enough that the rest of the journalism pool avoided them both for days.

Not her proudest moment.

The second time Ben had strayed, she'd done what she should have done the first time and confronted him. He'd sworn it would never happen again, and fool that she was, she'd believed him. She'd found out about the third time right before he'd been killed. The last thing she'd said was she'd wanted a divorce.

Did one have anything to do with the other? Had he taken a risk he shouldn't have taken and deliberately put himself in harm's way? She'd never know, and the unknowing ate away at her insides.

If she knew, without a shadow of a doubt, that she had nothing to do with his death, she'd be able to pick up a camera again.

And now this.

Tears fell on the white linen paper.

Outside of the moments after she'd seen him killed, when her keening wail brought soldiers rushing to her, she hadn't cried for Ben. In her family, emotions had never been shared, and she'd never felt close enough to Ben's parents to change that habit.

But now, she cried. Not sobbing tears of release but the steady stream of regret. If she'd been a different person, they might have survived or at least parted when they needed to. But now?

If she were smart, she'd never get into another relationship again. The only result was pain.

She swiped at her eyes then read the letter again. They were right about one thing—she needed some advice to handle the investments. She didn't need much for herself; she'd been frugal with her money. But it would be nice to do something for the ranch—maybe get Jarod a new tractor so he didn't need to keep repairing the old one.

The attorney they'd used to draw up the ranch documents had retired, but there was that sign she'd seen in town for Cassandra Sanders. It would be nice to throw work to a female lawyer. Trish had said her husband was an accountant. Maybe he would know someone good at financial planning.

She called and made the appointment with the attorney, then went back to the purgatory of her mother's office.

# # #

"CJ has the pictures you took," Nick said as Trevor hopped into the truck.

"Cool," Trevor said, his gaze lingering on a girl with long, brown hair standing by a struggling sapling at the edge of the schoolyard.

Nick had looked at CJ the same way when he was thirteen. If only things turned out the way he'd planned as a teen. He wished he could spare his son the inevitable heartache, but that wasn't the way things worked.

"I told her we'd stop by and pick them up," he said.

"Cool," his son replied again, reluctantly giving up on staring at the girl.

"How was school?" Nick asked as he pulled out of town.

"Okay."

"Got homework?"

"Yeah. A bunch."

"What?" Nick asked, almost used to the painful process of prying information from Trevor.

"Math. Like five pages of problems."

"That's a lot."

"Yeah."

"So who's the girl?"

That snapped Trevor's attention to him.

"What girl?"

"The one standing by the tree."

"Nobody."

"Uh-huh." Nick grinned at Trevor.

"Really. Nobody." Trevor went back to looking at the mountains. After a few moments, he said, "They really are kinda big. Not as big as Mount Rainier, but big."

"Highest one in the Bob is about nine thousand, four hundred feet."

"Why do you call it the Bob?"

Nick shrugged. "I'm not sure. It's just what everyone's called the Bob Marshall Wilderness since I grew up."

"Kinda like an in-crowd saying?"

"Yeah, the in-crowd of Montanans, all million of us."

"Hmm." Trevor said and went quiet.

Nick turned down the drive and followed the curve to the west side of the foothill where the ranch was situated, his heart beating a little faster. It had been a long time since he'd been here, and Jarod had kicked him off the property when he'd come to patch things up with CJ. It hadn't taken him long to realize Grace was a mistake, but when CJ wouldn't see him, he slipped back into the relationship, figuring it would only last until the end of high school.

He hadn't counted on Grace's determination to piss off her father.

Well, if Trevor was the result of his mistake, he was glad. His son was a good kid. A little lost right now, but he had to believe it would get better.

He came to a stop by the ranch house just as Jarod came out of the barn. They'd seen each other around town but hadn't done more than nod and keep walking. Once in a while Nick didn't even get that.

Jarod held onto a grudge like it was his favorite toy.

At the same time, CJ came down the ranch house steps, a purse slung over her shoulder. Trevor hopped out of the truck and Nick did the same.

Jarod stiffened when he spotted Nick, and increased his stride.

"Sturgis," he said when he reached the truck. "I thought we had an understanding."

"Give it a rest, Jarod," CJ said, getting to them seconds later. "That was two decades ago. This is Nick's son, Trevor. Trevor, this is my annoying *younger* brother, Jarod."

Jarod found his manners and held out his hand to the kid, who thankfully shook it.

"Nick, can you do me a favor?" CJ asked. "I've got a lead on a vehicle in town, but the ranch truck's in use. Can you take me to see it? I'm probably going to get it, but if I don't, it would mean driving me home again."

"No problem," he said.

Jarod took a step toward him, and Nick straightened his spine.

"Men," CJ said and threw up her hands. "I'll climb in back and you can sit up front," she said to Trevor, who was watching the two men, his mouth slightly agape. "Just ignore them. They're old friends who haven't quite grown up yet."

Trevor grinned. "It's okay. I'll get in the back."

After a few more barbs were tossed, Jarod gave one final glare and stomped to the house.

Nick shook his head and climbed into the seat. Seventeen years was one hell of a long time to hold onto anger. He'd do something to change it if he could, but that wasn't in his power. Each person was responsible for his own mojo.

"Where is this car?" he asked CJ as he turned on the motor.

"It's a Jeep, not a car."

"Whatever."

She gave him the directions.

The Jeep was in the southeast section of Choteau among homes that were built during or shortly after World War II when people didn't feel the need for big, sprawling mansions. There was comfort in neighborhoods like this, like people were content with what they had.

When had people become so empty that a roof over their heads and food on the table wasn't enough?

One of those questions he'd never answer, but it made for good mind fodder on the back of a horse in the wilderness.

"We should go on a fishing trip this spring," he said.

"You mean all of us?" CJ asked.

Damn, he'd been so lost in his own thoughts that he'd forgotten she was there.

"Um, sure. Why not?"

"With any kind of luck, I'll be back on assignment," she said. "But thanks for asking."

"Fishing is boring," Trevor announced from the back seat.

So much for that idea.

# # #

A fishing trip sounded like a great idea ... for a life she didn't have.

CJ climbed out of the truck and walked to the faded green door that matched the trim on the white house—also faded. The screen door opened with a squeal and she thudded the brass door knocker on the wooden door.

A diminutive woman in a blue sweatshirt dotted with vibrant splotches that looked like dried paint opened the door. Her gray hair curled around her head and her bright blue eyes were sharp and clear.

"You must be CJ," she said. "You have the same look my Bobbie used to have. Just let me throw on a coat and I'll show you the car." She disappeared behind the door and reappeared with a blue parka in her hand. "It's out back. I'm June, by the way." Glancing at the truck, she added, "Your husband and son can come along. Most men like to get under the hood before they buy anything." June waved at Nick, indicating he should come over.

127

"Oh, he's not my husband, just a friend."

"Too bad. He looks like a nice man."

"Yeah." Except for that one major slip in high school, he probably was. If she were staying, it would be nice to find out for sure.

Nick and Trevor caught up to them as June was pulling the tarps off the vehicle.

"Wow," said Trevor, "That's a great car!"

"Jeep," she corrected him.

He rolled his eyes in the non-verbal expression of *whatever*.

The white vehicle was pristine. June showed her how all the detachable parts were removed, making a great summer car. Should make it easy to sell when CJ was ready to leave. Or maybe Cameron would return soon and he could have it. An extra vehicle on the ranch would probably be welcome.

Nick popped the hood and stared at the engine, jiggling a few wires and rubber tubing. Like the rest of the vehicle, it was almost as clean as the day it rolled off the factory line. When she turned the key, the engine roared to life and settled into a smooth purr. She turned it off and got out of the driver's seat.

June's face saddened as she looked at the white car. "Bobbie bought it just before she went overseas. Said it would be the beacon to bring her home."

"What happened?" CJ asked gently.

"Their vehicle ran over an IED. It was armored, but ..." June shook her head.

"I'm so sorry."

The four of them were quiet for a few seconds and then Nick cleared his throat. "It's a nice Jeep, ma'am," he said.

And well worth the asking price.

"I'll take it," CJ said.

June nodded.

"Then you won't need a ride back?"

"No, but thank you for bringing me here."

"When you're finished, why don't you meet us at John Henry's for pizza?" Nick asked. "You can show us the photos."

Damn. She'd forgotten all about the envelope she'd stuffed in her purse. But having dinner with Nick—again—was a habit that wasn't a good idea. She was leaving, and she didn't want him, or his son, to imagine anything else.

She opened her purse to hand them the envelope.

"Please?" Trevor asked.

"Okay." She smiled at him. "Sure."

"See you in a few," Nick said and he headed back to his truck, Trevor dogging his heels.

"Seems like there's an opportunity there," June said before heading back to the house.

"I'm leaving soon."

"Oh? Then why do you need to buy a vehicle? You could just lease one, couldn't you?"

"Probably, but this seemed easier. Besides, when I'm done it'll still be a good vehicle for the ranch."

"Where are you going?"

"Back to the Middle East if I can get an assignment there. I'm a photojournalist."

"Dangerous." June shook her head. "Why go? You're not a soldier."

"No, I'm not." CJ pulled out her checkbook and wrote out the payment for the Jeep. "But I feel someone has to show the truth of what's happening over there. Not only the bad but also the people trying to survive and live with some sort of joy and purpose."

"It's a brave thing you're doing."

"I'm not sure about that, but thank you." CJ smiled and handed the check to June. "I really am sorry about your loss."

"Thank you. Bobbie was doing what she thought was right and she died for our country. I wept for several months, but the thing that heals me most is painting." She pointed to a picture of sunset over the mountains. "I imagine her there, just out of my sight, and it brings me comfort."

CJ nodded but stayed quiet.

"The papers are in the glove box. Here are the keys," June said. "Good luck. Let me know if there's anything wrong in the next month, and we'll be happy to check it out. Bobbie's brother has been maintaining it." The sad smile flitted across her lips again. "I think it's been his way of remembering his sister."

"I will. Thank you."

CJ got behind the wheel of the Jeep and savored her newfound freedom. It had been years since she'd had a car of her own. Maybe, before she left, she'd take a road trip north through Glacier National Park to Whitefish. Just her and the mountains.

Chapter Eleven

Nick breathed in deeply when he and Trevor walked through the door of John Henry's, and smiled. Garlic, onion, peppers, and a variety of other aromas generated only by good pizza surrounded them.

"What do you think?" he asked his son.

"It's okay."

So it was going to be one of those evenings. Good thing he had CJ as a buffer.

When they sat at one of the tables, a high school girl walked by and tossed menus on the table before continuing to her next destination. Through the wall, he could hear the thrum of slot machines and low conversations. Thankfully, smoke no longer seeped through the porous wood as it had when he was a kid.

They'd just started debating the merits of Hawaiian pizza against good old-fashioned pepperoni when CJ came in. Nick gave her a smile that was half admiration and half relief. Thirties sat well on his old girlfriend. She had a strength that she'd not had as a teen—they probably all did. And yet, there was still a softness he'd like time to explore.

She smiled back at him, but her expression was guarded.

It was going to take a lot of work to get through that armor, and there was no time to do it. He wished he had the chance, though. Some way to make up for the damage he'd done in high school.

He stood and pulled out the chair next to him.

She hesitated a second then pulled off her coat, threw it on a nearby hook, and sat down. "So what are we having?" she asked.

"How do you feel about pineapple?" Trevor asked with a half smile.

"On pizza?"

Nick struggled to keep from laughing. CJ had always hated that particular style.

"Yeah. It's good," Trevor said.

"It's gross," she replied. "Normal pizza, please."

"And by that she means sausage or pepperoni," Nick said.

"You guys are boring."

He and CJ laughed.

Then he made the mistake of looking at her and catching the glint of joy in her eyes. Maybe there was a way past all that steel and concrete after all.

They decided on pepperoni. He ordered a local brew for himself and CJ and a soft drink for Trevor. While they waited, CJ pulled the photographs from her purse.

"These are really good," she said, handing the envelope to Trevor. She also pulled out the piece of paper she'd used to track all the settings. "You framed your dad's face nicely, and your focus is steady."

Trevor studied the pictures.

"Can you see how changing the settings changed the picture?"

"Yeah. That's really cool." Trevor flipped through them again. "I like this one best." He held it up to CJ.

"I agree," she said. "Take a look at the settings."

He checked the piece of paper then frowned. "But most digital cameras don't have these settings," he said.

"The better ones do."

"Can I see?" Nick asked.

Trevor handed him the photos. As CJ had said, they were

nicely framed and in focus. He'd have to take some money out of his savings and get the kid a camera while he was here.

"How are you settling in?" she asked Trevor.

"It's okay. I'll be glad when I get back to Seattle though. No offense, Dad. It's just there's more to do."

"Yeah, Montana winters can be long." She took a long sip of her beer. "Do you play any sports?"

"I never did sports in Seattle and I had plenty to do." Trevor's voice bordered on resentment.

"Oh, I see." CJ seemed at a loss.

"He helps me with the horses and stuff," Nick threw in.

"Of course. I always found books helped me get through the dark time."

"I hate reading."

"Really?"

Trevor shrugged his shoulders and studied his soda.

CJ looked around the room, as if wondering how she got there.

He struggled with a safe topic of conversation.

They were saved by the arrival of pizza.

"This is good," Trevor admitted after a few bites. "I thought it was icky the last time I was here."

"New owners," Nick said. "I think the guy is from back east somewhere."

"And he wound up here?" CJ asked.

"Yeah. He went to school with someone from Choteau or something like that."

"It really is amazing how people get here." She took a bite of her pizza. "Different from how I remember, too," she said to Trevor. "Say, listen, why don't I bring the camera up to your dad's tomorrow? I can leave it with you so you have something to do."

"Don't you need it?" Nick asked.

"I have a couple of others," she said. She frowned for a brief moment then seemed to recover. "It would make me happy to know Trevor was using it."

"Sure, that'd be great. Maybe you can give me another lesson." Trevor smiled. He actually smiled for the first time since they'd gotten to the restaurant.

"Say, maybe we can go to Freezeout Lake soon," Nick said, trying again to include her in the invitation. "Birds should start coming through again sometime this month. Snow geese arrive early March."

"I'm hoping to be gone by the end of February."

"Well, let's go before then. You can take pictures, and Trevor can learn to get some action shots."

"That sounds cool," his son said, hope in his voice.

CJ's mouth drooped a bit. "We'll see."

Trevor shrugged and went back to his pizza.

Couldn't she see how much his son needed her around? Nick kept his gaze steadily on CJ.

She looked up from her pizza and shrugged her acquiescence.

"Okay," she said, "Let's plan a time—not this weekend, but next. It's a good idea."

Trevor looked up and gave her another grin.

"I'd like that," Nick said.

She smiled at him, but there was sorrow written on her face.

# # #

As a last-minute whim before she went to Nick's, CJ grabbed her oldest camera from the duffle bag where it had sat for the last two months, ever since she'd returned from the Middle East.

134

Maybe this time she could actually use it.

She had to get past this fear. It was ridiculous. Willpower had gotten her through every other problem in life, but it simply wasn't working now. Two sessions with the therapist hadn't brought any change.

Two more probably weren't going to change anything either. Geraldine Morgan didn't strike her as a woman who could be snowed by her protests that everything was fine.

If CJ wanted to get out of Montana anytime soon, she was going to have to muscle through this on her own.

The snow that had come down the Front during the night was tapering off as she traveled the back roads to Nick's cabin. He'd chosen a nice, if remote, spot to build. It was just like they'd imagined when they were teens. Did he realize he'd built their house for his ex-wife?

And what did that mean exactly? Did he still have feelings for her? Long after it had happened, Jarod told her Nick had shown up right before she left for college, desperate to talk to her. He'd escorted her old beau off the property.

What would have happened if Jarod hadn't intervened? Life was so many choices and decisions, but once they were made, there was no going back.

The Jeep easily made the hill to the cabin, and she pulled next to Nick's truck. She was half out of the car when she heard Trevor from the barn.

"We're in here!"

"Okay!" she shouted back. Gathering the cameras and canisters of extra film she'd brought, she headed to the structure, a far newer building than they had on the ranch.

Trevor held the door open and shut it behind her as she entered the floodlight bright barn. The usual odors of hay and manure emanated from the half of the structure dedicated to horse stalls. A roan she hadn't seen before nickered from one of them.

The other half of the barn contained neat racks of saddles and other horse gear, as well as stacks of supplies that could be packed into wilderness areas. Everything was in tip-top shape.

The horse nickered again.

Smiling, Nick came over to her. "She's not happy she's in here by herself, but she's due next month and it's a bit too icy out there for me to risk her falling."

"Yeah," she said. "It looks like it started out as freezing rain before switching to pure snow." They walked to the stall. "She's a beautiful animal."

"Thanks. She's got a great disposition. Perfect for trail rides."

Trevor was too close to feel comfortable asking the question that was on her mind: What was Nick going to do with his son when trips took him away for two or three weeks at a time?

"Did you bring the camera?" the teen asked.

"Sure did," she said, pulling the bag off her shoulder and handing it to him. "There's four rolls of film in there—two black-and-white and two color."

"Wow, thanks," Trevor said.

"That's very generous," Nick said.

"I won't be using it anytime soon."

"Why not?"

Shit. Before Ben's death, she'd used the traditional camera to capture desert scenes she thought would look better in film. Several of those rolls were still on her dresser at the ranch. "Too slow for news work," was what she finally came up with.

He eyed her, and she turned away, not wanting him to see the truth that she was afraid of what she'd see when she looked through the lens.

"Can you show me some more things?" Trevor asked.

"Okay, sure." She didn't have anything else waiting for her besides her grandmother's journal and the endless boxes of paper.

"I'll stay here and keep doing inventory," Nick said. holding up a clipboard.

This time, instead of showing how the settings worked with a close-up, she showed Trevor how to manipulate long-distance scenery. The sun had emerged, and the mountains to the west glistened with fresh snow.

"Can you take a look?" he asked after taking five or six shots.

She took the camera with a shaking hand.

"Something wrong?" he asked.

"No. I'm fine."

He gave her the same suspicious look his father had given her.

She could do this. She had to. Falling apart in front of a teenager was just wrong.

Steeling herself, she looked through the viewfinder for a few second, then pulled it away from her eye as the edges of the mountains started to morph into desert.

"I'm sorry," she said. "I ... well ... something happened and I'm having trouble taking pictures. Don't tell your father."

Great. She'd confessed her greatest failing to a kid and then told him to keep it a secret.

She stared at the Rockies, the camera loose in her hand.

Trevor tugged at it and she let it go.

"You know," he said. "I miss my mom a lot. It's not something I can talk about with Dad. Before they split, it was pretty loud."

"They argued a lot," she said, her attention refocused on him.

"Yeah." He twisted the camera strap then looked up at her.

"But she's still my mom, even though she doesn't want me anymore."

CJ's heart broke.

"I'm sure she still loves you," she said. "It sounds like she's disappointed in your actions."

He shrugged and looked away for a second, then back at her.

"It's tough when someone tells you they don't want you and don't give you the chance to … well, fix it," he said.

"Yes." She put her arm around Trevor and pulled him close for the thirty seconds she figured he'd allow it. "It's excruciatingly tough."

Oh, Ben.

# # #

"Where's CJ?" Nick asked as Trevor came back into the barn.

"She said she had to go home."

Odd she didn't come in to say goodbye.

"She's really sad," Trevor added.

Nick put down the clipboard and focused on his son. "I know. She had some bad things happen to her, and she's upset about it."

"Can't you make her happy? You're her friend."

Nick shook his head. "We're not really—" Then he stopped. "Yeah, we're friends, I guess." And he cared about CJ, more than he was ready to admit to himself, never mind Trevor or, god forbid, CJ.

"So what are you going to do about it?" Trevor asked.

One of the barn cats, a sleek black mouser he'd named Tim for no reason whatsoever, rubbed his head on Trevor's leg, and the boy crouched down to pet him.

"I'm not sure."

"Well, you're going to need to think of something. She's *really* sad."

"I'll think about it," he said. "How about we call it a day and watch some basketball?"

"What is it with you guys and sports?" Trevor asked.

Nick threw his arm around Trevor's shoulders as they left the barn. "It's a Montana thing," he said. "You were born here. You'll get it."

"Right," Trevor said.

After shedding their outer clothes in the mudroom, Nick riffled through the cabinets. "Popcorn?" he asked, looking over his shoulder.

Trevor was clicking on his phone. "Sure," he said. Putting his phone up to his ear, he said, "Mom?"

Nick felt a sinking sensation in the region of his stomach. He pulled the box of popcorn from the shelf and tried to pretend like he was ignoring the conversation behind him. All he got was low murmurs at first, but then there was an explosion.

"Why can't I come home? I hate you!"

Nick turned in time to see the phone land on the table and Trevor storm off down the hall. Seconds later, his door slammed.

He sighed and dug his own phone out of his pocket. Much as he wanted Trevor with him, his kid needed to know his mother still loved him. Grace could be a jerk about a lot of things, but she would never give up on her son, he was sure of that. She wasn't very good at explaining that though.

Before he could dial, the phone rang. He glanced at the number.

"Hi, Grace," he said.

"I'm sorry, Nick," she answered. "Trevor frustrates me so much. He expects me to believe he's changed after a month."

"I don't know," Nick said. "Maybe he wants to find out if you're ever going to let him come home. He's a fish out of water here."

"He didn't used to be. He loved all that manly stuff you used to do with him."

"Grace, he was nine. He's a teenager now who's spent the last four years in a huge city. He had a hard time adjusting to that, too, remember?"

"Yeah, but, Nick, you don't know what's been going on. He's hanging with the wrong crowd. His best friend was arrested for dealing meth, for god's sake. Pot is easy to get … I swear half the kids in his school are high all the time. And then he disappears for hours with that camera of his. I took it away hoping he'd stay home, but that didn't work."

Nick stifled his groan. Arguing with his ex-wife wasn't going to solve anything—they'd already proved that *before* the divorce.

"Say, can you box up the camera and ship it overnight to me?"

"The camera? Why?"

"There's a lot to take pictures of around here. It might keep him occupied until it starts to thaw." No way was he mentioning CJ's involvement in Trevor's photography.

"I suppose. Just be careful, Nick. You don't know how capable he is of lying."

Like his mother had been.

Nick mentally kicked himself for thinking that.

"I will. Thanks."

"Okay."

"And, Grace," he added, "can you maybe call him once in a while and show him you still care? He misses you."

She was quiet. She was either going to agree or fly into a fury.

"Sure," she said, much to his relief.

# # #

From Catherine's diary, August 1943:

"Everything is going well ... except ... I never realized how much I would miss home and Mom and Dad. There are so many little things that adults have to do. I never thought about it before. The boardinghouse supplies breakfast and dinner, but I have to plan lunch for myself. I've gone hungry more than once!

The news from the war is horrible. We've bombed an oil refinery in Romania. And the news says the Germans have left Sicily, in Italy. So many of our soldiers are dying. Stephen sent me a letter, but I couldn't read most of it. A lot was blacked out.

It all seems so far away. Here life goes on. I saved enough to buy one of those lipstick tubes—my first ever! It's called blush red. I haven't worn it yet. A group of us may go to the movies on Friday. Alfred Hitchcock's latest movie is playing.

I wish Stephen were here.

# # #

The next Monday afternoon, CJ climbed the narrow stairwell to the second-story law office over the hardware store. While the steps were worn with age, a gleaming maple wood table topped with a colorful spray of flowers anchored the landing outside the office. She pushed open the frosted-glass door and entered the polished and tasteful waiting room. Western-themed prints decorated the walls, mainly vistas of rolling hills and granite mountains, but there were a few of trim ranches nestled in valleys.

From beyond an inside door, she could hear someone on the

phone, so she took a seat in one of the guest chairs. The county courthouse had been a bust—no one remembered Jarod making a huge cash payment. In addition to answering the questions she had on the estate Ben had left her, maybe Cassandra Sanders could shed some light on what to do next to rectify the situation.

"May I help you?" A trim blonde, not a hair out of place, stepped from an inner office. She was about the same height as CJ, with the body of an athlete and the wardrobe of a big-city lawyer.

How had someone like her ended up in Choteau, Montana, population 1,691 at the last census?

CJ rose. "I called you for an appointment last week."

"Ah, yes, CJ Beck. Come on in. Cup of coffee?"

"That would be nice."

Cassandra walked to a credenza and poured black brew into a flawless white mug. "Cream?"

"Black. No sugar, thank you." She accepted the cup and followed the attorney into the inner sanctum. As she walked in, she noticed a small, black-and-white photo on the wall to her left. The rolling foothills leading to the Rockies reminded her of a spot in the far southeast corner of the Beck ranch.

"How can I help you?" Cassandra asked as she sat, well-crafted pen poised over a yellow legal pad.

"Well, it seems I've been left a rather large sum by my husband."

"I'm sorry for your loss. Might I ask the amount?"

Not even a breath between the two sentences. She may be an excellent lawyer, but her people skills could use a brushup.

"I'm not exactly sure. A lot of it is tied up in investments—British investments."

"Your husband was a Brit?"

"Yes."

"Then we're going to need to be really careful about how we go about this. You don't want to trigger British taxes. They are fierce."

"But I'm an American. Why would I be taxed?" CJ asked.

"If they can, they will. Can I see the document you mentioned when you called me?"

CJ handed over the paperwork and the attorney scanned it before looking up.

"I have a colleague in the Chicago office where I used to work. He's a tax expert on this kind of thing. Would you mind if I reached out to him before I gave you an estimate as to what it would take to untangle this?"

"Well, I guess not." Nothing like being wishy-washy. Did she want it fixed or not? She didn't need to *like* the experts—they just had to be good. "Sure. No problem."

"Good. I'll make a copy of this letter and get back to you in about a week."

"Thanks."

Cassandra went into a small room at the side of the office.

As soon as she left, CJ stood and looked at the photo more carefully. It sure looked like their property, but it was an old shot, probably back in the thirties. She slipped her phone out and took a quick snap before sitting down.

"So what brought you to Montana?" she asked when Cassandra returned.

"Oh, distant relations. I had an ancestor who lived here for a while before moving back to the Midwest. I decided to give it a try to see if I liked it better than Chicago."

"Quite a switch."

"Yes. My dentist told me I was a woman of extremes."

Cassandra smiled.

"And do you like it?"

"So far, yes." Cassandra handed the original letter back to her. "Was there anything else?"

"As a matter of fact, there is. I'd like to get your opinion on something."

Cassandra returned to her chair behind the desk.

CJ explained the situation, but at the end, the attorney shook her head. "It's one of the things I still haven't cracked in this town," she said. "The old boys'—and girls'—network in the county offices is still fairly strong, and sometimes it's tough to get people to trust you."

"That tends to be the case in much of the state," CJ said. "Montanans will take you at face value, particularly if you were raised here, but out-of-staters need to earn trust for the most part."

"Well, maybe next year I'll be able to help you, but for now I'd suggest an accountant. They're going to be more likely to know how to get answers."

"Thanks." CJ rose. "I look forward to hearing from you."

She traveled back down the stairs, mulling over the lack of an accountant. Without moving her car, she walked toward Bridges Coffee Shop.

Chapter Twelve

The coffee shop was almost empty when CJ walked in. A clean pine scent competed with the coffee and grease aromas. Mae must be getting close to closing. CJ checked the sign. Nope. It still stayed open until four-thirty, like she'd remembered as a kid. It was a long day for the older woman.

"Be right with you!" Mae sang out from the back.

CJ sat herself on the stool and took out her phone. A few messages from colleagues. Murmurs of concern about governmental pushback on investigative reporting, a trend that had landed one or two of her colleagues in hot water.

Nothing else of importance.

"Hey, CJ. I got coffee and I got pie. What's your pleasure?" Mae pushed a white mug toward her.

"Just coffee and maybe a little information," she said.

Black liquid poured expertly into the cup.

"What do you need to know?" Mae asked.

"I need a new financial advisor—someone an expert in taxes, estates, that kind of thing. I'd like someone who isn't all the way in the city."

"You already know him. Trish's husband—Brad Small."

She hadn't realized he was more than a CPA. Perfect. Brad was a lifelong Choteau resident. If he was still as easygoing as he was in high school, he wouldn't have a problem working with Cassandra.

"Great," she said, pulling out her phone.

"Don't bother," Mae said, riffling through a pile of business cards by the cash register. "He's my accountant. Here's his card."

CJ still took out her phone. "I have to call him, Mae."

"Oh yeah." She wiped the back of her hand across her forehead and still the skin on her face sagged a little from fatigue. "It's getting late in the day for me. I'm not always thinking straight about now."

"Don't you have any help? It seems a lot to do day in and day out."

"My son Jimmy's taken over the cooking, but he leaves after the lunch run to get supplies and stuff for the next day. I get a high school girl to help out now and then like when you were a kid. Other than that, it's me."

"It's as wonderful as it always was, Mae. I feel at home here."

"Then stay," Mae said, her gaze steady on CJ.

"You'd get tired of having me around." She forced a chuckle; she had an idea of what Mae was getting at.

"You know I don't mean that. This is your home, girl. Even though they may not say it, your brothers need you. Jarod goes to my church. I swear he looks like an old man every time I see him. He had too much pressure too young. And Dylan's the opposite— a tumbleweed. They need to have some free time, find a girl ... make some babies."

"And you think if I came home they could do that."

"Certainly wouldn't hurt. Come to think of it, you could find someone and pop out some babies, too."

CJ shook her head. "I can't have kids."

"Oh, I'm sorry, honey." Mae put her worn hand on hers. "It's always tough on a woman when she can't have one no matter what the reason."

"It's okay. It never seemed the right time to try, and then ... well, I made sure it could never happen."

"Oh. I'm so sorry."

Mae's sympathy pierced her core and she swiped at her eyes.

"Well, there's always some who could use a little extra mothering," Mae said, grabbing a coffeepot and topping off her cup.

Like Trevor.

She finished up her coffee and slid some bills on the counter without calling Brad. "Thanks for the info. I'll see you again soon."

"Remember what I said. This is your home. It's about time you realized that."

As she walked back to her car, she kicked the piles of snow that edged the sidewalk, just as she'd done as a child when things didn't go her way. The cold air chilled the tip of her nose, stealing away the warmth she'd accumulated at the coffee shop.

What did Mae know about her life anyway? Jarod and Dylan had made the choice to stay on the ranch. She'd urged them to sell and get on with their lives any number of times. There were only bad memories on that land.

But Jarod had just made it clear that the ranch was the top of his priorities.

Still his problem. She had her own life. She was doing important work—telling the world the truth.

But was she telling it to herself?

She shoved the thoughts from her head and climbed into the Jeep. Before starting the engine, she dialed Brad.

"Hello, sunshine!" he said after she identified herself. "Trish said you were back in town. I hope it's for good this time."

"Sorry, Brad. I'm only here for a little R and R."

"Too bad. How can I help you?" His voice took on a professional tone.

She told him briefly about Ben's letter.

Since he wasn't busy at the moment, she followed his

directions to a house tucked into the foothills west of town. The sprawling house was a dark-stained brown with red trim. Brad's office was at the northern end, and she could see a large extension with industrialized vents toward the back. It must be where Trish baked her pies. Her business was obviously bigger than she'd let on.

Brad's tall frame filled the doorway to his office. "Good to see you," he said and gave her a bear hug just as he had when they were teens. He'd never quite gotten political correctness, and it didn't bother her in the least.

He nodded as he read through the letter the attorneys had sent, and stayed quiet as she told him what Cassandra had said.

"I think it's a good thing you came to me, too," he said. "It will take both of us to sort through this for you and insure you pay the least amount of taxes and invest wisely for the future."

"You have no problems working with her? I know she's new in town," CJ asked.

"I can work with about anybody. You know that." He gave her the smile that had endeared him to all of the town's basketball fans. "She's a sharp attorney. A friend of mine went up against her in a divorce case and said it was a tough fight all the way. Better to have her in your corner."

"Good to know," CJ said. "There's another matter."

"Okay. Shoot."

She explained the missing tax receipt and the county's inability to find any record. "I'd really like to straighten this out before I leave. Do something for the family."

"That's odd. The county is usually pretty good at keeping track of these things, especially since they were audited a few years back."

"Well, it's not odd for Jarod. He thinks paper has only one

duty—to be used to start a fire in the fireplace."

Brad chuckled. "Yep. Sounds like him. Practicality is fused in every bone of his body. He's a good man. I've tried to set him up any number of times, but he always claims he's too busy."

Was he? Or was her brother too picky, as he'd told her? Or was it something else entirely?

No time to figure it out now.

"Anyway, I can check into it for you," Brad continued. "I know a number of folks there, including the head of the property tax department."

"Thanks. I appreciate that."

# # #

"What's this?" Trevor looked at the package his father had handed him.

"Open it." Nick handed his son the small jackknife he always carried in his pocket. True to her word, Grace had overnighted the camera.

Trevor meticulously sliced through the tape covering the box, folded the knife back to its place, and handed it to Nick. After the rustle of too much bubble wrap, he pulled out his camera. His immediate joy was snuffed out by a teenage act of unconcern. "I've already got CJ's camera."

Nick kept his reaction internal. "Even CJ has more than one camera. I thought with the trip to Freezeout, it would be good for you to have a color option as well as black and white."

Trevor tried to keep his expression blasé, but he couldn't hold it.

"That's a great idea, Dad. Thank you for thinking of it."

"You might thank your mother, too. She pulled it together

and sent it."

Trevor went still.

"Yeah. Okay. That was nice of her," he finally said.

A step. That would do.

"Good. Then let's plan the trip," Nick said.

"What do you mean?"

"Well ... what time should we leave? Do we need to have anything for breakfast? Lunch? Extra supplies? When do we head back home?"

"Like when you're planning an outfitting trip."

"Exactly."

"So, when do the birds show up?" Trevor asked, his eyes clear and bright.

"Hate to say this, but sunrise is pretty fascinating."

"Sunrise?"

"Uh-huh."

"That's like really early."

"Uh-huh."

"But it would be cool for CJ, wouldn't it?"

"Yep." Nick waited.

"Then I'll get up early."

"Okay."

"But I won't be happy," Trevor added.

"Fair enough." Nick took out a piece of paper. "Now what do you think we need for supplies?"

Trevor listed off a few overly salty and sugary items, and Nick indulged him on one for each meal. It was good to be doing something with his son that would help the woman he'd once loved.

The kid was right. CJ was hurting, like a wild animal that trusted no one, particularly the men in her life. Why should she?

The most important of them had betrayed her in one way or another. He didn't know if her husband had piled on, but from her skittishness, he suspected he had.

There was also the panic he'd seen with the camera and the fact he hadn't seen her shoot a picture since she'd been home. Would the trip to the lake change that? Or would it be one more failure for her? If it was, he'd need to be ready to support her.

"I think we need a trip to the store, Dad."

Nick looked over the list they'd made.

"Yep. How about we stop in and see your grandparents, too?"

"I suppose."

He hoped he lived long enough to survive his son's teens.

# # #

After picking up what they needed, Nick drove to his parents' store. The weather had held, but like it always did when they sky remained clear, temperatures sank twenty degrees. As they walked from the truck to the store, fat, fluffy birds glared from trees as if Nick and Trevor were personally responsible for their predicament.

"Brrr," he said, stomping his feet when he entered the store. "It's cold."

"Got hot coffee right here," his dad said. "And we can whip up some hot chocolate for Trevor." He gave Nick and Trevor quick hugs.

"Sounds good. It's frigid out there."

"You can sure say that again." His mother came from the center of the store, yellow feather duster in her hand. "Arizona is sounding pretty good right now." She embraced Trevor in a long hug. He made a brief effort then endured it.

"If you need a vacation, I can watch the store. Trips won't start up for another few months," Nick said. "Trevor can help after school."

His parents exchanged glances.

"We were going to ask you if you could do that," Mom said. "We really do need a break from the cold. It seeps more into my bones every winter." She looked paler than he ever remembered, almost like she was fading away.

"Any time, you know that," he said.

"C'mon in the back, Trevor," his dad said. "I'll get you some hot cocoa and we can pour a mug of brew for your dad. Looks like he could use it. You must be working him too hard."

"Thanks, Granddad." Trevor trailed his grandfather past jars filled to the brim with single-wrapped candy and licorice of every flavor. Heart-shaped candy boxes and flowery greeting cards stuffed racks near the register. A floral scent from nearby red candles tickled his nose. Faded red paper hearts framed paper doilies of the same shape—probably the same ones that had been put up for decades.

As he glanced around, Nick realized the whole place looked a little tired around the edges.

"What's up, Mom?" he asked.

She rested half on a stool by the cash register.

"The trip—it's not just a vacation," she said. "We're going to look for a place to retire ... perhaps one of those retirement places."

Fear stole his breath. "What's wrong?"

"Nothing serious, but we're getting on. Your dad, well, his ticker isn't working quite the way it should."

"That's not good."

"It's not, but with medication, diet, exercise—the usual

stuff—he should last a good long time. Maybe a little less coffee, too."

He smiled.

"Problem is, come winter, we're stuck inside too much. We never were those winter-loving, cross-country skiing types. Hunkering down by a fireplace with a good book is more our style. We figure if we can get a house or townhouse where they take care of stuff —provide meals if you want them, entertainment , other people our age—we'd be more active."

"Are you going to sell the store?"

"We're not sure what we're going to do. Henry has his own life up by Valier. You have your outfitting business. But, Nick, if we're not around, we can't help you with Trevor. What are you going to do with him while you're on trips?"

"I don't know that he's staying, so I'll cross that bridge when I get there."

"Grace hasn't made up her mind?"

"Nope."

The air was heavy with their silence.

"If we do anything, it won't be til summer, so you won't have to figure anything out until fall." She looked at him with something resembling hope. "Unless you want to take over for us," she added.

Staying inside all day had never appealed to him. Some ancestor had bequeathed the outdoor-in-the-winter gene to him that had skipped his parents. Still, if Trevor stayed with him, he'd have to think about doing something else ... something besides the life he loved.

No wonder CJ was so desperate to get back. It was sort of the same situation.

"I'll think about it." He grinned. "Taking over the store for a week will let me know if I'm still capable of doing the job."

"Oh, you'll be great at it, like you always were."

Only problem was, capable of doing and wanting to do were two different things.

# # #

Before the sun rose on Saturday morning, CJ got up and pulled a few things together for the trip to Freezeout. Her camera sat on her childhood desk, the proverbial snake ready to attack. She needed to take it with her. She should take it with her, prove to Trevor that even bad things in life could be overcome. She'd be fine as long as she didn't look through the viewfinder.

And how in hell was she supposed to pull that off?

She could just click the shutter without looking. Okay. That was a plan ... sorta.

She stuffed it into her tote, along with the food Birdie had insisted on preparing.

"Nick's an outfitter," she'd tried to tell the housekeeper as she sliced homemade bread, pealed a few pieces of limp lettuce, slathered mayo, and added turkey and cheese to each. "He'll know what to bring."

"They are men. You'll all be outdoors. No matter how much he brings, you can always bring more. It'll make you feel like you're pulling your own weight."

And so there were sandwiches, chips, and cookies along with three bottles of water already stashed in the bag.

She zipped it closed, slung it over her shoulder, picked up her tripod, and crept downstairs. The house was eerily quiet except for a gentle snore from the room where Jarod slept. Coffee aroma snuck out of the kitchen as she got closer. Birdie had set the timer and put out two to-go cups.

CJ left one. Whatever else, Nick would have brought his own coffee.

Bundled in her coat, scarf, hat and gloves, she waited on the dark porch. Sunrise wasn't even a thought.

Headlights carved a path through the black-and-white night. She handed Trevor her bag then climbed into the passenger seat.

"Not too bad out there," she said.

"Nope."

Silence from Trevor.

She smiled. Waking up early as a teenager had never been something she'd enjoyed.

"Thanks for driving," she added. "I'll chip in for gas."

Nick grunted, neither confirming nor accepting.

She let it go.

"I brought some donuts," he said.

"I can see you are giving your child healthy, nutritional food," she joshed.

"You say that because you've never tried to feed a teenager when you get them up before noon."

"Touché."

He tuned into the local country station, and they settled into a comfortable companionship, sipping coffee and making the occasional comment about the weather, the latest sports rankings, and the rural economy—all standard Montanan fare. The chocolate-covered donut hit the spot.

The sun was edging the eastern sky when they pulled off the main highway and onto the dirt roads of the wildlife management area surrounding the lake. They weren't alone. A few dozen pickups and SUVs lined the area where people already lined the main lake, cameras ready on tripods or steadied against their vehicles.

In front of them, lumps of white bobbled on the open water—thousands of them.

"You need to find something on this side of the lake," she said, "so Trevor and I aren't shooting into the sun."

"Bossy for this early in the morning," he replied, but he managed to find a good spot.

Trevor roused enough to climb out of the back seat but still didn't have much to say. In addition to the camera she'd given him, he had a fairly expensive digital camera around his neck.

"His mother sent it," Nick said when she glanced at him.

"Good," she said. "Now you've got two choices. If you look out there, you can see one or two begin to stir." She pointed to the east. "Sun's just about to come up. I'd say go with the digital because right now it will have the faster focus. Brace yourself against the truck and figure out what your shot is—the flock as they come off the lake, an individual bird? Then go for it. Don't think. They aren't going to give you time for that."

Already the restlessness had increased. The geese's honks sounded as loud as cars in a city traffic jam.

CJ slid the legs on her tripod open, attached the camera, and aimed it at a reasonable point in the air while shutting her eyes as she put her face to the viewfinder. There. That should do. Nick's focus was still on Trevor.

The squawking increased and the birds rose as one, a defining noise produced by white feathers with a flash of black wing tip here and there. She got caught up in the spectacle. So many birds seemingly flying in random directions until they began to sort themselves out. Several were close enough she should be able to get a shot. She bent down to the viewfinder but couldn't open her eyes. She clicked anyway, fighting back the tears that threatened to spill.

"How's that working for you?" Nick asked. "Don't you have to look to frame a picture?"

"I ... I can't," she whispered.

"How much do you trust me?" he asked.

She gave him her best version of her "You've got to be kidding" look. Must have worked.

He chuckled for a second then became serious. "Let me help you."

"How?" She looked over at Trevor.

"He's fine. He pretty much told me to beat it," Nick said with a rueful smile. "I won't let anything bad happen to you," he added, his gaze steady on her. "How about if I touch your back so you know I've got you covered?"

He was taking her seriously, not trying to tell her it was all in her head.

Okay. Maybe this could work. She could trust him for this one thing, couldn't she?

The air had chilled her cheeks, and her insides quivered with fear. If she didn't get past this though, she was going to be stuck at the ranch for a long time.

"Let's try," she said.

Before she bent to the viewfinder, she looked around for the best shot. One of the snow geese was lingering at the edge of the reeds, looking like it had slept in after a hard night before. Even it was beginning to stir, though. She shifted the camera to get the shot she wanted.

"Okay."

Nick stepped closer and put a hand on her back, heavy enough that she could feel it but not so heavy as to interfere with her movements.

She took a deep breath and put her eye to the viewfinder. Where was it? Ah, there. She focused the lens, framing the white bird in the reeds. *Squeeze the shutter. Yes!*

Again? He, or she, was beginning to honk and stretch her wings. Money shot. The bird's wings ascended, but its beak turned into a lit cigarette.

No, no, no!

She shoved the camera away.

Chapter Thirteen

Nick grabbed the tripod with his left hand, saving the camera from tumbling into the snow. With his right, he pulled CJ close to him. Her body trembled as she gasped for air.

An older man and his wife turned toward him. "You okay?" the man hollered.

"Yeah, thanks," he shouted back. "I got this."

He guided CJ back to the truck.

"I'm such a fool," she muttered over and over again.

There was no point in arguing; she wasn't really at the lake but lost in a far different, traumatic place. Was that therapist doing anything at all for her?

He needed to get her warm.

She didn't resist when he helped her into the truck's passenger seat.

"What's wrong?" Trevor asked.

"She isn't feeling well. I'm going to warm her up." He handed the tripod and camera to him. "Can you disassemble this so I can stow it in her bag?"

"Sure, Dad."

Nick retrieved one of the blankets he kept in the lockbox in the back of the pickup and wrapped it around CJ. The air in the cab had chilled in the half hour they'd been at the lake.

He hopped into the driver's side and started up the truck.

Turning up the heat full blast, he grabbed her bag. She'd said something about water and sandwiches. "Here," he said when he found the bottles, "drink this."

Staring out the windshield, she held out her hand, but there was no attempt to take it from him. He wrapped her fingers around the bottle and guided it to her lips. She drank and seemed to revive enough to grasp the bottle.

There was a knock on the door. Trevor.

With her bag in his hand, Nick turned off the truck and got out, closing the door behind him to ensure the heat stayed in the cab.

"She going to be okay?" Trevor asked. "Do we need to go to a hospital or something?"

He took the tripod and camera from his son. "I think as soon as I warm her up and get some food in her, she'll be okay. Thanks for taking care of this." He put the camera in the tote. "You hungry? She's got some sandwiches." He pulled one out. "Looks like homemade bread, too. Must be Birdie's doing."

"Who's Birdie?"

"The housekeeper at the Becks' ranch."

"Doesn't her mother do anything?" Trevor asked.

He was going to have to talk to his son about sexism, but now wasn't the time.

"She's dead, kiddo," he said softly.

"Oh. That's too bad."

"Her father's gone, too."

"Oh." Trevor took the sandwich and a bottle of water. "Okay if I go back to taking pictures?" he asked.

"That'd be fine."

Nick hopped back in the cab.

Life had begun to return to CJ's eyes.

"I'm such an idiot."

"So you said." He held out a sandwich. "Eat this."

"I can't." She pushed it away.

"You've had a shock. You need to raise your blood sugar."

"Donut?" she asked with a small smile.

"Too *much* sugar." He moved the sandwich toward her.

"God, you're worse than Birdie."

"I've never had a better compliment."

As she slowly chewed and swallowed, he watched Trevor. He'd given up the digital to use the film camera, balancing himself as he shot photos of reeds, snow, lake, and whatever birds were in the area.

Following Nick's gaze, CJ stared in the same direction. "He needs a tripod." She gave a tiny laugh. "He also needs to figure out that developing film costs money."

Just as she said that, Trevor stood and shook his head as he stared at the back of the camera. With a shrug, he put it back in its case and picked up the digital again.

"He'll get it," Nick said. "He's only thirteen."

"Were we ever that young?"

"Of course. It was only two decades ago." But he knew she wasn't talking about numbers but a loss of innocence. "It was different then. Before the Towers came down, before Iraq. These kids are born knowing the world isn't safe. We had to learn."

"Wish it hadn't gone that way," she said. "War is the suckiest thing I've ever seen. What is it they used to say in the sixties? 'War is not healthy for children or other living things.' They got that right."

"It must have been pretty horrible."

"It was." She took a deep breath and drank more of the water.

"Think you'll ever get to a point where you can live with it?" He didn't ask if she would get past it. No one ever got past trauma as ugly as what she'd experienced, both here and abroad.

"I hoped I would. Maybe."

161

"Just not quickly enough."

"Nothing is ever quick enough for me," she said, looking at him for the first time since she'd had the panic attack. "You know that."

Her eyes were clear and steady and her chin lifted as if defying life to take her down. She was amazing. If only ...

He cleared his throat. "Ready to go back?"

She shook her head. "Would it be okay if I sat here and watched the birds for a little bit? You could see how Trevor is doing."

"Sure. Are you warm enough?" He tucked the blanket around her a little more.

"Yes."

Once again, he got out of the truck. He'd give her about fifteen minutes of solitude and then check again, both on her and the warmth of the truck.

Like Trevor, photography had been the thing that held her together after the deaths of her father and mother. If she didn't have that, how would she cope? He had to help her somehow, but to do that, he had to gain her trust. She'd given him a moment only because she was desperate. Hopefully, there would be a time in the near future when she'd be able to trust him again, without all the drama.

# # #

"Thanks for the day ... and everything," CJ said as Nick pulled before the ranch house. "I'd forgotten how amazing Freezeout could be with the snow geese." She glanced at him, feeling shy, almost vulnerable. He'd seen how broken she was. She'd probably never see him again.

In the back seat, Trevor was intent on scanning his photos. How would he handle it if she disappeared from his life? A lot of people had already abandoned him.

"Hey," she said anyway, touching Trevor's propped up knee.

"Hey yourself," he said with a grin.

"Can I see?" She held out her hand for the camera.

"Okay."

As she scanned the photos, she was once again impressed by the efforts at composition. The kid had an eye. She paused at one that captured strong lines of light, lake, and black-tipped wings in triple parallel lines. "This is amazing."

"Let me see." Nick leaned forward and took the camera. "Wow." He looked back at his son. "That *is* amazing."

"Thanks." He smiled and handed a roll of film to CJ. "Can you get this developed for me?"

She reached for it, but Nick intercepted the transfer.

"How about you text me the address and I'll take care of it."

"I don't mind."

"I'd rather do it." Nick's words were harsh, but he softened them with a grin. "That way I can get him to work it off."

"D-a-a-d," Trevor whined.

They chuckled.

"Are you still looking to be out of here soon?" Nick asked.

"I'd planned ... hoped that I'd be leaving in a few weeks. But ..." She tilted her head at him and shrugged. "I don't know. The therapist wasn't encouraging on Thursday."

"You'll figure it out." Nick touched her hand.

Her first instinct was to pull away, but she forced herself to stay still. He didn't mean her harm; he'd proved that.

"Anyway," she said, "thanks for the day."

"Can you come up some time and show me all the focus and

speed stuff on the digital camera?" Trevor asked.

"I'd like that." She glanced at Nick.

"That'd be great. Let me know. We both appreciate it." He leaned toward her slightly then backed off.

She shoved open the door.

Movement in the corral by the barn caught her attention. A saddled horse, Prince maybe, danced in the center of the space, his head flicking the reins that hung down from his nose. Everything else was still around him.

Where was her brother?

Without shutting the truck door, she walked toward the fence railing, her pace slow so she didn't startle the animal. Behind her, a squeal told her Nick had opened the driver's door.

The horse tossed his head even higher.

She glanced at Nick and went back to working her way forward, finally getting to a point where she could see the full saddle.

A boot was wedged in the stirrup. Its owner's leg slopped toward the ground

Her heart went to her throat as Nick came up beside her. She looked at him and he nodded.

"Trust me," he whispered in her ear.

Could she? Twice in one day?

Her brother needed help. She couldn't let her own fears get in the way of saving him.

The horse had stopped shaking its head and was gazing at them intently. Overhead, several geese squawked, their V-shaped line snaking its way north. Sun glinted on the icicles as they dripped from the barn eaves, seemingly a normal winter day.

"Okay," she whispered.

Nick climbed through the rails and took a few steps forward.

The animal focused on him. Steadily, Nick walked and stretched out his hand in the universal sign of supplication. A breeze ruffled his hair and the horse's forelock.

She held her breath.

Trevor came up next to her, his gaze intent on his father's movements.

The horse stomped a hoof.

Nick froze.

The tableau remained for a few moments before Nick whispered again and made his slow motions forward. Soon he reached the horse and allowed it to sniff him. Snorts and head shaking accompanied this inspection.

Then the animal shied a few steps away, dragging whoever was attached to him with him.

CJ's hand flew to her mouth to keep her involuntary gasp from escaping.

Nick went through the motions again, and again the animal shied. The third time he was able to stroke the hairy chin. As he stepped right, she saw he'd gathered the reins in his left hand but still kept his movements deliberate as he reached for the stirrup to free the foot and cradle it to the ground.

As soon as he was free, the horse backed away from the scene. Nick turned and waved her toward him. She started to run, but he held out his hand and pumped it down.

She slowed to a walk as Nick led the horse to the fence and hitched him to a rail. He got to Jarod about the same time she did.

Her brother didn't stir and his leg didn't look right.

# # #

"It's going to be a long night," CJ said to Nick when she saw Trevor falling asleep in the chair. "Why don't you take him home?" She gestured to the boy. "Dylan can give me a ride home."

"Are you sure?" Nick asked, touching her arm. "I don't mind. Trevor's got tomorrow to catch up on sleep before school."

"Thanks, but you've done enough, and Trevor needs to be in his own bed." She grinned but took a step to escape his touch.

He dropped his arm.

"Okay. Keep me posted."

"Will do," Dylan said, shaking his hand. "Thanks again for everything. If you hadn't found him, he'd be in worse shape."

After they'd gotten the horse away from Jarod, Nick had called 911 and wrapped her brother in blankets as best he could without moving him. She had to tamp down the fear that they couldn't stay where they were. It was the ranch she'd grown up on, not a war zone.

The sun was hazy behind the high clouds but still gave off enough warmth at the high elevation to provide some comfort. Settled, Prince gave the occasional nicker and side glance before Trevor took him into the barn, took off his gear, and placed him in the stall.

The EMTs had arrived in a half hour and bundled Jarod off to Benefis Teton Medical Center. The emergency room doctor said he had a mild concussion and a broken leg.

"I've set it, and we'll keep him overnight. He should be awake by morning."

"And if he's not?" she'd asked.

"I'm sure he'll be fine." He'd raised a hand like he was going to pat her shoulder, looked at her expression, and thought better of it. "I'll let you know if there's any change."

Once Nick and Trevor left, Dylan and CJ settled themselves

into the worn chairs of the waiting room. She picked at the nubby fabric until her brother glared at her.

Sighing, she selected an out-of-date fashion magazine and flipped through it. The latest styles and makeup tips had never fascinated her and they still didn't.

She'd let her family down ... again. If she hadn't gone off to Freezeout to try against all odds to get a photo, she would have been there and could have gotten to Jarod earlier. And she had only one picture to show for it.

Avoiding relationships with other people was the only solution. They were better off without her. Ben would still be alive—

"Stop it," Dylan said. "I can see the smoke coming out of your ears. It wasn't your fault."

"If I'd been there—"

"You might not have seen it happen. I was there, remember? But I was painting—not even a thought about what anyone else was doing."

"What is Jarod doing with that horse, anyway?"

"I can't get him to tell me anything concrete," Dylan said. "You know how rodeo crazy he was when we were growing up. All he wanted to do was rope calves."

"Yeah." Like a lot of things, the dream had gone down the drain when her father died.

"I think the current plan involves training horses to be calf ropers, either other people's horses or training and selling."

"Starting with a rescue was risky."

"It was a cheap horse."

Ah. Money was always an issue. Not that there wasn't enough but that it had to be managed.

"We've got a bigger problem than that," Dylan said.

"What's that?"

"Calving season is coming up. I doubt that leg'll be good enough to handle the work. Plus, Jarod had 20 percent more cows inseminated this year over last to try to make up for some lost revenues."

"When do you think they'll start dropping?" she asked.

"In a few weeks. Then we'll need to watch them, vaccinate them, ear tags. You know the drill."

She did. It was hard, exhausting work that allowed little sleep. While the ranch wasn't huge, it was going to take two people to handle the intense workload.

Based on her conversation with the therapist, she wasn't going anywhere soon. "I can help out for a few weeks. The therapist isn't satisfied I can hold it together yet."

"You sure you remember how?"

"To hold it together?"

"No, to wrestle a calf without mama kicking you in your butt."

"Oh, that. Sure." At least she thought she did. It had to be easier than holding herself together.

"I guess we're going to find out," Dylan said.

# # #

From Catherine's diary, October 1943:

"The war seems to go on and on. There are hardly any men left in Montana. A lot of them come to the new army air corps base to train, but then they're on their way. It's no fun to be young in the forties when your man's gone.

I sound like a whiner. Buck up, Catherine! At least I have a job and friends. Mom went from her father's house to Dad's. All she's ever done is cook and clean. She says she's happy though.

When am I going to get married? I'm ready to start a big one. All Stephen has to do is come back. He's told me we'll get married the first time he's furloughed home so everyone knows I'm his girl.

What if he doesn't come home?

Heavens to Betsy! What a silly thought. Montana boys are tough. They'll all make it home.

# # #

"Is this Mr. Sturgis?" a stern female voice asked when he picked up the phone Monday morning.

"Yes, ma'am. How can I help you?" Nick replied, just as his mother had taught him.

"Trevor's father?"

"Yes, ma'am. What's this about?"

"This is Mrs. Helms, vice principal of Choteau High School. I need you to come to the school for a conference regarding your son."

"Now?"

"Now would be good, Mr. Sturgis. He will be in the office until your arrival. How soon do you think that will be?"

"Uh ... a half hour."

"We'll see you then." The phone disconnected.

What the ...?

Without buttoning his coat, Nick strode to the truck and got into the driver's seat, buckling the seat belt as the truck headed down the long driveway to the main road.

What had Trevor been thinking? Hell, what had he done to annoy the vice principal?

He got to the end of the drive and waited a tad too long to apply the brakes. The truck skidded into the intersection and shuddered to a stop.

Nick's heart raced. Getting himself killed wasn't going to help his son. He took a deep breath, made the turn, and headed into town.

Mrs. Helm's office was in the same room as it was when he went to high school. The furniture had been updated and the framed photos showed different people, but it was still the no-nonsense space he remembered.

Trevor was already in the other guest chair.

Mrs. Helms, a curly-haired woman probably in her forties, gestured to the remaining chair.

He sat then cleared his throat. "What seems to be the problem?"

"Your son was fighting on school grounds."

He wanted to ask if it would have been okay if Trevor had been fighting off school grounds but instead, he said, "I'm sure there's a good explanation."

Mrs. Helms smiled in a way that reminded him of a cat ... a large, hungry mountain lion.

"There *is* no good explanation for fighting," she said.

He flicked a glance at Trevor, who was pointedly staring out the window.

"Don't you even want to know what happened?" he asked. His son wasn't going to be railroaded by a vice principal, no matter how correct the charge might be.

"I already do. The morning duty teacher saw the whole thing. Trevor hit another boy in the stomach, the boy retaliated, and it escalated from there."

Trevor shifted in his chair but continued to stare out the

window.

"Who is the other boy? Is he in trouble, too?"

"He will be taken care of, Mr. Sturgis. The person you need to be worried about is your son. I'm giving him a three-day suspension. Talk to him about violence. I expect him to comply to school rules when he comes back." She signed a piece of paper, tore off the top two copies, and gave the bottom one to him.

The air in the room seemed to be seeping through the cracks. All he could smell was an overly floral scent, but he couldn't tell whether it was from an air freshener or the woman herself. All he knew was that it was time to get Trevor out of here.

"Let's go," he said.

Mrs. Helms rose from behind her desk. "Thank you for coming in." She didn't extend a hand.

He nodded and left, sensing Trevor behind him.

They were silent on the walk to the truck and silent on the drive home. Nick couldn't think of anything to say except to yell at his son and ask why he'd been so stupid.

Even he knew that wasn't recommended parenting.

Chapter Fourteen

When they got home, Nick said, "Hang up your things and then sit at the table. We need to talk."

A grunt was all he got.

He grabbed a mug of coffee, sat at the table, and waited, sipping while he did. The acid brew scoured an already roiled stomach, and he put the mug down.

Trevor thumped into the chair.

"So tell me, what happened?" Nick asked.

"You heard her. I punched a guy." Trevor looked anywhere but at his father.

"I want to know why."

Trevor shrugged. "He's a jerk."

"Lots of people are jerks. We don't go around and randomly hit them. What did he do?"

"I don't want to talk about it."

"He must have done something." Nick leaned forward and tapped on Trevor's arm to get his attention. "I know you. You don't hit people without a good reason."

"You don't know me. You haven't been around for the last four years. Gerard never complains about anything I do, and at least he's there. I don't need you, and I don't want to be here."

Only a kid could slice through a man's jugular so easily.

"We're not talking about the last four years. We're talking about right now, when you are here. I'm still your father, no matter what the circumstances. Now tell me what happened."

"I told you. I don't want to talk about it." Trevor took out his phone.

"The phone," Nick said.

"What about it?"

"Give it to me. You get it back when you go back to school."

"No."

Nick simply held out his hand.

"I'm not giving it to you."

God help him and give him the strength and patience he needed.

"Fine. Have it your way." Trevor tossed the phone on the table with a clank, pushed back his chair, and stomped to his room.

Parenting sucked. Big time. Best to let the kid cool down before tackling him again.

He slid Trevor's phone into a top kitchen cabinet, slid his own in his pocket, threw on his coat, and went outside to the barn to muck stalls.

An hour later, he'd burned off some of the energy he'd accumulated in Mrs. Helm's hot little room. Too bad that Trevor was on her radar now. He'd have less leeway to mess up.

Nick perched on a hay bale with a glass of water he'd poured from the big jug he kept in the barn and took out his phone. "Hi, it's Nick," he said when CJ answered. "How's Jarod?"

"Grumpy."

Nick chuckled.

"He's out of the hospital and making lists for everyone," she continued. "You'd think no one had ever lived on a ranch before. He's driving Dylan and Birdie crazy."

"And you?"

"I could use a break, too."

"Well, I may have just the thing." He told her about the

situation with Trevor.

"Wow. He must have had a good reason. I can't see him hauling off and belting someone like that," she said.

"Me neither. But I can't get him to tell me what happened."

"And you think that he might open up to me while we're taking pictures."

"Something like that."

She was silent for a few moments.

It was a stupid idea. Trevor wasn't her kid. Why should she care?

"Look," she said. "I've got an appointment at one. Why don't I come up after that? By that time he may be ready for diversion."

"Sounds good."

After Nick hung up the phone, he leaned against the wall behind him. Had it really been the best idea to contact CJ? He was already getting used to having her around. So was Trevor. Yet she'd always been up front that she'd be heading out again as soon as she was cleared.

What kind of fool's errand was he chasing?

He snagged a piece of hay and chewed on it for a while, hoping enlightenment would strike while he was sitting there. Did all parents muddle through like this? Probably. Should he call Grace and discuss the problem with her? Probably.

Crap.

# # #

"Seems like I just saw you," CJ said as she settled herself in Gerri's office. "I hope you didn't expect much between last week and now."

"It only takes a moment for clarity to strike," Gerri said,

perching in her black chair, pen poised over her pad.

"I don't think I've found that split second yet."

"Yet you seem to have found a sense of humor."

"I suppose. I guess I've accepted that you aren't going to let me go yet, and if you don't, the doctor in Great Falls won't, and if he doesn't ... It's like those lines from Shakespeare—one of those king plays."

"For want of a nail?"

"Yeah. Except in this case it's for want of a picture."

"Have you made any progress with that?" Gerri asked.

CJ fidgeted with her purse, unsure how much to share. What if the therapist believed this was a huge leap forward and expected more from her? Or would she think that the effort it had taken to get this *one* picture wasn't enough? With a trembling hand, CJ brought forth the print of the photo she'd taken.

Somehow, she'd managed to capture the swan just as it was lifting its wings.

"This is amazing!" Gerri said when she saw the photo. "Freezeout?"

CJ nodded, feeling like a shy child who'd shown her first drawing.

"So, tell me how this came about," the therapist said.

"Well ..."

"It's okay," Gerri said. "You're safe. Nothing goes beyond this office."

"Tough to do in a small town."

"You don't know the half of it," the woman said with a grin.

The tension in CJ's body dissipated a fraction.

"I went with Nick and his son. I'm teaching Trevor about photography. It's something he's interested in. Anyway." She picked up a throw pillow, put it in her lap, and squished it with her hands. "Nick … I mean … I was taking a picture … and … well, he knows the problem. He offered to help." More pillow squeezing. "He put his hand on my shoulder and that steadied me … well … enough for one picture." She gestured at the paper Gerri held in her hand.

"He made you feel safe."

"For a bit."

"Then what?"

CJ told her about the panic attack.

"It may seem like a little step to you," Gerri said, "but for me it's an enormous leap in two areas. First"—she ticked them off on her fingers—"you took a picture. Second, you allowed a man—not just any man, but your high school sweetheart—to help you and to touch you. Big steps."

"I guess so."

"What would you say to someone who told you what you told me?"

"I'd tell them pretty much what you just told me," CJ admitted. "I guess I'm pretty hard on myself."

"Yes." The therapist was quiet.

Her high school sweetheart. And the first man who'd broken her heart. Yet she'd let him get closer to her than any man since … well, since forever. She never would have let Ben help her like that. More proof she'd never really loved the man.

How could she take his money?

Something she'd have to think about later.

"So, now what?" CJ asked.

"More of the same."

"That would mean spending the rest of my life around Nick," she said with a grin.

Something that didn't sound too bad.

"I don't think you need to go that far. Find safe spaces. Safe places. Your brothers?"

"Jarod isn't safe for anyone right now." CJ filled the therapist in on the accident. "But Dylan might be okay."

"He's a painter, isn't he?" Gerri asked, checking her notes.

CJ nodded. Dylan would understand.

# # #

A half hour later she was on her way to Nick's, unsure if participating in a problem between father and son was a good idea. It implied an intimacy that didn't exist. What would Grace think? Of course she'd been the one to abandon Trevor in the first place. What kind of mother did that?

Probably one who was at their wit's end.

Up until this point, Trevor had been easy to work with. What would happen if he thought he was being manipulated? She tried to think back to her own rages when she was a teen. She didn't want to see anyone about anything.

Of course, that had been when she needed her camera most.

She knocked on Nick's door and let herself into the mudroom. Knocking again, she waited for his hello before she opened the door and stuck her head inside.

"How about I take him down to the ranch?" she asked. "Do you think he'd like that?"

"No clue. I can ask."

Nick disappeared down the hallway.

She leaned against the doorway. The ranch would be neutral territory for Trevor. Even Jarod, cantankerous as he was at the moment, would be nice to him, which meant a respite for her.

"Dad says you want to show me your ranch," Trevor said,

looking like he'd woken from a nap.

"It would help me out, actually," she said. "My brother's been a grump ever since the accident. If you hang around he'll be nicer."

"You sure about that?" Trevor sounded doubtful.

"Yep." Well, mostly. "I figure you could bring your digital and we'd work on taking pictures of some of the horses moving."

"Cows, too." An element of excitement entered his voice.

"I don't think you'll get much movement out of them."

"Okay."

"What time do you think you'll be back?" Nick asked, as if nothing major had happened that morning.

"Hour or so. Sun will be going down. It's too cold for night photography."

"I'll get my things," Trevor said.

During the ride to the ranch, she asked him about his life in Seattle and what he'd taken pictures of. It sounded like much of his time was spent roaming the streets and getting grab shots of people.

"That's why I want to learn black and white," he said. "I think I can catch more of a person's expression than I can in color. Like Margaret Bourke-White."

"You know about her?"

"Yeah. There was an exhibit in Seattle. Mom took me. She did some rad things with black and white."

"She certainly did. You can make your digital camera shoot black and white, you know."

"Yeah, I figured that out. I just can't get the contrast right."

"I'll show you when we get to the ranch."

# # #

A few hours later, CJ was exhausted.

Jarod had been civil but reminded her of the chores she still needed to do. Trevor started to help but then decided he'd rather take pictures. She'd shown him how to access the black and white features and pointed him in the direction of the horses. Instead, he'd decided to take pictures of her working. "I really like taking pictures of people," he'd said.

As she did her chores, he had her stop and pose. It felt like he made these demands every few minutes.

"You know," she said when she sat down on a hay bale to rest, "you're going to need to learn to take pictures while people are moving. Not everyone's going to stop and pose for you while they're working."

"I know. I was working on framing—like we talked about last time."

"I suppose I can't ask you to learn everything at once," she said. Heaving herself off the hay, she opened Jarod's fridge. "Coke?" she asked.

"That'd be great. Thanks."

She handed it to him and popped one of her own. Ungodly sweet. She may never reacquire her taste for American pop. Probably just as well. She was getting of an age where every calorie counted. Hell, she'd put on five pounds in the few months since she'd been home.

"Can I see?" she asked.

He handed over the camera.

Once again she was struck by his ability. He had a real future in the field if he stuck with it. But first, he needed to get through his teenage years. And life was throwing him a bunch of curveballs.

"He's a bully," Trevor said, as if answering an unasked question.

"Who?"

"The guy I hit."

"Oh. Does the school know?"

"Yeah. But they don't care. His dad's on the school board. Donates a lot to the basketball team. The guy I hit is a big shot on the team."

"Oh." She knew how that went. For a long time bullies seemed to disappear, but they'd had a resurgence almost everywhere she looked. People in positions of power too willing to throw their weight and money around.

"So what pushed you over the line?" she asked.

"He wanted to date this girl in my class. She said no. He wasn't happy."

CJ waited.

"I can't believe the things he said about her. Mainly online but also where she could hear him. Said she'd ... you know ... hook up." His cheeks turned red. "Trashed her reputation."

"Did people believe him?"

"The ones who wanted to, sure. Some didn't. But then he put his hand on her ... um ... you know ..." Trevor waved his hand around. "His friends all grouped around him so no one could see. I was at the edge of the building. He didn't see me. He told her that she was too small and to ask her daddy to buy her bigger ones."

Ugh. No girl needed to go through that.

"So why didn't you say anything to the vice principal?"

"Are you kidding? I'm the new guy. No one's going to believe me."

"Maybe. But if no one stands up to these guys, they aren't

going to go away."

Trevor looked at her incredulously. "I punched him in the stomach. Isn't that enough?"

She laughed, finished her soda, and stood. "Violence is the easy way out, I'm afraid. And you suffered the consequences— you're on suspension." She shook her head. "With all the wars I've seen, I haven't seen one that really solved a problem yet. It's conversation and listening that does that." She picked up the bin of ear tags she'd collected from various spots around the barn and thrust it on a shelf. "I think I'm done. Let's get you back home."

He stood up. "What do you think I should do?"

"Tell your dad what you told me. He might be able to help you sort it out. He never did have much tolerance for mean people."

"Okay." Trevor's voice still held some doubt, but he'd have to work it out himself.

The bitter tang of garlic and sweet smell of sautéed onions greeted them when they walked into the cabin.

"Hungry?" Nick asked. He was at the stove, stirring a mixture with a wooden spoon, and he turned his head to give them a grin that was everything a woman could want—appreciation, safety, and a hint of sexual availability.

Damn. Thinking of him that way led directly to heartache. Nothing else.

Trevor disappeared down the hallway.

She looked away. "I should be getting home."

"C'mon," he said, putting the spoon on the counter. "It's a beautiful trout I caught last summer with some roasted vegetables. Ice cream for dessert. How can you turn that down? Besides, I owe you for working with Trevor."

"I enjoy it," she said. "It's not work."

He turned around, and once again she was struck by how

good he looked. It was as if her eyes had suddenly been opened. For the first time since the beginning of her marriage with Ben, heat stirred within her.

That was all it was. And it wasn't something to explore with Nick. When she got back out on the road again, she'd indulge. Not until then.

"Well?" he asked, holding up a glass of white wine.

What the hell.

"Sure," she said. She took the glass.

"How did it go?" he asked.

She glanced down the hall. "He's got talent. It should be encouraged."

"How?"

"Ask to look at his pictures. Maybe use them for your website. Encourage him to take pictures for the yearbook or whatever they do these days."

Nick nodded.

"Any word from Grace about what's going to happen?" she asked.

"No. I called to tell her about the fight and it was basically, 'I told you so.' She thinks he's acting out—talking about sending him away to school. I told her she was jumping the gun and to give him a chance here. But it's going to be an uphill battle."

"There's more going on than that." She smiled. "I think he's more like you than Grace wants to see."

"Did he say something?"

"Yes, but I think he should tell you himself."

Nick looked at her as if he was going to disagree but then said, "You're probably right. You guys have a good relationship. No use in spoiling it."

"Right."

"Why don't you sit on the couch while I finish assembling this and put it in the oven?" he asked.

"Sounds good," she said.

She settled down into the comfort of his well-padded couch. The evening sun colored the sky. A few hawks, probably red-tailed, swooped on the air currents, their sharp eyes searching for unwary prey.

Like humans, their eyes were in the front of their face. Hunters with a greater ability to search and destroy. The difference was, hawks limited it to going after food and defending young. Humans seemed to have another agenda all together. Would they ever figure out that mutual destruction made no sense?

Probably not. Her job, revealing the truth of what was going on in a far-off world, didn't make a difference.

With a sigh, she took another sip of wine.

The sky embraced the colors of evening ... first the pinks and baby blues, then the bright yellow brought the deeper reds, oranges, and purples as the sun started its slow slide behind the granite mountains.

"It really is amazing," Nick said as the couch sagged with his weight.

"Yes." She should take a picture. But her camera was at home.

She did have her phone. Maybe with Nick here ...

"I want to take a picture," she said. "Do you think you could stand close to me?"

"Of course. Where do you want to go?"

"How do we get to your porch?" she asked.

"Door's over there," he said, pointing to an alcove by the kitchen area. "It's cold outside. Do you need a jacket?"

She shook her head. "I just want a few pictures." She looked at him and smiled. "More than one without freaking out would be an achievement."

"I get that."

Once they got to the porch she framed the piece of sky she wanted in the camera and stared for a few moments.

Nick was inches away.

She was safe.

She pressed the shutter button.

A deep breath.

She framed another part of the sky and clicked again.

Two pictures.

The reds in the sky changed texture in her mind's eye.

She was going to muscle through this. Ben's death was not going to defeat her.

Another deep breath.

Three.

"I think that's about it," she said, lowering the camera and turning to Nick.

"I'm glad I can help you do that," he said softly. "It feels good to see you coming back to life."

His gaze was soft, and she felt the tug of awareness. Her pulse became more rapid, and the cold that had been seeping into her bones retreated. She stared at him, her lips slightly parted.

He stroked her cheek once with his hand then rested it on her chin for a few seconds before he dropped it.

"As desirable as you are and as much as I want to kiss you right now," he said, "I don't think it's a good idea. Too many decisions coming up for you, and I have Trevor to think about." He sighed. "But don't for a moment think I wouldn't like it."

"I'd like it, too." She shivered. "But I understand. Let's go inside, shall we? It's cold."

"Yeah. Dinner should be about ready."

As she followed him indoors, the might-have-beens made her heart ache. It was foolish though. If Grace had never appeared, she and Nick still wouldn't have stayed together. Too much had happened.

Maybe the therapist was right—the answer to her happiness not only lay in forgiving herself for the recent past but in letting go of all the resentment she held toward everyone in her past.

"Nick?" she said after they got inside.

Trevor still hadn't emerged from his bedroom.

He turned, his forehead in a small frown, as if he were trying to wrap his mind around something.

She plunged ahead.

"I wanted to tell you ... I mean ... I forgive you for high school ... for dumping me, that is."

God, that sounded lame.

She opened her mouth to try again.

"Hush," he said, a smile reframing his mouth. "I get it. Thank you. It means a lot to me." And then he did kiss her. Just a brush of his lips against hers, but it felt like a tsunami hit her.

More, her greedy little soul whispered.

Chapter Fifteen

Instead of kissing her again, Nick walked to the stove and lifted the lid on dinner at the same moment Trevor walked into the room. Nick's son looked more relaxed than he had during the day. His shoulders had reached their natural level instead of being hunched to his ears, and the lines between his eyebrows, so like his own, had disappeared.

He walked to the stove. "Smells good," he said.

"It's about ready. How about setting the table?"

"Okay," Trevor said. "And Dad?"

"What, kid?"

"I'm sorry."

Nick glanced at her and said with a grin, "Wow. Two confessions in the space of ten minutes. I'm a lucky guy." The smile faded a bit. "Seriously, thanks. That means a lot." He gave Trevor a brief but strong hug.

Dinner was delicious. The fish, cooked to perfection without being dry, lay on a bed of onions, garlic, olives, and fennel. The wine Nick had given her enhanced all the flavors.

"How'd you get to be such a gourmet cook?" she asked with a smile.

"Outfitting," he said. "A lot of my tours, particularly the nature tours and fishing, come with those extra touches that make them popular with the more well-heeled tourists." He grinned. "I've got an awesome liquor cabinet, too. Of course, I pack it into reusable containers so the horses and mules don't have to tote glass, too. They're pretty flat when we pack back out."

"And you do this all by yourself?"

"No, John and Grant, my assistants, help me with the packing, the trip, the unpacking."

"I can help now, too, can't I, Dad?" Trevor asked.

"Sure, just remember these are paying guests. Even if we don't like them or their politics, we need to be nice."

"You mean I can't punch them in the stomach."

"Exactly."

"About that, Dad ..." Trevor told his father what he'd previously told CJ.

She could see Nick was having a bit of trouble keeping his temper under control.

"I'm glad you told me," he said when Trevor was done. "Tomorrow I'll call Mrs. Helms and make an appointment to see if we can straighten this out."

"What if she doesn't believe me? I'm the new kid—and I did punch him first."

"Oh, don't get me wrong, you're still in trouble. But you were right to be upset. Saying nasty things about someone because they won't do what you want or believe what you believe isn't right. Nor is touching someone when they don't want it. Fighting isn't the answer, but there has to be a way."

CJ hoped he was right. Some days it felt like the bullies of the world were getting the upper hand and hanging onto it tight.

Time to worry about the state of the world another time. Right now, it was important to enjoy being home for a while and guard her heart against the man who was most capable of breaking it for a second time.

# # #

CJ climbed up the steps to Cassandra's office the following

Wednesday. While Jarod hadn't said anything about the taxes, a few weeks had gone by and she hadn't heard anything from the attorney. She had to show her brothers she could pull her own weight at the ranch—not only physically, but in ways they hadn't imagined.

Jarod was old-fashioned, tended to do things the way they'd always been done, and who knew where Dylan's mind was half the time. They weren't used to dealing with bureaucracies. She was—governments, non-government organizations, and hangers-on of all stripes, mercenaries, religious charities, and the like. The Teton County tax department was simply a different version.

She'd gone to Cassandra to expedite the process, but if the lawyer couldn't handle it, she'd tackle it herself. Ben's estate was a different matter. She needed to make sure that was handled the right way. There was a time when using professionals made sense.

As before, there was no one in the waiting room. For some reason, the air was stuffy, with a hangover of sandalwood. She normally liked the scent, but this was too sweet and cloying. She coughed.

The inner door opened.

"Oh, hello," Cassandra said. "You're early. I wasn't expecting you for another—" She glanced at the polished gold wall clock. "Oh, I guess you're right on time." She gave a sharp look toward the door. "I just need to straighten up some things and I'll be right with you."

"Okay." CJ settled into a chair, her senses on high alert, like they'd been before air strikes in war zones. Probably her imagination, but it would be a good idea to learn more about the attorney and where the picture in her office had been taken. Unfortunately, that would need to wait until the snow cleared.

"I can see you now," Cassandra said.

In the inner office, the sandalwood aroma was even stronger; it almost smelled like a man's cologne. If someone had been wearing it, where was he? And why had the attorney kept it secret?

As she took her seat, CJ glanced at the spot where the landscape had been the last time she was in the office.

It was gone. In its place was a black and white photo of tulips in a vase, totally different in nature from the rest of the artwork on the walls.

"So, here's what I've learned," Cassandra began. "There's a lot confusion at the tax department. Apparently, someone was working there who was not following procedures. There's a suspicion she may have even been skimming from some of the tax payments—particularly those in paid in cash. She'd pretend to be without a receipt book and promised to mail it to the property owner."

"And this being Montana, people believed her."

"Yep. Seems her husband had been diagnosed with colon cancer and they didn't have any insurance, barely had enough money to pay their bills every month."

"So we're not the only ones in this predicament," CJ said.

"No. My understanding is that the county has hired an outside forensic accounting firm and the woman has been removed and told to retain a lawyer."

"Are you representing her?"

"No. My area of expertise is tax and estate law. Since she doesn't have cash, she's going for a public defender."

It was a sad story. Too many people were being backed into hard corners lately.

"However," Cassandra continued. "There's a good side and a bad side to the accounting review. My understanding is the tax department has experienced a lot of cronyism over the past hundred years."

"Hard not to, with a small town."

Cassandra picked up a mug and took a sip.

"Oh!" she exclaimed. "I've been so scattered, I forgot to offer you coffee. Would you like some?"

"Yes, that would be nice."

Walking to the credenza that held a fancy one-cup coffeemaker, the lawyer pressed a few buttons and put a mug on the shelf. While the machine hissed and steamed, she turned back toward CJ and leaned against the piece of furniture.

"Do you know if your family owns the mineral rights to the ranch?" she asked.

"Why wouldn't we? We own the land, don't we?" Or did they? She remembered something her dad had mentioned once in passing. He'd been hungry for cash. Gas and oil companies were willing to pay a small fortune to drill on their land, but he couldn't find any documentation on the family's mineral rights.

"In Montana, landowners can sell or lease the right to drill or mine on their land. Anything the owner of the mineral rights takes from the land is theirs—oil, gas, silver, copper, or any of the trace minerals that are so valuable now."

"Yes, I remember that now. I don't know if we own them or not."

"However, the mineral rights owner is also responsible for any taxes the county or state levied on mineral rights—something Teton County just voted into existence."

Crap. They could get an extra tax.

"How do I find out about the mineral rights?"

"There should be a record in the county property office. I could do a title search for you." Cassandra gave her a bright smile.

"I'll look into it myself." No need to pay someone to pry any further into their personal business. Besides, there was something hinky about the rights ... if only she could remember what it was.

"How about the estate?"

"I think we have that about finished. Brad is great to work with—thanks for introducing me."

CJ half-listened while Cassandra told her what to expect. The other half of her brain, at least the part that wasn't being eaten away by guilt, was trying to remember what her father had said about the mineral rights. So many things to figure out. Would she find the answers before she returned to her real life?

# # #

CJ had made an appointment with Brad Small the same day to discuss what to do with the money coming her way. Much as she wanted to refuse it, the ranch could use an infusion of capital, and wise investments would make sure she had someone to care for her when she grew old. There wouldn't be any children, and she doubted there'd be a husband.

No man she knew would put up with the career she had, and she wasn't about to change it. The sooner she got out of Montana, the better.

The meeting was brief, resulting in more questions that needed answering—mostly by her. She thanked him, stuffed his list in her purse, and headed back out into the cold. The temperatures hovered near zero again, belying the brief taste of spring that had tempted them at Freezeout.

"CJ!" Trish's voice stopped her just as she was about to get into the Jeep. "C'mon in for a cup of coffee. I just took a peach pie out of the oven."

Coffee would have gotten her inside, but the idea of a slice of hot, oozing pie sealed the deal. She slammed the door closed and trudged to the family side of the structure.

"Brrr," Trish said as she closed the door behind CJ. "Now's about the time I get tired of winter."

"At least another month, maybe two to go," she replied.

"How are you handling it? After the desert, I mean." Trish took CJ's bulky coat and hung it on a nearby peg before leading the way down the long hall to a spacious kitchen in back without bothering to wait for an answer.

Everything gleamed with stainless steel, from the walk-in freezer to the multiple ovens and racks of waiting pies. The space was redolent with the aroma of sweet fruit and spices.

"Today's my baking day," Trish said, pouring steaming liquid into a mug advertising Glacier National Park, before topping off her own. "I prep all week, store them, and then bake from dawn til dusk. Tomorrow I'll deliver them."

"Sounds exhausting," CJ said, watching her old classmate cut generous slices from the still-steaming pastry.

"I love it. I've always enjoyed baking and crafts like knitting—the domestic side of things. Cleaning? Not so much." She laughed. "But when Brad started his own business, I got the bug, too. Two kids derailed me for a while, but as soon as they were old enough to help, I started. A few years ago we saved enough to build this wing."

CJ took a sip of coffee and cut off a bite of pie with her fork. Respecting the steam rising from the utensil, she blew on it for a bit.

People changed so much as they became adults. While she'd pictured Trish and Brad getting married, it never occurred to her in high school that they'd each start businesses. But whoever thought about that kind of thing as a teen?

"Is it successful?"

"It's steady. I'm not going to become a millionaire, but it sure helps with the bills, and with college for our two on the horizon—even if they go to a state school, it's a chunk. Well, let's just say the money is spent as soon as it comes in."

College ... then Trish's kids, too, would be entering the adult world of jobs, businesses, and families. Time was going too fast. And all CJ had to show for it was a few grains of desert sand.

She better figure out what she was doing with her life.

"So what's changed in town? Any more of our class hanging around?"

Trish filled her in on the local gossip. Between the sweetness of the pie and the warmth of the conversation, CJ relaxed.

"And how about you?" Trish finally asked. "How are you adapting to being home?"

"There's good and bad," CJ said.

"Isn't there always?" Trish asked, her smile soft. "I remember thinking as a kid that if I planned enough and stuck to it, did the right things, and went to church on Sundays, nothing bad would ever happen. That worked fine until life happened." She plucked crumbs from her shirt. "The first big blow was when I lost Nathan."

CJ wrinkled her forehead in confusion.

Trish turned back to her. "Nathan was my firstborn. He was born with a heart defect. They tried their best but ..." Trish splayed her hands in a helpless gesture.

War wasn't the only place tragic things happened.

"I'm so sorry."

Trish swiped at her eyes. "It was a long time ago, but sometimes it seems like yesterday." She seemed to shake herself out of her reverie. "More coffee?"

"A little, then I need to go." CJ made a face. "Your husband has given me homework."

"He's good at that." Trish laughed.

Suddenly, CJ wanted to know. Brad and Trish seemed happy, in spite of their loss. How did that happen?

"And you and Brad get along well?"

"More than I'd ever imagined. He's turned out to be one of the good ones. Even when we disagree, he's willing to work it out. Sometimes I need to go somewhere to calm down first, but it's a commitment we made in the beginning—we were going to do what it took to make it work."

Something she and Ben hadn't done. They'd been more like two comrades in arms, flitting from adventure to adventure in the good times, going solo during the bad. A prescription for the disaster their marriage had been.

"You'll figure it out," Trish said.

"I'm afraid that ship has sailed." CJ took a few more bites of the amazing pie in front of her.

"That's not true." A timer dinged and Trish pulled more steaming pies from the oven then slid a few more into its cavernous space. "When you find the right person, it will all fall into place, no matter how old you are."

CJ's thoughts flicked to Nick. At sixteen, they'd thought they'd been destined for each other. Now they were more than twice that age. She had to admit, the spark was still there. There might be a possibility ... if only their work didn't keep them thousands of miles away from each other.

"Do you have to work in the Middle East?" Trish asked, as if reading her mind. She was prepping pie boxes. "I mean, there's plenty of trouble right here." She stopped and leaned against the counter. "Drugs, human trafficking, especially on the reservations, and environmentally we're slowly blowing ourselves up. Come home, CJ. We need your talents right here."

"That would mean coming back to Montana."

"It's not that bad." Trish laughed and went back to folding boxes. "We're not any more isolated than the desert, even if we're a tad colder."

"A tad?" CJ let a chuckle escape her lungs. It had an odd, disused sound.

"Well, maybe more than that."

"It's not the cold that keeps me away. You know that." Something about the older Trish made it possible for CJ to be truthful. Maybe it was her open expression, or the confession of her own loss. Who knew?

"That was a long time ago, CJ. It's time to move on. Your dad messed up—he was imperfect, like most of us. He just managed to do it in a big and tragic way that affected a lot of people."

But that wasn't all of it, she wanted to protest. But she was being ridiculous. She'd told Nick she forgave him for high school, but what did that mean? They were just words ... she'd have to let go of a little of her lifetime of resentment, too, and who knew where that would end? Would she find the strength to forgive Ben? Her father?

Herself?

"You're thinking too hard," Trish said, handing her a box with pie. "Here, go find a sweetheart and celebrate Valentine's Day tomorrow." She grinned. "I hear there's one of your old ones on the loose."

"With a growing teenager who would do a lot of damage to this pie," CJ said, allowing herself a smile at the idea.

Maybe it wasn't a—she almost groaned aloud—half-baked

idea. It had been decades since she'd celebrated hearts and flowers. Ben hadn't believed in the holiday.

"Thanks," she said. "And not just for the pie. It was good talking to you."

"Me, too," Trish said. "Come by again."

"I will."

# # #

From Catherine's diary, February 1944:

"The hardest things to watch at the movies are the news reels at the beginning. Stephen is over there ... somewhere. He still can't tell me. Italy is almost liberated, but there are Germans in Rome still. Russia has defeated the Germans in many places there. Maybe this war will end soon.

It's been over a year since I've seen Stephen. One of the men at work likes me, I think. Holy Toledo, who am I kidding? I know he likes me. He gave me a big heart-shaped box of chocolates for Valentine's Day. I shouldn't have taken it. But it's been so long since I've had good chocolate.

Last night, George—that's his name— kissed me. Only on the cheek. I wouldn't let him do any more. But I want to. I'm so tired of waiting to get married. A few girls at work have sent 'Dear John' letters to their beaus overseas. I could never do that to Stephen. No, I'll have to wait until he comes home.

I hope I can be strong until then.

# # #

"I'm going up to Nick's for dinner," CJ told Jarod Thursday

when she took him to the doctor for his checkup.

"I need you at the ranch," Jarod growled. "We gotta get those cows off the high ground. Some of them are early calvers—just can't seem to wait til decent weather."

"Decent weather doesn't come until April," she said, trying to hold her temper. The longer Jarod had a cast on, the more demanding he became. "I seem to recall all the calves were born late February or March."

"That's the point. We gotta get them down. We need you to do it. I can't ride—can't even get on an ATV."

"Doc said six to eight weeks, right?"

"Yeah."

"What would you do if I weren't here?" she asked as she maneuvered the Jeep into a parking spot near the medical center.

"Couple of guys I could hire," he said, thrusting open the door and hopping out to land on one leg.

"You shouldn't do that. What if you fell again?" She pulled the crutches from the back and handed them to him.

"I got it," he snapped.

It was going to be a long six weeks. And what if Gerry released her before then? Would she feel okay going?

"Look," she said. "When I go up to Nick's, I'll ask him if he can help out—"

"Don't need Sturgis's help."

She sighed as her brother maneuvered himself up the walk. Why was stubborn the only gene that all of the Beck siblings had in common?

Jarod had already settled himself in a blue plastic chair, leg stretched out, crutches propped beside him when she walked into the waiting room. His attention was seemingly on an ancient issue of *Outdoors*, but she knew better by his furrowed brow.

She sat down next to him.

"Nick and I have made our peace," she said. "It's time for you to do the same."

Jarod turned the page.

"Stop acting like you're a teenager," she said. "You ... uh, *we* need the help. I'm sure Nick will be willing. It'd be good for Trevor to help out, too."

"He seems like a good kid," Jarod admitted.

"He's got a couple of assistants. Maybe they can help, too."

"Do whatever the heck you want," Jarod said, dropping the pretense and glaring at her. "You always do anyway."

"Jarod Beck?" the nurse called from the doorway. "The doctor is ready for you."

CJ waited until her brother hobbled out of the waiting room, then pulled her phone from her purse and texted Nick. She hadn't actually made plans with him, but she'd hidden the pie from her brothers in hopes he'd be open to the idea.

Her fingers hesitated over "send" button. It was Valentine's Day. What kind of message was she actually sending? She couldn't have it both ways. If she were hell-bent on leaving, it wasn't fair to Nick or his son to get any closer. But without Nick, she wasn't sure she'd be able to get completely over the hurdle of taking pictures again.

What if it was all a mirage? Sure, birds and shots of the mountains were possible, but what would happen when she was faced with the blood of war? Would she freeze again? How would she be able to find out?

Too many weighty questions. Right now, her family needed help—help that Nick could hopefully provide. She had a bribe. May as well use it. She'd deal with the rest of it later.

Chapter Sixteen

"How was the dance?" Nick asked his son after Trevor got into the truck. The boy had a dreamy smile on his face, the kind that was only brought on by a girl.

He was way too young.

"Fine," Trevor answered.

Nick was silent as he drove through the few streets toward the grocery store. How did a parent talk to a kid about a school dance? He remembered his first one, full of agony and goofball actions, particularly from boys who didn't know what to do with the females who had morphed from pals into something different—something they couldn't quite wrap their heads around.

And tears. Lots and lots of tears.

"Did she dance with you?" he asked as he pulled into the parking lot.

"Yeah." Trevor's answer was drawn out, as if he'd been on pot for the last hour. Then he looked around. "Why are we here?"

"CJ's coming for supper."

"On Valentine's Day?"

"Appears so." The driver's side door shut with its familiar whine. He really needed to get that fixed.

"Does that mean she likes you?"

He didn't know what the hell it meant. Could be that she simply forgot the significance of the day. Although she had mentioned she was bringing dessert.

"Don't know," he said, striding toward the store, Trevor a few steps behind.

The small space was lit up as if it were trying to dispel the entire winter gloom by itself. Nick's mind raced as he stalked the aisles. Steak? Chicken? Some highly creative pasta dish with cream? Maybe someone went to Great Falls to get fresh fish off the plane.

Chicken. That was it. Poach it with some herbs and wine sauce and serve over rice. Steamed peas with rosemary on the side. And some wine. Right.

He turned and almost ran into Trevor.

"Are you getting anything?" the boy asked. "Or finding out what they have? Looks like the same stuff since I've been here."

"Yeah. I'm getting there." He started through the store again, this time with a plan in mind. He was approaching checkout when he saw a rack of red hearts, the kind filled with bad chocolate, next to a rack of pawed over greeting cards.

"You should get her some chocolate," Trevor encouraged with all the wisdom of a thirteen-year-old boy.

"She's bringing dessert," he replied.

"That's lame, Dad. You need to get her something. It's Valentine's Day."

With a groan, Nick wheeled the cart to the display. He scanned the cards. Mush. All of them. Not the message he wanted to send. As pricy as they were, the red cellophane-wrapped hearts felt cheap.

A lone bouquet of pink carnations caught his eye. It's what he'd gotten her for the one and only Valentine's Day they'd spent together. Would she remember?

Before he could change his mind, he snatched them up and stomped to the checkout.

It took him less time than normal to drive the distance between the town and his place in the foothills. The main roads were dry, and he didn't hit icy patches until he was close to home. The shadow from the hills never let some parts of the road get clear until spring. Like most Montanans, he took account for it during the winter months.

"Doesn't it ever get warm here?" Trevor complained as they entered the mudroom and sloughed their gear.

"April, maybe."

"Ugh. I can't wait to go back to Seattle."

"What about the girl?"

"There are girls in Seattle," Trevor shot back. But the goofy expression returned and he added, "They aren't as nice, though."

As soon as the groceries were unloaded, he started to head to his room, backpack slung over his shoulder, phone in hand.

"Homework?" Nick asked.

"Did it in study hall," Trevor called back.

So far, the kid's grades were good, so there was no point in hassling him.

CJ arrived while Nick was in the barn, seeing to the horses.

"Need a hand?" she asked.

He looked up from the tack he was oiling.

Even with the oversized Carhartt and knit cap pulled over her hair, she drew his attention. She'd lost the innocence of youth, but her face still had the strong lines of her Scandinavian ancestors, including the strong set of her jaw. When she wanted something, she went after it these days.

Who was he fooling? He and his Montana life weren't on the list of things she desired anymore.

"I got it," he said. He gestured at the box in her hand. "One of Trish's pies?"

"Peach. I'll put it in the house, okay? Trevor around?"

"He's here, but I think you've been replaced."

"Oh?"

"Valentine's Day dance. There's a girl."

Her laugh was far more relaxed than he'd heard it since she'd returned home. "In that case, I'll be right back."

"You don't …" His words were lost in the air as she walked out the door.

He tried to concentrate on the job at hand, but it felt like a thousand steel balls were ratcheting around his body.

When she came back, she looked around, shed the coat, and then picked up another rag and a nearby halter.

"You really don't have to help," he said. "You could take pictures or something."

"First of all, it's too damn cold to take pictures. Second, I'm here to bribe you."

"Oh? The pie would have been enough."

"I want to make sure to seal the deal." Her hands were sure as she oiled the bridle, not seeming to care about the mess it was making of her hands. Grace had always refused to help with the dirty chores.

"And what deal might that be?" he asked.

"We need some help." She put down the rag and leaned forward. "Jarod can't ride and it's getting time for the first set of cows to calve. We have to get them moved from one of the far pastures to a smaller space closer to the barn. Dylan and I could do it, but it would be a lot faster if there were another person or two."

"How many cattle?"

"About seventy-five."

"I'll be there." Regardless of what happened between them personally, most Montana ranchers lent a hand when needed. They all knew their day would come when they needed help.

"We're thinking about Saturday. Would that work?"

"Yep. I'll bring my own horse—easier that way."

"What about Trevor? Maybe he can help, too," she said.

"He's never done anything like this."

"Well, isn't it about time he learned?"

"I'll ask. I don't want to push him." Nick hung up the halter he'd completed and grabbed the next one. "I feel like he's finally settling in."

"Any word from Grace about what happens next?"

"Nope. It's frustrating the crap out of me."

"Doesn't seem fair." CJ hung up her piece and grabbed the next on the rack.

"Kids don't come with parenting instructions." He may not always like the choices Grace made, but CJ was an outsider—she'd never had a child. "Ever think about having children?"

She was silent.

Shit. Maybe she couldn't have them. That could devastate a woman. Sally, his sister-in-law, had had a hard time conceiving and it was a tough time for his brother.

"I'm sorry," he said. "None of my business."

"No, it's okay."

He let the silence drift, punctuated only by the rustling of cats in the straw and the movement of leather being oiled.

"I wanted to establish my career," she said. "It didn't seem fair to be dragging a child into dangerous places or leaving her in a stranger's care while I did my job."

Should he respond or let her tell it in her own way? He kept quiet.

"Ben and I planned to have kids one day ... but things happened. Then I started taking a good look at what was going on in the world."

The pain in her voice tugged at his heart.

"Ben and I really hit the skids. I was getting older. I went to London and had my tubes tied. He didn't know. I never said anything." She looked up at Nick. Her eyes were glistening. "Then it was too late." She returned her attention to the leather. "It's for the best. All the reasons for my not having a child still exist."

"I always wanted two or three," he said. "Enough to keep each other company like Henry and I did. You always need someone in your life who knows what a turd you were as a kid."

Her smile was weak, but it was there.

"But everyone has to make their own choices in this life," he said. "I understand why you did what you did." He hesitated. "It can be reversed, you know. The tubes can be put back together."

Her smile was genuine this time, almost reaching her eyes, which still held a trace of sadness. "There would have to be a powerful reason for me to do that, and I can't think of anything. Even if I fell in love with"—she looked away—"someone, I don't believe I want to have a child. They'd have to accept that."

He swallowed. "I see." A profound sense of sorrow swept through his body.

Why should it matter to him? They weren't involved. They weren't going to get involved. As soon as she got the all clear, she was gone.

"So what's on the docket for dinner?" she asked.

He told her.

"Wow. Sounds wonderful. Hard to believe you're still on the loose, Sturgis."

"Women love the cooking, hate the job," he replied, hanging up the halter, capping the oil, and folding the rag he'd been using.

"Have you ever considered anything else?" she asked.

"Grace and I were talking about it. Like I said, I wanted more kids. She wouldn't do it unless I found a new occupation. I was trying to decide what to do, when ... well, she decided on another option."

"I see." CJ folded her rag and handed it to him.

Their hands touched. There wasn't a spark, but a familiarity gave him more comfort than any lustful charge would have done.

"I'm sorry it turned out that way for you," she said, looking up at him.

She was close. Too close. In spite of the years and disasters she'd seen, her eyes still held the same clarity they had when they were young.

Her lips parted.

It would be so easy to kiss her again—only this time like he meant it.

He lowered his head. Just a taste.

She didn't back off, and when he felt her lips beneath his, it was as if he'd never kissed anyone before. It wasn't an aggressive need but a desire all the same. Exploring her lips, he tasted her experience, her life that no longer held innocence. She was totally present.

He pulled her closer, and she slipped into exactly into all his nooks and crannies. His heart thumped faster and he kissed her more greedily, driven by a want he never knew he had. He could explore this woman for the rest of his life and discover something new every time.

Except he'd never get that chance.

He forced himself to slow down and release her.

They stared at each other, not needing words to clarify why they had to stop.

"Maybe dinner is a bad idea," she said.

"Trevor will know something is up, and he's riding me about

you already."

"Okay. Then I'll be nice and neighborly—strictly professional."

As he watched, she transformed without changing a thing except shuttering the longing that had been in her eyes. She pulled on her jacket and headed for the door. "Coming?" she said without turning around.

"Yeah," he said, his heart full of regret.

# # #

She was playing a dangerous game.

CJ tried to remain calm as she accepted the glass of chardonnay Nick handed her when they got inside his cabin. She avoided touching his fingers and walked over to the window the moment the glass was secure in her hand.

"No matter what time of day it is," he said, coming up behind her, "I'm in awe of that view. To think I get to sit here and look out at God's creation any time I want. In the warmer weather, I sit on the deck with my cup of coffee and listen for the songbirds. I have no idea which one is which, but I can tell they're different by the sounds they make."

"Sounds lovely."

"It is. It's one of the reasons I was having so much trouble coming up with a second career. I love this place, the lifestyle. And when I'm out in the Bob or another wilderness area, it's even better. It's like every sense I have comes alive again."

"I know. I've felt that in the desert. Like I'm seeing the world as the ancients saw it."

"Yeah. Well, I better get dinner started. Enjoy the view."

She sank into the couch as pots and pans rattled from behind her. It really was an incredible view. How was he going to handle Trevor, though, if he went off for weeks at a time—particularly during fall hunting season when the kid needed to be in school?

It was the same dilemma she'd faced: some careers didn't mesh well with parenting.

"Did you give them to her yet?" Trevor's voice made her turn around.

"Give me what?" she asked.

"The—I can't tell you. They're Dad's surprise. For Valentine's Day, you know." Trevor's face was full of eager innocence.

She glanced at Nick. His lips were pursed as he returned the glance, like he regretted something he'd done.

"Not yet, kid," he said.

"What are you waiting for? Valentine's Day is almost over!"

"You don't have to give me anything," she said. "It's a sweet idea, but—"

"I do want to," he said, "but now's not the time. I'm in the middle of cooking."

"But—"

"Later." Nick's voice was firm. "Sorry," he said to CJ.

"No problem. Like I said—"

"Got it." He walked back to the stove and Trevor walked back down the hallway.

The atmosphere disturbed by currents she didn't—or didn't want to—understand, she returned to her perch on the couch. Soon savory aromas tickled her nose.

Damn, that man could make a meal.

He could probably do other things just as well if that kiss was any indication.

She sighed. Time to get her head on straight. She knew what she had to do, and it didn't involve getting any closer to Nick than she already was. She'd been a fool to show up on Valentine's Day.

And what message was she sending to Trevor? That adults toyed with one another and then left each other hurting when it ended? He had already seen that lesson in action with his parents.

"More wine?" Nick asked, holding out his hand. "Dinner is almost ready."

"A little, thank you." She handed him her glass. "Can I help with anything?"

"No thanks. Just grab a seat at the table and I'll bring the plates over."

"Sure."

After pouring the wine, he walked down the hall. A minute later, he returned with Trevor a few steps behind him.

"I'm starved," the boy admitted as he took his place at the table.

Nick laid plates of steaming food down on the table. Poached chicken was nestled next to steaming rice and bright green broccoli.

"Looks wonderful," she said.

"Dig in," he replied and lifted his glass. They all clinked, the sound tickling a memory from her childhood when she used to believe home was a safe and loving place. If only she could believe that again, selectively let go of the past hurts while remembering the good parts.

She glanced at Nick, who was discussing some intricate math problem with Trevor. The past was the past—good or bad. Why was she letting it dictate her present life? Gerry was right. It was time to deal with it and let it go.

Who knew what her future would hold if she could do that?

"Well, you look like you've discovered something wonderful," Nick said.

"I'm not sure if that's true, but I may be ready to look at life from a different perspective."

"Oh?" Nick asked.

"Nothing certain ... just thinking." She grinned at Trevor. "Figure out your math problem?"

"Not really. Dad keeps trying to tell me the way he used to do it, and it doesn't make any sense to me."

She chuckled. "It seems to be a perpetual problem. My parents never understood my math either."

"Were you any good at it?"

"Pretty good," she said.

"Can you help me after dinner?"

She shouldn't get in any deeper. "I'm afraid I need to get back to the ranch. Long day tomorrow preparing for the roundup. Did your dad tell you?"

"Tell me what?"

"CJ's family needs help rounding up some cows and getting them closer to home," Nick said.

"How come?" Trevor asked.

As they finished their dinner, CJ told him about cows, calving, and the perpetual cycle the market required. Nothing was left to nature anymore. Leery at first, Trevor gradually grew excited about the idea of doing some actual "cowboying."

"Makes me realize how much he's missed," Nick said as she helped him clear the table. "When we were growing up, learning to rope a calf was as natural as breathing."

"Maybe for you and Jarod," she kidded. "I seem to remember being the one who was the calf."

He chuckled. "Yeah, you're probably right. It used to piss you off no end."

"I was the older, more sophisticated one." She mockingly

flipped her hair. "At least to Jarod. I could never believe how you liked to pal around with my younger brother."

"We had common interests—the outdoors, family, horses—and it was a handy excuse to hang around you without seeming to care."

"Oh, I knew you cared," she said, smiling with the memories. It had all been so easy when they were Trevor's age. Hormones were only stirring, and tragedy was still at bay.

"Good times," Nick said as he washed the plates and put them in the rack.

"No dishwasher?" she asked.

"Uses too much water," he said. "I think that was one of the breaking points for Grace. Dishpan hands and all that. And for just me?" He shrugged. "Not much point."

"The women in the desert gather by wells to do their dishes, especially as more and more dwellings were destroyed and families lived among rubble. I took a lot of pictures of them when I was allowed."

"What happened to the pictures?" Steaming hot water rose from the sink as he attacked the skillet he'd used for cooking.

"Nothing. No one wanted them. Too much women's business. Not enough of the male-dominated actions of war."

"Hard to believe that kind of thinking still exists in this day and age."

"A lot of misogyny, racism, and religious hatred simmers under a lot of people's skin—people we'd never even think of being that way."

"Yeah." He nodded toward the hallway. "Maybe in his lifetime."

"Hope so." She stepped away from the kitchen area. "Thanks for dinner. I had a lovely time. See you Saturday."

He turned from the sink, drying his hands rapidly in a towel.

"Thanks for coming, and the pie." His gaze searched her face. "Sorry for ... earlier."

"Don't be. It was nice to forget for a while."

Nick cleared his throat. "Trevor!" he yelled down the hallway. "CJ's leaving."

Pounding feet ran down the hallway.

"Did she like them?" The kid looked expectantly from one of them to the other. "D-a-ad! You forgot!" He trotted back down the hall a bit and emerged from a room with a vase in his hand.

"Here."

Pink carnations. Why the hell did it have to be pink carnations? She still had the dried petals from the ones he'd given her during their first dance in a mason jar in her room somewhere.

The panic she thought she'd conquered rose again.

"I ... can't ... no ..." She ran from the room, pulled on her gear, and left.

Chapter Seventeen

CJ watched as Nick's pickup and horse trailer pulled up next to the barn, steeling herself to act professionally. In spite of her resolve, she'd cried herself to sleep on Valentine's night, the pain of Ben's death compounding the ache of lost teenage love. By morning she was all cried out but felt more cleansed than she had in a while, as if she'd finally let a small chunk of the past retire to where it belonged.

Trevor practically bounced out of the cab, waved, then scurried over to her.

"Dad wants to know where we should unload the horses."

"We're going to drive them closer to the south pasture," she replied. "My brother is hitching up our trailer and bringing it around now."

"How can Jarod drive with a broken leg?" Trevor asked.

"My other brother, Dylan," she replied as she stowed her field camera in the horse's saddlebag. The buckskin mount had become her favorite since she'd returned home. Joey had patience and stamina.

Trevor patted Joey's neck. "CJ says we're driving the horses south somewhere," he said to his father.

The ranch pickup and trailer bumped around the corral and pulled to a stop next to Nick's rig.

"Hey, Dylan," Nick said when her brother hopped from the truck. "Good to see you."

"You, too. Thanks for helping out." Dylan shook hands with him. "I figure we'll truck 'em down to the south pasture and drive the cows north to this pasture here." He gestured to the south side of the barn. "Then we'll go back and retrieve the rigs."

"Sounds good."

CJ helped Dylan load their horses. The day was chilly but not as bad as it had been. Patches were beginning to thaw, exposing grasses for the first time in months. Blue skies arched overhead, and several hawks circled on thermals in the distance.

Good day to be alive.

Once they were mounted, Dylan gave out assignments. She and he had the flanks of the herd, while Nick and Trevor would drive the middle. The strategy would have worked well, except the cattle had other plans.

As they rode toward the animals, the cattle began to stir, lowing sounds grumbling their discontent. The cows shuffled here and there, and began to drift toward the north.

CJ pulled out her camera to try take some grab shots as she rode. Joey was a steady mount, not prone to shying, hopping, or any other ungentlemanly behavior. Maybe if she snapped fast, she could get away with it without her vision blurring into a desert scene. At first she took long shots, relaxing into the steady rhythm of Joey's gait. The heat from the horse and the squeak of leather seemed natural, a gentle pace from earlier times.

As the cattle moved, she kept her horse at a steady walk in line with Dylan on the other flank. Nick and Trevor were slightly behind them, pushing the stragglers with the rest of the herd. Nick's face was relaxed but concentrated, shadowed by the brim of the cowboy hat he wore. Trevor's expression held nervous anticipation, his obviously new hat perched on top of his head. From the easy way he was sitting, his riding muscle memory had returned.

She leaned back and took some close-ups of their faces, then a photo of Nick's hand lying on his blue-jeaned leg.

The edges of her focus began to blur. She'd pushed it too far. Time to give it a rest, so she stowed the camera back in the saddlebag.

Suddenly, Dylan swung from his routine walk. One of the cows had decided to take a detour to a tuff of newly exposed wheatgrass. Her brother tried to cut off the cow, but she was having none of it, determinedly walking to her destination, ignoring the man shouting curses and flailing his hat.

Then another decided that it, too, needed to taste the delectable morsel instead of the old hay they'd distributed to lure the cattle north. She urged Joey into a trot and headed it off. More docile than Dylan's miscreant, the animal headed back to the herd.

One by one, the cattle randomly walked off to whatever imagined delight appeared in their dim brains. One by one, they brought them back while Trevor and Nick kept up the steady pressure from the back.

She couldn't blame the animals. Even her human nose caught the scent of change in the air. Springtime in the Rockies was competing smells: mud, fresh blades of grass, the sharp tang of new pine branches wafting from the west. Nowhere else on earth compared to it. She'd been born to it.

It's where she belonged.

"Turn around!"

Trevor's strained voice caught her attention. He'd moved away from his father as his section of the herd had ambled farther ahead of the others. One of the cows had decided they were headed in the wrong direction and turned a hundred and eighty degrees, directly confronting the raw kid.

Neither of them was budging, but the cow was getting restless, waving her head back and forth.

CJ squeezed her legs and pointed Joey in the direction of the cow. "Hah!" she yelled, waving her hat up and down and slapping it on her leg. A path parted before her, but the cow in front of Trevor stayed rooted to the ground.

"C'mon, you lazy animal!" she shouted, coming as close as she could then landing a kick in the flank.

The cow turned on her with a bellow. CJ circled around behind her and yelled to Trevor, "Get on that side and keep her from turning that way!" Then she circled again and yelled at the animal.

After shaking herself, the cow seemed to notice the rest of the herd drifting away and trotted to catch up.

"Thanks, CJ," Trevor said.

"No problem. Now let's get the rest of these animals back. I'm over the roundup thing—how about you?"

"Yep." He urged his horse into a trot and forced the rest of his lot forward, looking like he'd been born into a saddle.

He was a good kid, the kind she'd have been proud to claim as her own.

For the next few hours they pushed, prodded, and chased the reluctant cows toward the new pen. By the time they returned to the ranch house with the rigs and taken care of the horses, the supplies Birdie had packed were long gone.

She was ravenous.

"C'mon inside," Dylan said to Nick and Trevor. "Birdie promised a feast. You can wash up in the guest bathroom."

"That'd be good." Nick laughed.

Fortunately, she had her camera in her hand and was able to catch the grin on his sweat- and dirt-stained face before panic set in. It was an expression of joy—satisfaction at a job well done and a day spent in mountain air. God, she'd miss this when she went back.

Bit by bit she was pushing against her fears. It was only a matter of time before she'd be back to who she'd been before the tragedy.

Well, not quite. Ben's death had irrevocably changed who she was at her core.

They trooped into the house, except for Dylan, who walked over to his cabin. That left her to deal with Jarod, who was pacing the living room as best he could with crutches.

"Well?" he asked as soon as he saw her.

"We got it done. They were an ornery bunch, but we convinced them we were badass cowboys and they finally got the idea." She chuckled.

"Thanks, CJ. And thanks for getting Nick. We couldn't have done it without them."

"Then maybe you'll cut him some slack, let bygones be bygones?"

"Yeah." Jarod shook his head, but there was a smile on his face. "We Becks sure do have a hard time letting the past be the past."

"You can say that again. I'll be down in a few. Go pester Birdie or something."

She dashed up the stairs, feeling lighter than she had in many years. There was a place for her in this family—they needed her as much as she needed them. When she went back overseas, she'd put time and money aside to return home on a more regular basis.

Showered and in clean clothes, she joined the others around the big dining room table. The meal reminded her of childhood Sunday dinners with roast beef and chocolate cake and plenty of laughter around the table. She'd forgotten how good it was, overlaid by the bad memories of her parents' deaths.

At the end of the meal, Dylan insisted on helping Birdie clean up, with a noble but ineffective assist from Jarod.

"How did your pictures turn out? Any problems?" Nick asked as she walked him and Trevor to the door.

He wasn't talking about focus.

"A few, but I worked past them." She grinned. "It felt really, really good."

"There's a bunch of elk up in the foothills a little north of my place. Just off one of the major trails. I thought I'd take Trevor up there on snowshoes to see what he could do with action shots. Want to come?"

"Sure," she said without thinking it through, experiencing a stab of conscience after she'd spoken. Trevor didn't need to be any closer to her.

"Good. Which day works for you?" he asked.

They agreed on the following Thursday when school was closed for some teacher event, and then Nick and Trevor walked out the door. She watched as they loaded the horses in the rig and drove off, an unfamiliar pang of loneliness in her heart.

# # #

"These are really neat," Gerry said as she scrolled through the photos CJ had taken during the roundup. "You've captured a real sense of what it means to ranch in Montana. Can you identify these folks? I think I know Jarod, but the others?"

CJ rapidly pointed out the people. When Gerri got to the shot of Nick grinning, she stopped. "He looks really happy—and nice. Have you made your peace with him?"

"Yes. He's got his life and I've got mine."

Gerry studied her. "And you're sure about that."

"Absolutely."

"And you didn't have any problems taking these photos—no flashbacks or anything like that?"

"A little." She explained how she'd managed the camera using long-range shots at first and keeping the photography to short bursts.

"I see."

CJ's heart began to beat faster in anticipation. Was she finally going to be set free?

"And your brothers?"

"I think we're better," CJ said honestly. "I guess I realized I've got a role to play in their lives. I need to be back here more often, not just for weddings and funerals—not that I showed up for those anyway."

Although the only wedding there had been was hers. What was going to move her brothers along in that department?

"So your family needs you."

"In a way. The same way I need them." She picked up one of the throw pillows, played with the tassels at the corners, then put it back down. "We have shared life experiences. We know what happened. Over time, we'll be able to put it to rest."

"So you haven't put your parents' deaths behind you."

"I don't think any of us have, really." CJ took a deep breath. "We bury it away, like something that happened to someone else."

Gerri nodded. "That happens a lot." She looked through her notes and nodded. "While I think that you'll need to unbury those feelings and come to peace with it in order to be truly happy, that wasn't the purpose of this therapy session. It was to make sure your mental health was strong enough to return to the field, if that's what you still want to do."

"Yes," CJ said with a confidence she wasn't entirely feeling.

"Then I see no problem with referring you back to Dr. Wikowski. He should be back from his trip by now. I'll send him my report tomorrow and then you can contact him to schedule an appointment."

"Thank you. I really do feel better than when I first started. And it's nice to be able to take pictures again."

"I'm glad." Gerry stood. "Someday, I hope you'll come back so we can finish the rest of it."

CJ rose as well with a chuckle. "Maybe ... but I'll probably let sleeping dogs lie. I'm feeling happy enough."

"Well, okay then." Gerry held out her hand. "If I see you on the street, I'll say hello. We can pretend we met while fishing or something."

"In January?"

Gerry shrugged. "Ice fishing?"

CJ smiled then shook Gerry's hand. "Thanks." She put on her coat and walked out the door. The sun was shining as if celebrating her victory with her.

She should go back to the ranch. Or call Birdie to see if she needed anything in town.

But she was free.

After a quick text to Jarod to let him know she'd be gone for the afternoon, she turned off her phone and headed north out of town. The roads were clear and the mountains sharp against the sky. The prairie slid by, building to small hills and descending to tiny valleys with iced over potholes. Mallards and goldeneyes bobbed in what little open water there was.

As she crossed into the reservation, bright-colored houses and mobile homes dotted the landscapes and scattered cattle grazed in the fields, some closer to the barns than others. Every rancher was marching to the same tune: calving season was coming soon.

She rounded a hill and came down into the valley that held the seat of the Blackfeet Nation—Browning, a scattered tableau of schools, churches, and dwellings in various conditions. Double-wides that had been there for decades, and looked it, perched next to sharp-looking mobile homes. A cement teepee, which apparently housed a coffee shop, anchored the ninety-degree turn to the west. Across from the museum, a quilt shop had opened since she'd been here last.

That had been a long time ago. She'd come up to Glacier the summer before she'd left for college, working as a boat guide on Two Medicine Lake. Like others her age, she'd partied and hiked, and partied some more, trying to forget the worst year of her life.

Jarod had not been happy, but it was the best thing she could have done. She needed that transition.

As she followed the road west, the stark granite mountains rose straight up from the prairie. She'd known their names once, but all she could remember now was Dancing Lady. Almost to the small town of East Glacier, a herd of fenced-in bison ranged beside the road. On a whim, she pulled over and braced herself against the side of the Jeep and took a photo of one of the animals framed by the mountains and blue sky behind him.

It was a perfect day to be alive. Her photos came easily; she'd deal with the panic over time. She sent up a prayer of gratitude to Nick for helping her over the hump. She was going to miss him.

After crossing the bridge over the chasm created by the Two Medicine River, she pulled into the small town—really a few blocks of buildings on the left side of the highway. She'd missed lunch, but the Two Medicine Grill was always good for a hamburger.

She entered the narrow hallway that passed the kitchen and

counter, immediately hit by the smell of decades of grease built into the walls of the old diner. Three men in cold-weather overalls, separated by two stools each, hunched over coffee and burgers. She headed to the back where the seating was more traditional.

As she waited for her order, she skimmed her phone and idly listened to the women behind her talking in the singsong rhythm of the rez.

"They found that one girl, up toward Babb," one woman said. "Shackin' up with her boyfriend, that one. Her mother was steamin' mad. Only sixteen. What are they thinking?"

"They're not," another voice chimed in. "With all the girls missing, how could she do that to her mother?"

"Well, it's that kinda family," the first one said. "Them Coyotes have been ignoring peoples' feelings since forever, y'know."

There was a general chuckle.

It was a different world. CJ had heard something about the Native American girls that were going missing from reservations. There were suspicions of human trafficking, but nothing that could be proven. Some had been found, used up and dead.

Thrown away.

It made her heartsick.

Too much like the young girls in the Middle East who were used as pawns in conflicts and family bargains, but happening here. What else was going on in the States that she'd been ignoring in her rush to cover world events?

The railroad underpass had received a new coat of paint recently. The bright blues and reds gave way to a narrow dark tunnel that opened on the splendor of the lodge built from local timber in the early 1900s. The building was dark and snow covered the long lawn, but during the summer she'd been there, it had been alive with tourists.

The twisty turns to the lake were as she remembered, and she followed the road through the park as far as she could before pulling over to the side. During winter the park service pulled the gate across the road because they couldn't keep up with the snowfall in this small section. She pulled out her camera, walked behind the barrier, and continued up the road.

Snow draped on the fir trees and laced the rough bark of the aspens. She took lots of close-ups of patterns, some in black and white, some in color. An eagle soared overhead before landing high in a tree and glaring down at her. Backing against a tree, she steadied herself and captured his white-headed majesty with her lens. Then she continued on.

When she got back into the Jeep and turned on her phone, she was startled to see how late it was. The words spoken in the diner came back to her. She didn't need to add to anyone's worry, but there weren't any service bars. Time to head back.

Carefully, she drove back out of the mountains to the prairie. The light held until she was almost at the ranch. When she got home, she leaned back against the vehicle and stared at the sky. A bright star—Venus?—gleamed over the barn roof. Cattle lowed not far away. A barn owl swooped from one of the barn's loft openings, ready for its nightly hunt. Everything and everyone was where they needed to be.

Why was she so eager to run away?

Chapter Eighteen

Thursday continued the streak of blue skies, but with a drop in temperature of about ten degrees. Nick readied the equipment they needed to snowshoe up the trail to the elk. It was a bit of a hike, but Trevor was toughening up and CJ looked as fit as she ever had.

He needed to stop inviting her places. She was leaving and Trevor was too attached already.

So was he.

But having her around was like finding something he'd forgotten that was essential to living, like he'd spent the last decade breathing incorrectly, and now his lungs were full to capacity. He had his son and the woman he loved.

The woman he'd once loved. *Be careful to make that distinction, Sturgis.* How much breaking could one heart take? He didn't want to find out.

Where were the damn poles? He had a set for Trevor that he'd picked up, along with a set of snowshoes, from a Craigslist ad. It had taken some digging to find his own shoes, but he couldn't find the poles. Methodically, he started at the back of the shed and looked through everything, which gave him time to think through Grace's phone call last night.

She'd suggested Trevor go back over spring break. She and her new husband thought that it was time for some family therapy. Probably a good idea, but he could see his time with Trevor coming to an abrupt end again, just when the boy was settling in. They needed to find a way to stop jerking the kid around.

But what kind of argument could he put up for keeping Trevor in Montana? As she'd pointed out, his outfitting business was going to pick up again, first with folks who were winter-crazed and ready to get back out to the wilderness and then with fishermen.

There was only so much kid care his parents could give. And even they may not be around much longer. His father had said this might be the last Montana winter they had in them. Would they sell the store? Should he offer to buy it?

He shuddered with the thought.

His life was in upheaval all around him. It was enough to make a man grumpy.

Ah, there they were.

Piling the equipment in his arms, he left the shed and dumped it in the bed of the pickup.

CJ's Jeep crested the slight rise to the cabin.

In spite of his resolve, his heart beat a little faster.

"Hey there," he called out to her as she got out of the vehicle.

"Hey, yourself," she said, a lazy smile forming across her face; her gray eyes focused on him. "You ready to go?"

"Just about. I figure we'll take my truck." His voice should have been strong and confident.

It wasn't.

"Okay. I'll put my gear in the bed while you finish up."

Ten minutes later they headed down the drive, Trevor and CJ talking animatedly about f-stops and shutter speeds—Greek to him. But if Trevor was happy, he was happy.

Once they reached the trailhead, they slipped on their gear and headed up a slight rise to a saddle that led into the national forest. Sometimes the land cooperated like this, providing a smooth path into the wilderness convenient for both animals and people. Most of the trees around them were short: stunted cottonwoods, small groves of aspens. Discarded branches thrust limbs through the snow, giant arms pleading for help from the battering winds and freezing snow.

He was becoming fanciful. Probably because he'd stayed up the night before reading the last book of short stories by Rick Bass, a master of poetic language describing the west.

"Look," he said, pointing to a place where the snow was churned up enough to reveal the mud beneath it. "They're around." A few seconds later another track caught his eyes. "Unfortunately, so are the wolves."

He led them to the track. "It's the time of year when the older elk are fatigued and hungry. Exactly the kind of prey wolves want."

"Will they hunt us?" Trevor asked.

"Given the opportunity, they might," he answered honestly. His feelings were complicated when it came to the reintroduced animal. He admired their wildness and their place in the ecosystem. He also knew they played hell with the cattle that were the livelihood of ranchers.

"We'll keep an eye out," CJ said. "I brought my pistol and bear spray."

"Ditto," he said.

"You guys have guns?" Trevor's voice was a shriek.

CJ chuckled. "Yeah. It's a good idea in the wilderness."

"What about me?" he asked. "Why don't I have a gun?"

"Because no one has trained you to use one," Nick said. "Do you want to learn?"

"Um, maybe … nah. It wouldn't be much use in Seattle."

A pang hit Nick's heart. Trevor hadn't talked about going back to the city in a long time. What had Grace said to him? With

CJ here, it wasn't the time to bring it up.

"Let's be quiet," he said.

"Have your camera ready?" CJ asked Trevor, readying her own gear so that it was handy.

His son pulled out the camera, checked some things, and held it to his eye before nodding. His face held concentration, clear eyes scanning the landscape around him in a way that reminded Nick too eerily of his own habits.

Carefully, they ascended the next section of trail that led around the western side of a small hill. The churned up snow continued, but they didn't see any more wolf tracks. Nick's breath eased. As they emerged from the shadow of another hill, he saw the herd. The bull elk stood above his hare, and spotted them immediately. He stared at them for a few moments but must not have been too worried about their presence as he moved his massive head to scan other parts of the horizon.

"He's magnificent," CJ whispered.

"Can you get a shot?" he asked.

"We're a bit far and I didn't bring a tripod."

"Let's see how close we can get. They seem pretty calm. Probably more interested in getting at the grass the thaw revealed than us." The easy nature of the bull elk also meant the wolves had headed off in another direction.

He led them around the second hill toward a more rocky section. Isolated granite boulders scattered the landscape. Eventually, they rounded the top of another hill and were able to see the herd from a closer vantage point.

"Perfect," CJ said. "The rocks will allow us to steady the cameras for more long distant shots." She showed Trevor how to brace himself. As he studied the herd through his lens, CJ stretched out in the snow and steadied her elbows on the ground, cradling the camera in her hands.

Nick stayed silent, his gaze focusing on the herd and the actions of the bull elk. The big male was keeping an eye on them. He had several long scars on his hide, and from the size of his rack, he was one of the older bulls. Probably why his herd was the size it was.

Movement near the herd caught his attention, but as he focused his eyes, he realized he was looking at four or five young males, hanging out on the fringe. The following fall, the old fellow was going to have a battle on his hands.

CJ stood up and brushed herself off before pulling a bottle of water from her bag. She offered some, but Nick shook his head.

"I've taken the first step toward freedom," she said.

"What do you mean?" he asked.

"My therapist said I was done. Now all I have to do is convince the shrink in Great Falls and I can go back to my old life."

A sick feeling rose in his stomach. *Suck it up, Sturgis. It has been her plan all along.*

"I'm glad for you," he said. "When do you think you'll head back?"

"I don't think I can leave until Jarod's back on his feet—not with calving season and all that. The doc told him another month and he should be able to remove the cast. That should give Max just enough time to find me placement."

He couldn't help himself.

"So no thought about staying here then."

"Not at all." She seemed surprised. "What would I do? I'm not a rancher. That life seemed ... I don't know. Too repetitive."

"Not enough adrenaline." He grinned at her.

"Yeah, I am a bit of a junkie that way."

"So nothing else could keep you here." He deliberately looked at the elk, not wanting her to see any truth that might be there.

She was silent for a moment then gestured for him to step away from where Trevor snapped photos.

"Are we talking about things or people, Nick?" she asked softly.

"Both, I guess," he said, still not looking at her.

It was so still he imagined he could hear her heart beating as she stood beside him.

"I'm not going to deny there's still an attraction," she said. "I know you feel it, too. But is it enough to sustain a life change? I don't know. Besides ..." She toed the snow with her boot. "In spite of being set free to go back to my career, I don't think I'm able to love anyone yet ... if I ever was. There's been too much betrayal."

"You can move on from the past."

"I'm not sure about that. Working with the therapist showed me that in order to deal with the past, I have to look at it honestly. I'm not sure I'm ready to do that."

"You were able to get past us."

She touched his arm, and he finally looked at her. Her chin was resolute, but her eyes were shiny from something other than the glare of the sun on the snow. "That one was easy," she said. "I could look at that and know we were just kids. Even dealing with Jarod and Dylan has been less stress than I thought it would be. I guess I finally realized we *are* a family, and I'm part of it."

"So what's holding you up from letting the rest of it go?" he asked.

"The oldest answer in the world." Her chuckle was bitter. "My parents. They never dealt with anything—they just avoided the truth and went on like nothing was happening. My dad had affairs and my mother had her knitting club. You could feel the searing pain between them, but we were too young to know the cause." She shrugged. "I haven't the faintest idea how to have a conversation with anyone other than a therapist about what's really bothering me."

"Yet here we are, doing that very thing," he said.

"Oh." She fell silent again.

Their conversation wasn't finished for good, but he sensed it was time to let it go for now. He scanned the horizon again and pulled out his binoculars to get a closer look at several dots moving on one of the western hills.

"Wolves," he said, handing the instrument to CJ.

She looked through the lenses. "Damn. Now I really miss my tripod." She handed them back to him. "You should show Trevor."

"Yeah, and then we should move on. They're still far away, but they're headed in this direction. At the very least, they'll spook the herd. And if they get one ... I'm not sure I'm ready for Trevor to see that."

"Okay."

The moved slowly to his son, and Nick showed him the wolves. Even though they were far —probably too far —Trevor snapped a few shots. Nick didn't say anything. Learning from experience was better than someone telling him what to do.

Then quietly, almost stealthily, they moved back to the trail.

"That was amazing," Trevor said. "I've never seen a wolf before. I wish we could have gotten closer."

Nick glanced at CJ.

"That was probably close enough for now," he said.

"With the lens you have," CJ added, "it would be difficult to get a good shot even if you were closer."

"Would yours work?" he asked.

"Maybe, but only if I had my tripod with me. And even then

..." She shrugged. "There's a lot to learn. The more you learn, the more gadgets you might want. But the most important thing of all is your eye—how you see the world. And you have that one already."

"Really?"

"Yes."

Trevor's smile was so big it almost broke Nick's heart. How was his son going to take it when CJ walked out of their lives?

# # #

CJ refused Nick's offer of dinner when they returned. There were still chores to be done and Jarod was already riding her for her continued absences. He was grumpy enough when he was well. When he was sick, he was unbearable.

Besides, she wanted to get back to her grandmother's diary. Her grandfather's name had been Stephen, so he must have come home, but he'd died shortly after she was born. What had happened between them? Had her own father's infidelity been a by-product of watching *his* parents?

Family dynamics could be weird.

After she completed the chores her brother had laid out, she returned to the house. Jarod was in the ranch office, and from the grunts coming through the open door, things weren't going well. Against her better judgment, she leaned against the doorway, crossed her arms, and stared.

A big furrow of concentration was across his forehead, barely visible under the black hair that had lengthened from its usual military cut. He stared at the computer screen, pecked a few more keys, and shook his head again.

"Come to gloat?" he asked.

"Not at all. Need help?" she asked.

He held up an official-looking letter. "It seems they found our tax money—it was part of the embezzled funds."

"Well, isn't that good news?" She walked behind the desk and pulled up a chair so she could sit and see the screen.

"It would be if I could figure out how to enter it in this darn program," he said. "Before he retired, the accountant insisted we use it, but it makes no sense to me. And, of course, I keep flipping numbers, so that doesn't help."

It wasn't until his teens that Jarod had been diagnosed with a numbers dyslexia, but knowing why he did it didn't keep him from doing it.

"We need a bookkeeper," she said. "Someone who can enter all that stuff for you."

"It's probably a good idea, but we can't afford it."

"I can."

"Oh?"

"Ben left me some money, and I want to put it into the ranch—handle some repairs, a bookkeeper, whatever we need."

"We don't need your blood money." Jarod's voice was harsh. He hadn't liked Ben when she'd brought him back to Montana after they'd married.

"Stop. Don't think of that. Besides, we've got bigger problems on our hands."

"What's that?"

"Any idea who owns the mineral rights to our land?"

"We do." Jarod's voice was matter-of-fact. Then he looked at her. "Why? What's up?"

"Do you know where the deed is?"

"Not offhand," he said. "I'm sure it's around here someplace."

"According to our attorney, it's not recorded at the county."

The nagging worry at the basis of her skull was beginning to throb. What was it she'd overheard Dad say about the mineral rights?

"Does it matter? Doesn't it automatically go with the land?"

She shook her head. "The county is going to be adding another tax to the mineral rights."

"You mean on top of the land tax?" Jarod spoke slowly, like he'd finally started understanding the problem.

"Yep. And they're going to tax us for mineral rights ... even though they don't have a record."

"D—" Jarod stopped himself before the swear left his lips. "We can't ever get ahead."

"There must be some documentation in the boxes in Mom's office, but I haven't had time to finish going through them since you've been down and the cows have been dropping calves."

"I seem to remember an old family Bible," Jarod said.

"Yeah." It had been thick and worn, its black cover cracked and broken. Thin script in faded blue ink lined the beginning and end of the text. Bibles served as family recordings in the 1800s and beyond because they were routinely handed down. "Any idea where it is?"

"I think it was in Mom's bedroom for a long time," he said. "Most of that stuff we packed up when she died."

"I didn't find it in the office, but I haven't been in that room since I got home," she said.

"We don't use it very often."

"Maybe I'll tackle it this weekend—see if I can come up with the Bible. If someone else owns the rights, it's something we ought to know."

"Does that mean someone could drill on this land? Every time he comes home, Kaiden goes on about how we could make a fortune drilling for gas or oil or some such thing." Jared said with a frown.

"And ruin the land."

"Yeah." The chair creaked as he turned to her. "Cattle aren't always the best thing for the land either."

"What? You turning vegetarian on me or something?" She grinned at him.

"Not in a heartbeat," he said, returning the smile. "But I've been reading about new techniques that damage the land less. Every once in a while, I think about bison, but that's a whole new species that requires a lot of learning."

"Where does Prince fit into all this?"

Jarod hesitated.

"Never mind ... you don't have to tell me," she said.

"I'd rather not. I'm still thinking it through."

"Oh." She was disappointed, even though she'd given him an out.

He clicked a few more keys and the monitor went black. "I'll finish this up tomorrow. What are your plans? Dylan said he could sure use your help."

"I'll be here."

"For how long, CJ?" Jarod's voice was flat, as if he expected the worst but wasn't going to give the universe the satisfaction of letting it know.

"I'm not leaving until you're back on your feet," she said.

"Even if you're cleared to go?"

"Even if."

Her brother let out a long breath of air. As he did so, she took a good look at him. He had aged much more than a man who was thirty-four should have. "Much Too Young (To Feel This Damn Old)." Except conservative Jarod never would have used the word *damn* like Garth Brooks had. But the truth was the same.

Something needed to change for him.

"Cameron's calling Saturday," Jarod said, pushing himself to his feet and grabbing his crutches.

"It'll be good to hear from him."

"Yeah, I hope he comes home for good soon. We need this family together, not scattered across the globe."

"Someone should have a wedding—seeing anyone, Jarod?" She poked him in the ribs and suddenly the time fell away and they were two siblings, joshing around before fate dealt its one-two punch.

"When would I have time to do that?" He swung himself around the desk and headed for the door. "A woman would have to be dropped right in front of me to have that happen."

Well, that could be arranged. Especially if she came with bookkeeping skills.

# # #

From Catherine's diary, June 1944:

"Our troops have invaded mainland Europe. Hundreds of thousands killed. Where is Stephen? Among the living? The dead? I haven't gotten a letter in so long.

When will this wretched war end?

And what will I do when it ends?

George has been my steady companion. A few kisses here and there. I shouldn't, but I'm so lonely. Life seems to be standing still in Montana. Everyone is waiting. We aren't moving forward. We're only waiting for life to begin again.

I like George well enough. But he isn't my Stephen. He doesn't know anything about small-town living. He grew up in

Chicago.

And I'm missing Choteau and my family more every day. About now, the spring wildflowers will be in the mountains— shooting stars and glacier lilies.

I want to go home.

Chapter Nineteen

Cameron's face was indistinct, like whatever pixels they were using to transmit his visage had been scrambled and not put back together quite right.

"Still there, CJ?" he asked when the transmission settled down.

"Yes. Not quite ready to return to all that action and adventure," she replied. Like Jarod, Cameron was getting old before his time.

"You're not missing anything," he said. "Same old thing, day in day out. Gear up, get in a hot vehicle, figure out the latest maze of mines."

"You could always come back and do the same ol', same ol' of cows, cows, and more cows," Jarod drawled.

As he was expected to do, Cameron chuckled, but then he became serious. "Actually, my days about to become a little more interesting. A bunch of us are being sent on a mission. We'll be gone for a while."

"How long's a while?" Dylan's slow question was the one they all wanted answered.

"Unclear," Cameron said.

Silence at both ends of the video screen.

"But when I come back," Cameron said with a half-smile, "I'll be close to the end of my time. And I've decided not to reenlist. It's time for me to come home."

"Hallelujah!" Birdie shouted.

They all chuckled, and a tiny bit of the tension in the room lifted.

"Sold any paintings yet?" Cameron asked Dylan.

"Not yet, but I've got some interest from a gallery in Helena," her brother replied, not looking at anyone in particular.

"Oh?" CJ asked. It was the first she'd heard about it. Judging from the expression on Jarod's face, he didn't know about it either.

Dylan waved a hand. "No big deal. I've learned the hard way. Can't count on anything until someone puts down cold, hard cash. Besides, I've been too busy chasing cows dropping calves to worry about art. With Jarod out of commission—"

"What'd you do to yourself, big brother?" Cameron asked.

"Got off a horse the wrong way," Jarod replied.

Cameron shook his head. "Yeah, I better get home soon to keep all you yahoos safe from your own selves."

Another chuckle. The conversation drifted to ranch matters and CJ's attention wandered. She was half here and half gone. Limbo. It was as if all the pieces of her personality had never been fully integrated. She'd spent the last two months doing everything she could to get back to her job, but now that the time was close, she wasn't 100 percent sure it was what she really wanted.

How the hell was she supposed to figure that out?

She was beginning to sound like her grandmother, waffling between two men who represented two different lifestyles. How had Catherine finally made her decision?

And where was that Bible?

# # #

The next morning, after Jarod and Birdie went to church and with Dylan holed up in his cabin, CJ slowly pushed open the door to her mother's room. Originally, it had been the master bedroom, but her father had moved to the guest quarters, the suite Jarod now occupied, long before her mother got sick.

Why had they even stayed together?

Different times. Values that she didn't quite understand. Marriage was sacred so you didn't end it, but cheating was somehow different?

The room still held a faint scent of the perfume her mother had always worn—something that smelled like spring. The room had been closed up too long. Memories needed to be swept away and new life infused.

She crossed to the far side and swept open the heavy drapes. Chill immediately made her shiver as the cold that had built up between the windowpanes and the fabric came into the room. For a few seconds she stared out over the land, the view that had been her mother's only lens for the last years of her life.

CJ was becoming maudlin.

Shaking it off, she looked around the room. Would the Bible be something her mother had kept near her or tucked away? Her parents had been churchgoers, and Mom had attended Bible study before she'd gotten sick, but she'd kept a smaller volume for her personal use.

May as well start with the closets.

She pulled open the closet door. The walk-in was empty of clothes, thank god. Birdie's doing, no doubt. Her brothers wouldn't have thought about it. She lifted one of the boxes in the far corner and put it on the bed.

Pictures. Stacks and stacks of unsorted photos. She'd never have time to go through them.

She picked up a few—photos from happier times, when all of them were little. Smiles lit almost every face, except when they were getting yelled at by Mom or something tragic, like dropping an ice cream cone, had happened. She stared for a long time at a little girl with raspberry stains all over her face, and could almost taste the sweetness of the jam they'd been canning.

There *had* been good memories growing up.

The bed sagged a little as she sat down and pulled more pictures from the box. A half hour passed before she stopped. She'd label the box and deal with it later.

Three more boxes of photos were labeled and set in a corner. They needed to go up in the attic with the generations of old stuff already up there.

A box of books excited her for a few seconds, but they were women's fiction from the year her mother lay in bed. No Bible.

Doors opened in another part of the house, and she could hear the faint murmur of voices. She opened a few more boxes and sorted through the books. Still no luck. At least these boxes could be donated to the library or stacked in one of the take-one-leave-one bookcases around town.

"Any luck?" Jarod asked from the doorway.

"Not really. Found some old pictures and a few boxes of books but no Bible." She flashed him a grin. "But there are plenty of more places to look. I'll finish up here today then do a little more work in the office. Eventually, someone will need to tackle the attic."

"I appreciate this," Jarod said, his voice wistful. "I wish you were staying for good."

"I know, but my life is somewhere else. I have to go back."

"Do you?"

It was the question everyone kept asking her ... and the one that kept her up late at night.

"Yes," she said. It was the only answer she had.

# # #

The next two weeks passed too quickly for CJ's comfort. The first lot of calf births were coming to an end, and the older animals had the good sense to start drifting down to easier pastures where she and Dylan could slowly push them into the calving pens.

When she wasn't cattle ranching she tried to help Jarod sort through the bookkeeping. While not a total mess, it left much to be desired. He didn't like the idea of a bookkeeper—it meant admitting a defect in his mind, and he wasn't always willing to let CJ help either.

In her spare time, she finished going through her mother's room, looking for the Bible without success. Every once in a while she had to stop. She'd lay on the large queen bed covered with a few white comforters and let the memories flood over her. When she was little and woke with a bad dream, she'd sneak from the room she shared with Jarod and baby Dylan across the hallway and slip into her parents' room. They'd groan, snuggle closer together, and make room for her before they'd all fall back to sleep.

There'd been love in that room once, before the growing family took over the upstairs and her father moved his things out.

When she finally finished sorting through her mother's bedroom on the third Friday in March, she sat on the bed again. Winter still clutched much of the land, but the days had more than twelve hours of sunlight and the sounds of returning geese filled the skies. Tuesday was her appointment with the psychiatrist in Great Falls. Like the earth, her life was going to get a restart.

Her gaze swept the room. Her poor parents.

She lay back on the bed and closed her eyes, letting the memories and the tears ooze out of her. They were gone. What was done was done. She'd spent most of her life running from her past and making decisions on what her parents had chosen to do. What a waste. She may have made the same choices, but maybe not.

Nick.

It was his betrayal on top of the mess at home that had driven her away. If she'd had a normal family, would she have done the same, or would she have been able to deal with it, grieve, and move on?

She'd never know.

Her grief emptied from her—sorrow that her mother had died, resentment at the life her father had taken from them all, and deep anguish that they'd all lost so much.

She lay there for a half hour, until she could cry no more. Then she drifted to sleep. When she awoke an hour later, she looked at the room with new eyes. It was sad, tragic ... and gone. It was time to revitalize this room.

"Birdie?" She dashed into the kitchen where the woman was drinking yet another one of her interminable cups of coffee and watching her afternoon television. Dr. Phil was lecturing a man about some sin he'd committed.

"What!" Birdie sloshed coffee from the mug. "Oh lord, you scared me. Has there been another accident? Everyone okay?"

"Yes. Sorry," CJ said. "I was excited, that's all. Got a minute?"

Birdie's gaze reluctantly left the screen.

"I've got some ideas."

She led Birdie back to the master bedroom. "It's time to liberate this space from the ghosts that have been living here," she said with all the authority she could manage.

"You talked to Jarod about that?" Birdie asked.

"I have just as much right as he does to make decisions," she said. "Besides, he knows I'm cleaning. I'm just ... um, going a little bit further."

"Okay." The housekeeper sounded dubious.

"First thing is to get rid of all this fabric—the curtains, the bedding, everything. Throw it away, give it away, I don't care. You decide and I'll help you do it. Then we clean like crazy. Make sure all the personal stuff is gone, disinfect, dust, vacuum ... I don't know, maybe burn some sage."

"Sage?"

"Yeah, I'm getting carried away." But maybe she wasn't. Maybe for the first time in her life she was ready to break through the barriers and discover something new. Whatever it was.

It took the rest of the day to clear out the linens. Jarod poked his head in the room once to see what they were doing, waved a hand as if he wanted no part of it, and turned around. By the time she joined her brothers at the kitchen table for the heaping dishes of spaghetti, CJ was ready to eat.

"You want to explain what you're doing?" Jarod said after they'd each chowed down a third of their noodles combined with the oregano-rich sauce.

"With Mom's room?" she asked in all innocence.

Dylan looked up.

"Exactly," Jarod pressed.

Birdie got up and poured herself another cup of coffee.

"A fresh start." CJ pushed her plate forward and leaned on the table. "It was horrible, but it all happened a decade ago. We're all still mired in it. Nobody but me got married, and we see how mine turned out. We have to bury the past so we can get on to the future."

A frown crossed Jarod's face.

"Sooo," Dylan drawled. "You think just because you decide to come home again after five years, you get to tell us what to do in our own home."

Dylan objected? The brother who seemed to just roll with the easterly winds?

"It's my home, too," she said.

"She's right," Jarod said. "I'm not crazy about it either, but it already feels different, like something heavy has been lifted from the house."

Jarod was talking about *feelings*?

The world was spinning the wrong way on its axis.

Dylan shoved back his chair. "She should have asked."

Seconds later he was gone.

CJ and Jarod stared at each other.

"What was that about?" she finally asked.

"I have no idea. I didn't even know he cared one way or another. Heck, he hasn't lived in the house for years." He twirled his spaghetti for a few seconds but didn't eat any. "Keep doing what you're doing, CJ. It's time." He stared down at his plate then slid his fork back on the plate. "Sorry, Birdie," he said. "I'm not hungry anymore." He shuffled to a stand with his crutches and headed out the hallway.

CJ looked at Birdie.

The housekeeper shrugged. "It went about as well as it could have." Then she picked up her fork and dug in.

# # #

The small window in the psychiatrist's office gave a glimpse of the puffy, white clouds hurrying east across the prairie, driven by the wind in Montana's gustiest city. This was where airline pilots learned to take off and land in extreme wind conditions.

Dr. Wikowski had obviously spent time in the sun, tan all the way to the edge of his receding hairline.

"Tell me about your family," he asked.

She smiled at the familiar question.

"They're doing well," she said. "Jarod is almost recovered from his broken leg, Dylan has almost forgiven me for cleaning out the master bedroom, and Kaiden is knee-deep in oil and mud. The only worry is Cameron who is off on patrol somewhere."

The psychiatrist nodded. "At least they have names now," he said, looking down at the notes on his clipboard. "Before they were just four brothers. And the housekeeper?"

"Birdie is the same rock she's always been. A little slower, but I don't know what we'd do without her."

"Sounds like you have your family back. And more importantly, they have you." He riffled through the papers again. "Ms. Morgan says you've returned to taking photographs, that you're not as affected by your husband's death. She says you've done some amazing nature work. A new career path?"

CJ stuck with the answer she'd decided was the right one. "My career is in photojournalism. I'm going to continue to do that. I've let Max know to start looking for something for me ... pending your approval, of course." No use in antagonizing the man. He was the key to getting back to work.

"What about relationships? Family?"

"I've already promised Jarod I'd stay til he's back on his feet. And I'll make more of an effort to come back. I didn't realize how much I missed them. As for the rest ... that doesn't seem to be in the cards for me right now." She shrugged, trying to avoid thinking of Nick. "If it happens, it happens."

If only her heart didn't feel like it was an empty shell.

Dr. Wikowski studied her.

Was he going to accept her statements? Or insist on more therapy?

"I certainly hope that you are happy with your decisions," he finally said.

"I'm sure I will be." She could either be a photojournalist or hang out in Montana hoping the spark between her and Nick could become a flame. A binary choice. She couldn't do both. She'd made her decision and she was sticking with it.

He pursed his lips and stared at the material. Time for this to be over. Once she got going on her life again, it would all sort itself out. It had to.

"I agree with Mrs. Morgan," he finally said. "There are still areas of your life that I believe you would be better off dealing with, but they aren't enough to prevent you from doing your job safely. I'll let your bureau chief know."

"Thanks." She stood. "I appreciate that. I do feel better, actually, like I've got a stronger link with my family."

He nodded and stood as well. "I wish you luck, Ms. Beck. I hope you win an award someday."

Her step was lighter as she walked to her Jeep. Finally, she was free. Jarod's leg should be healed in the next few weeks, and by then Max should be able to find something for her. Treating herself to lunch before heading to the ranch store seemed like the right thing to do.

As she drove down the back streets of Great Falls, she idly noted the houses. Most were basic working class, here since the war. Was the old boardinghouse her grandmother had lived in even standing?

She'd finished the last entry in the volume she was reading and was having trouble finding the next one. It wasn't in the box with the others.

Frustrating. While Catherine had ultimately married Stephen and had CJ's father, it wasn't clear how, or even why, that had happened. What had been the final event to turn her away from the life George offered to become a rancher's wife?

She needed to find that volume before she left.

As she turned a corner toward downtown, a young woman, probably not much older than sixteen, ran into the street, her black hair streaming behind her. A young man ran after her and caught up to her in the middle of the street. Giving her a swift slap across her face, he dragged her back to the sidewalk.

CJ yelled at him, but there was no way he would hear her.

A horn beeped behind her so she finished the turn, desperately looking for a place to park. The conversation she'd overheard in Glacier came back to her. Was this one of the native women who were missing?

By a miracle, there was a spot. She slid the Jeep in it and, on an impulse, grabbed the camera on the seat next to her. Flinging the door closed, she raced to where she'd last seen the woman.

There! They went down an alley.

CJ sped after them, catching up as the man pulled open a door. No key, so it hadn't been locked. The girl pushed back as he tried to drag her inside, giving CJ the time she needed to reach them.

He yanked hard and the girl screamed as she was pulled in.

"Stop it!" CJ yelled.

"Get out of here!" he yelled back, his face distorted with rage. "This isn't your business."

She thrust the camera to her eye and snapped, the door framing his anger against the pale terror of the young woman behind him.

"I'll kill you for that!" he screamed and charged toward her.

CJ turned and ran toward the end of the alley, footsteps heavy behind her. She barreled down the street and slid into the front seat of the Jeep, thankful she'd forgotten to lock it. His hand reached for her rear bumper as she screeched from the spot, horns blaring behind her.

She was halfway to Choteau before she stopped trembling enough to think straight. What had she seen? Better yet, what had her camera captured?

She pulled onto the shoulder, turned off the Jeep, and steadied her breathing. Ahead of her stood the Rockies, solid in the test of time. When her heart had stilled, she picked up the camera and looked at the picture.

Money shot.

If only it weren't so tragic. The girl definitely looked Native American—long, dark hair, dark skin.

Something needed to be done.

She'd do what she always did—send the picture to Max. She also send him a note saying she was cleared for work. It was time to get back into the proverbial saddle.

But not before she did something about what she'd seen. She turned the Jeep around and headed back to Great Falls.

###

The officer on the case was Captain Lisa Howard, a veteran of the Great Falls department and a member of the Cascade County Human Trafficking Task Force. Her short, auburn hair was close cut and her face serious after CJ showed her the photo she'd taken.

"Yeah," the captain said. "He's been on our radar. So's that hotel—got a broken lock on the back door we can't convince the owners to fix. Can I get a copy of this?"

"Sure," CJ said, removing the memory card and handing it to her. "Anything to help catch this creep."

"Photos like this"—Captain Howard clicked the memory card on the counter—"are invaluable. Not only to help us take him off the street, but to show the public that this stuff is real."

"I'm a photojournalist," CJ said.

"Well, keep at it. The public needs to see what's actually going on."

"Actually, I'm headed back to the Middle East—the war."

"Too bad," the captain said. "All the bad guys aren't overseas." She held up the memory card. "I'll be right back."

If CJ believed in a higher deity, she'd believe he was trying to get her attention. This was the second or third time she'd been told that there were problems in the States that her work could help expose. But no matter.

"Here you go." The captain handed her the memory card. "Thanks for coming in. We've got officers headed over there right now. I've got your contact information if we need to get in touch."

"Will you let me know if you save the girl?"

"Sure, I can do that."

CJ had stopped for gas when her phone buzzed.

"Girl is safe. Thanks again," the text read.

Almost immediately, her phone buzzed again.

Max.

"Have a great gig in Iraq," it read. "Ready when you are in about a month."

CJ grinned and fist pumped. She was back in business. Six weeks from now she'd be back in the world she knew.

She cranked up the radio and headed down the road, singing as loud as she could.

Chapter Twenty

"Max has something for me!" CJ practically shouted into the phone when Nick answered. "The timing is perfect. I can wait until Jarod is back on his feet and then I'm off to Iraq!"

"I'm happy for you, CJ," Nick said, although his voice was mildly warm.

"How about I pick up dinner and we can celebrate?" she asked. She wanted to share her happiness.

Nick cleared his throat. "How about I take you out to dinner instead?"

"What about Trevor?"

"He'll be fine. There's pizza in the freezer. A night without his old man hovering wouldn't be the worst thing. I'll see you at John Henry's about six?"

"Okay."

"Good." He hung up.

Something was going on. Had Nick and Grace decided to get back together after all?

That was a nonsensical thought. They hadn't seen each in years, never mind having time to hook up.

She checked her watch. It had been a long day already with the doctor visit, the chase in Great Falls, and Max's news. She phoned Birdie to let her know her plans but didn't say anything about going to Iraq. She'd tell them all together.

"Well, that sounds nice," the housekeeper said. "You and Nick sure are seeing a lot of each other."

"We're just friends," CJ replied. "Anything else died years ago."

"Uh-huh. Drive careful coming home."

"I will."

She was going to miss Birdie's gentle admonitions. Overseas, it was each man, and woman, for themselves. Sure, they pulled each other out of harm's way, but it wasn't the same.

Grabbing a magazine she'd picked up in Great Falls, she headed to the restaurant. May as well enjoy a local beer while she waited.

Nick was early.

"Hey," he said, pulling up a chair across from her.

"Hey, yourself," she said with a grin. "We got to stop meeting like this."

"Sounds like we'll be doing that soon enough." His voice had an edge of betrayal.

"Nick, you knew I was leaving."

"Yeah."

"What can I get you to drink, Nick?" The waitress brought him a menu.

"I'll get a Golden Bobcat," he said, naming a beer brewed in Great Falls.

"Good choice. It's what CJ's having, too."

"Is it?" Nick asked. "We always did have similar tastes."

She smiled at him, but she held back her enthusiasm. This was not going the way she expected.

"So tell me about the job," he said.

"Max emailed me a few sketchy details, but it's similar to the last job I had, only a different desert and a different war."

"Sure wish we could get out of the war business. It's been going on half my lifetime."

She didn't have an answer to that.

The waitress took their order, and CJ finished giving him the information about the job—at least what she knew. He responded like he was listening, but it was polite murmurs, not engaged at all with what she was saying.

Ben had been the same—so had most of the guys she'd worked with in the field. It had never bothered her before, so why did it disturb her so much now?

Because it was Nick.

Her burger was flat. All she could taste was the onion she'd added along with the lettuce and tomato. During dinner, Nick talked about an upcoming fishing trip he'd just booked, including how his parents were going to watch over Trevor.

"It's a little tough on them, and not a permanent solution, but it will have to do for now—at least until Grace and I can figure this out."

"I'll still be here then. I can help out. Maybe he can stay at the ranch for a few days. We have plenty of room. And I don't mind taking him to school and picking him up." She warmed to the whole idea. She liked Trevor, and it would be fun being a doting aunt figure.

"I don't think that would work," Nick said.

"Why not?" She wiped the extra ketchup off her fingers and leaned forward. "What is going on?"

"You're leaving."

"You *knew* that."

"Yeah, well ..." His voice trailed off and he stared off in the distance. The vacant look in his eyes told her he wasn't really seeing what he was looking at. Then he brought his focus back to her. "I've discovered there's a problem with that."

"A problem with what? My leaving?"

"Yeah. It's just that somewhere along the way I discovered I still ... well ... have some feelings for you. And the way Trevor looks at you, I know he cares a lot about you, too. He's going to be hurt when you leave."

Her mind chewed on his words. *Fuck.* He had *feelings* for her. Not what she planned at all. This was supposed to be a laser operation—get home, get right, get out. And, in her gut, she knew he was right. A thirteen-year-old boy wouldn't understand—especially right after his own mother had sent him away.

She'd made a mess of things.

"I'm sorry. I didn't intend for that to happen," she said.

"Yeah, well. Life happens. I guess you owed me one after Grace."

"I didn't intend that at all," she snapped. "Give me *some* credit."

He shrugged. "Doesn't matter. The end result is the same. Look, I know you're going to be here another bunch of weeks, but I think it's better for me and my son if you just attend to your business."

"You mean not see you or Trevor again. Not even to say goodbye."

"I'll explain it to him."

Why the hell was her heart aching so badly? Getting back to her job was what she wanted.

"Whatever you think is right."

"This is it." He stared at the half-eaten burger and half glass of beer, then pulled out his wallet and threw some bills on the table before standing. "I'm sorry, CJ." His voice broke. "I'd hoped you'd reconsider, realize that your heart really belonged here at home ... but I guess all I can do is wish you a good future."

He slid on his coat, picked up his hat, and walked out of her life.

# # #

The door on his pickup gave its familiar squeal when Nick got in and slammed the door shut. He hung his hands over the steering wheel and stared at the non-descript restaurant in front of him. He could have been in any small town in Montana. Except he was cursed to be in the one occupied by CJ Beck. And doubly cursed to have opened his heart to her again.

Unrequited whatever this was—it was a bitch.

He started the motor and headed out of town. As he drove, snow came down, slowly at first, then more intensely, and the wind picked up. Soon it was difficult to make out where the road was. Reflectors on either side of the road kept him going in the right direction, while rumble strips on the edge and in the middle kept him in his lane.

His back ached as he hunched over the wheel. No wonder his parents wanted to get out of the state. What would he do without them to help with Trevor? Although winter wasn't his busy season.

What if he ran the store for them during his slow season? He could bear it for a few months. Financially, it would be a good fit too. His parents could help out with childcare during the shoulder seasons, unless Trevor visited his mother for school breaks. They could figure out the summer schedule together. If they'd be willing to work part time instead of totally retiring, he might be able to cobble together coverage for Trevor for the next five years.

It just might work.

Thunk, thunk, thunk.

He yanked the steering wheel to the left and felt the back tires slide to the edge of the road. He swung the wheel back to the right, keeping his touch light on the steering wheel to sense how the truck was reacting. As soon as he got the car straightened out, he focused on the road ahead, forcing all other thoughts away. They weren't important right now.

"Trevor," he called out when he entered the main part of the house.

"In here, Dad," Trevor's voice lofted from his room.

His son was lying on his bed, his fingers tapping on his phone. A plate with the remains of a pizza crust sat on the table next to the bed.

"I thought I told you—"

"Not to eat in my room. Sorry. But I was careful." Trevor looked up for a brief moment and grinned. "Really. Careful."

"Don't do it again," Nick said with all the seriousness he could muster, which wasn't much. He'd done the same kind of thing while he was growing up.

He cleared his throat. "Look, there's something we have to talk about."

"What?"

"You need to put the phone down."

"Is it Mom? Is she going to make me go back?"

"No, it's not. But would that bother you—going back?" Nick sat on the bed, which was covered with a forest-green comforter.

"Kinda. I mean, I'm just getting to know kids here. And, well, there's this girl. I kinda like her."

"The same one you got in trouble over?"

"Yeah."

While it probably wouldn't last, first girlfriends had a powerful sway over teen boys.

CJ's influence had never entirely left him.

"I'll keep that in mind when I talk to your mother. But that's not it. CJ got her clearance. She's going back to the Middle East in a few weeks."

"What? I thought ... Well, you and her are old friends ..."

"That's all it was—is. Friendship. She's got her own life. And she's going back to it."

"Oh." There was a powerful hurt in that one word, a pain that echoed in his own heart.

"She's got a lot of stuff to take care of," Nick lied. "So we won't be seeing her again."

"Not even to say goodbye?"

"I gave her my best wishes already," Nick said.

"But I didn't. She helped me a lot. I want to see her."

"We'll see," Nick said.

"Yeah, right." Trevor picked up his phone.

Nick let it go and walked out the door, torn about the best course of action. Letting Trevor see CJ again would give him some kind of closure, but it would also mean ripping open the wound to his heart.

Damned woman. Why couldn't she let down her defenses? In the times they'd spent together, he'd seen the yearning in her eyes for the land of her birth and the family she'd had before everything went haywire.

How could anyone leave Montana for good?

Yet, that's exactly what she seemed hell-bent on doing.

He slammed the flat of his hand against the wall, causing a few of the pictures to rattle on the wall.

"You okay, Dad?" Trevor poked his head out of his door.

"Yeah. Sorry. Didn't mean to scare you. I'm okay."

As okay as anyone could be with a hole in his heart.

# # #

From Catherine's diary, August 1944:

"Stephen is hurt ... oh, my heart aches.
He will be home in a few months. I must get back to Choteau.
Do my duty.
Oh, God, let him live."

That was where the diary ended.

CJ closed the volume. It was so frustrating not to know what happened. Her memories of her grandmother were of a woman with spunk who missed her husband greatly once he was gone. How had she gone from that last entry to the deep love that CJ remembered between them?

Life was so tangled. If only there were a clear path forward to where happiness was guaranteed. She was so tired of being heartsick.

"Jarod says you're leaving again." Dylan sat in a nearby chair.

In spite of meaning to tell them all together, she'd blurted out Max's news to her brother as soon as she'd seen him. He'd immediately told Birdie and obviously mentioned it to their brother as well.

The afternoon light lingered, giving the living room an almost otherworldly feel.

"Once he's back on his feet, yes, I'm headed back. Max has a good assignment for me."

"Aren't you tired of running away?" Dylan's voice was harsher than she'd ever heard it.

"I'm not running away. It's my job."

"But *why* is it your job? We need you here. We need to be a family again."

"We'll never be a family again," she said. "Kaiden's gone with his career and Cameron's fighting overseas. How come they get to do what they want, but I'm not supposed to follow my dream."

"Really? I don't remember you dreaming about filming bloody battles and never seeing your family."

"I always wanted to be a photographer. You know that."

"This is different." He leaned forward, scowling at her.

His face, weathered by sun and the ever-present wind, made him look older than his thirty-two years.

"Yes, but I discovered I'm really good at this. I want to make a difference, show the world what hell war is."

"It's not the only place that's got problems ... there are plenty of people being killed here—school shootings, snipers, all of it—if you absolutely need blood and gore."

"It's not like that." Damn him. "What would you know? All you've ever done is putter around with your paints on this ranch."

"Low blow, CJ."

He was right, but she wasn't going to give him the satisfaction.

"We all were affected by Mom and Dad's deaths," he said. "Not only you. Yeah, you were the oldest, but look at Jarod. He's taken over the ranch, trying to keep it together for the family—and that includes you. He gave up his rodeo dream for us."

"No one made him do that."

"That's who he is." Dylan shook his head. "I don't know how to get through to you anymore." He looked down at his fingers, the nails stained with darkened pigment. "All I know is that my brother gets older and sadder each day. Along with the rodeo dream, do you know that he was in love with someone from high school? They were quiet about it, but they were planning to get married after high school—wanted lots of kids, just like Mom and

257

Dad."

"What happened?" So much she didn't know. She swallowed hard.

"He kept putting it off. He wanted to have enough money for them to be secure." Dylan shrugged. "Ranching isn't always the best way to accumulate cash quickly." He sighed. "She eventually moved on. Now she lives up in Great Falls with a guy who works as an insurance agent. They've got five kids."

"Jarod's dream."

"Yep."

They sat in silence for a few minutes. Everything was a mess, but she couldn't see how her giving up her career would change anything. Eventually, they would move on. They'd have to. Trevor and Nick would figure out their lives, and so would her family.

The best thing she could do for them would be to go on alone and avoid permanent relationships like the plague.

"Well," she finally said. "I'm sorry about all of that, but it's something he's going to have to figure out on his own. It's not like we can get a mail-order bride for him."

"It's not funny, CJ."

"What do you expect me to do about it?" Her chest clenched with frustration.

"Stay. Help us out."

"What if there was another solution?" she asked.

"Like what?"

"Ben left me a lot of money. I'll give half of it to you and Jarod to run the ranch. That way you can hire some hands and you won't have to work so hard."

"We don't want your blood money." Dylan stood, his fists clenched.

She pushed herself to her feet and took a step toward him.

"It's not blood money!" Her stomach churned with anger. "It's the best way I can help out."

"No, it's not. And if you can't understand that ..." He shook his head. "Then there's no point in continuing this conversation." He walked out of the room.

She stared at his back for a few moments then sank back into the chair. The ranch world continued outside. Winter was slowly losing her grip on the land, but nighttime still brought chill.

Jarod balanced on his crutches and worked Prince in the fading light. He'd gotten the horse to perform on command—forward, left, right, backing up—not always smoothly, but it was there. Jarod had skill and patience. Dylan was right. He deserved a chance to reclaim his dreams and find happiness.

But it wasn't her fault he was tied to this damn ranch. She never asked him to do that. Dylan had no right to blame her. Jarod stayed because he was Jarod. If they accepted the money, then her conscience would be clear. She could live her life and they could live theirs. Her family would be fine without her.

A door slammed. Seconds later, Dylan stomped across the porch and down the steps toward the corral. Jarod walked Prince over to him. By the way Dylan was gesturing with his hands, he was relaying their conversation. Jarod glanced up at the house, shrugged, and said something to their brother.

Dylan stomped off toward his cabin.

Jarod lifted the loop of rope holding the gate closed and pushed it open. With a last glance at the house, he led Prince into the barn.

She let her gaze drift off to the landscape beyond the barn.

Come spring, the grasslands would be covered with flowers that would creep up the foothills to the mountain valleys. Bear grass, shooting stars, and glacier lilies would briefly carpet the space in yellow, purple, and white. All the flowers were delicate blossoms, ironic given the harsh conditions that surrounded them.

They were stronger than they looked, something she'd always believed about people, particularly her family.

But what if that wasn't true? What if too many wounds wore a person down so they no longer had the resiliency to fight back? Would that happen to her brothers?

If only they'd take Ben's money. It would help, wouldn't it? She didn't want or need all of it. She'd never asked for it in the first place.

The memory returned with full force.

One of their fellow journalists, a nasty Brit who looked like he'd graduated from Eton but had the ethics of an alley rat, had told her about her husband's latest affair. She could still see the words spilling from his mouth.

"He's chasing American tail," the Brit said. "Got a fondness for the dark ones." He smiled and place his hand around her arm, the back of his thumb touching her breast.

She pushed him off her, slapped his face, then walked back to her quarters, spine as straight as she could make it.

God, she wished he was wrong. But he wasn't; she knew the signs.

That night, she feigned sleep until Ben slipped from their bed.

"Where are you going?"

"Out. I need a smoke."

"You're going out to see that woman." She slammed her feet on the floor and stood. "This is it, Ben. I'm done.

"You're a raving lunatic, CJ. All I want is a smoke." He walked out the door and down the steps to the street below.

She threw on her pants and a jacket and followed him.

"Ben!" she yelled.

"Shut up, lady," a soldier hissed. "The enemy is out there and you're pinpointing our location."

"Yeah." She stalked after Ben and grabbed his shoulder.

He twirled on her. "Give it a rest a CJ."

"This is the third time, Ben! I'm over it."

"It's not like you're all pure and innocent," he spat out.

"I only did it once."

"Yeah, right. Once that I know about. Leave me alone. You don't love me. You never really loved me. You are totally incapable of loving anyone."

"I want a divorce." Her voice was shaky, but she'd said it. God, it tore her apart to give up on her marriage, but he was destroying what little of herself she had left.

"Whatever you want. I'm tired of trying to reason with you," Ben turned and stalked off, pulling his cigarette pack from his pocket as he walked away.

She stood and watched in anger as he leaned against a wall and lit the damn thing.

Moments later, there was a sound like *pfft,* and Ben slid to the ground, almost in slow motion.

CJ sat in the chair and played it over and over again in her head. The endless loop taunted her. She should have done something different. Said something different.

She should be a different person.

Her phone pinged.

Max: This is good stuff.
CJ: What?
Max: The picture you sent of the girl. Can I submit it?

CJ: Whatever.

What did it matter? For that one girl the cops had rescued, there were thousands more. Thousands she was powerless to prevent from being victims.

What use did her photography actually serve?

Max: It's a GOOD photo. What's up with you? I thought you were okay to go back.
CJ: I'm fine. There's just stuff. You know. Life. Family.

Her total worthlessness at doing any of it.

She needed to put on a better front. Otherwise, Max would send her back for another round of psychobabble.

CJ: Just that time of month ... you know.
Max: Uh. Okay. Later.

She let her lips curl up a little. Mention female troubles to most men and they disappeared like a shot.

Nonetheless, she needed to do something constructive.

Chapter Twenty-One

CJ assigned herself tasks—anything to feel useful.

Up at five with her brothers, she helped out with the calving. Jarod did as much as he could, but the bulk of the work fell on her and Dylan. Newborn calves and mothers near the barn needed to be checked, then CJ went with Dylan to the outer pastures to tag as many calves as possible. It was a never-ending cycle of circling the herds in the pickup and ATV, finding calves, tearing them away from their fierce mothers long enough to tag, and handling the little ones that didn't make it. She had to keep tallies—all the detailed recordkeeping of modern ranching.

However piqued Dylan was with her, it never showed as they worked. They developed an easy rhythm and an ability to quickly communicate without a lot of discussion.

After a quick shower, she dove into her mother's office. The past was the past. If she cleared out all this crap, they'd all have a chance to move on. Besides, somewhere in all of this mess had to be the information on the mineral rights and the next set of diaries.

This chore was less satisfying than handling the cows. Her mother had kept a lot of junk, including old love letters from her father, tied with the traditional pink ribbon.

CJ stood for a long time with the bundle in her hand. She didn't want to read them; she knew the tragic end to the story. But destroying them didn't seem right either. One of her brothers might have children someday, and the letters should go to them.

They would never go to her children. What a stupid decision that had been. It had seemed so right at the time. She could either have children or go on adventures around the world. Five years ago it had seemed a no-brainer.

Life was a series of choices. She made the first by going to Kentucky for school. Everything else flowed from that. No matter what the advertisements said, it was impossible to have it all.

She put the letters in an empty box. When she was done, she'd label the boxes and get one of her brothers to put them in the attic, along with the things from the first Jarod Beck.

Moving the boxes had freed up the right-hand bottom drawer of the desk. She tugged it open.

A Bible.

She snatched it up and opened the cover.

Catherine Beck was written in the same familiar hand as the diary entries had been. Not her mother's Bible, but it might have the information CJ needed. She flipped through the first few pages.

There it was—the family tree going back to Jarod and his wife Elizabeth. The family founder had had two sons: Jacob and Seth. She could trace Jacob's line to her father, Daniel. But Seth's side ended in the 1930s with two question marks—one where his wife would have been and one below them. Next to the second question mark, someone had noted "Alice."

Whatever happened to baby Alice?

She'd need to hire a detective to figure that one out.

No, not her. She'd recommend it to Jarod. And she'd offer to pay for it. Maybe he'd accept her money then.

Closing the Bible, she went back to cleaning.

After several more hours of sorting and tossing papers, she gave it up for the day and headed to the kitchen.

"Need any help?" she asked Birdie.

"No thanks. I got it."

Even Birdie was cooler since CJ had told her that she was heading back to the Middle East. The boys ignored her most of the time, except when they needed her help. Jarod seemed to be getting better. Maybe she should leave earlier than she'd planned, spend a week in New York and see a play and do some shopping. She had money now.

"I'll be outside," she said, picking up her camera.

The air was cool but not the frigid temperatures of the depth of winter. She could almost taste spring. When was the last time she'd experienced a real change of seasons?

Raising her lens to her eye, she snapped photos of the structures she'd known all her life. It was almost like seeing them for the first time. The blue sky framed the weathered boards of the barn. The corrals glinted where new wood had replaced old railings. Fence posts leaned this way and that as barbed wire extended to enclose a small pasture for cattle at risk. Beyond that, on hills still blotched with white snow, dark dots indicated patches of Black Angus, the ranch's signature beef.

She moved off the porch, angling to be out of Jarod's line of vision. Using the telephoto lens, she focused on the left side of his face, shadowed by the Choteau Bulldogs cap he always wore. Could she capture the absolute reliability of her brother in a still photo?

After taking a number, she widened the shot. He bent, but his frame was covered by the bulk of his coat. Giving up, she moved to the corral and examined Prince. She squeezed off a number of shots before Jarod joined her.

"He's turning out okay," her brother said. "In another six months, I might be able to sell him as a reasonable calf roper. Too bad you won't be around."

"Why? I've never pictured myself roping calves. That was you and Nick." A slight pang went off in her chest when she mentioned his name.

"Me either." Jarod's chuckle was genuine. "No, I meant to take pictures of him for a website I want to build."

"Really? A website? You?"

"Just because bookkeeping baffles me doesn't mean I don't understand technology." He took his hat off, thumped it against his crutch, and perched it back on top of his cropped black hair. "I had to trade in my rodeo dream for a ranch, but I've been thinking about a new one. Prince is the experiment."

"You've made your decision. You're going to train calf-roping horses."

"Yep." Jarod nodded. "Hope to train some riders, too."

When was he going to have time to do all that?

"Let me give some of Ben's money to the ranch. Please. That way you can hire some hands and have more time for the dream."

"Thanks, CJ, but that money's yours. I'll figure this out on my own. It's better that way." He shuffled away from the rail. "See you inside." He maneuvered back toward the ranch house.

Tears stung her eyes. They weren't going to let her give them anything.

Except herself.

The one thing she couldn't let them have.

# # #

Nick stomped to his truck. Trevor was in trouble.

Again.

This time he'd sassed a teacher and refused to do his work. Not once. Not twice.

The third time he'd done it, the teacher had called the office and they'd gotten in touch with him for a parent conference.

What had gotten into his son?

The truck bucked a bit as he flipped too fast from reverse into drive.

Settle down, Sturgis.

Maybe it was simply spring fever.

Probably not.

In his heart of hearts, Nick knew Trevor's problems were the same as his. CJ was leaving.

April first was the perfect day for recriminations. He'd been a fool thinking that the woman would ever stay in one place again. He'd had his chance with her a long time ago, and he'd blown it.

Although she might not have stuck even then. Between her father's death on an icy Montana highway after a visit to his latest mistress and her mother's slow demise due to cancer, CJ hadn't stood much of a chance at happiness in a relationship.

He may not have been able to provide it to her either, but damnit, he'd wanted the chance. CJ fit him far better than life with Grace, real or imagined, ever had.

When he stopped for the sign before the turn onto the main highway to town, he took a moment to gaze at the prairies rolling east. They seemed to go on forever, bigger than the humans that had been tromping across them for centuries. Like the rest of the planet, they were in danger of destruction, a problem too big for one man to solve.

Better stick to the ones he had a shot at handling—like his son. The planet and CJ would have to solve their problems on their own. But, damn, it was hard not to play the knight errant.

He swung onto the highway just as a semi came out of nowhere, hauling ass north. He slammed on his brakes. A woman who looked like she should be home baking cookies for grandkids gave him a glare worthy of a seasoned trucker.

Nick took a deep breath and focused. With one more glance to the south, he completed his turn and headed to town. A half hour later, he was back in the vice principal's office, feeling like he hadn't made it out of high school.

"Mr. Sturgis," the vice principal, Mrs. Helms, began.

"Nick," he said. "Please call me Nick."

"Of course. So what we have here," she gestured toward Trevor, "is a young man who, up until a few days ago, seemed to have turned himself around and was heading down the right track. He's personable and a good student. But this week?" She shook her head. "It feels like we're dealing with a very different person. Teachers tell me he's refusing to work, or doing shoddy work. The social studies teacher, who is our baseball coach, said he isn't coming to practice—"

"Wait a minute," Nick said, turning to Trevor. "If you aren't going to practice, where are you going after school?"

"Nowhere," Trevor said with a shrug.

"A lot of the kids head downtown," Mrs. Helms said. "He might go with them."

Nick looked back at Trevor.

His son was staring out the window.

"What else?" Nick asked.

"He walked out of English class," she replied.

"It was a dumb assignment," Trevor said.

"That doesn't give you the right to get up and leave."

"Why not? Everybody else walks out when they don't like what's going on. You, Mom, CJ ..." Trevor's green eyes turned as icy as emeralds with pain and anger.

"Nobody is leaving you," Nick said, even though he could see how it would look different to Trevor.

"Yeah, right." His son turned back to the window.

"It sounds like this has been a tough time for Trevor. Maybe it's for the best that he take a day off and think about his behavior."

"Are you suspending him?"

"For one day, yes. We can't have his attitude affecting the other students."

That was a lot of bullpucky.

"I'll talk to him."

"That would be good, Mr. Sturgis."

Nick tried to formulate the right words as they drove home.

Your mom loves you ... Nope. Not when she hadn't shown much lately.

I'm here for you ... But he was a stranger.

CJ ... ah, damn it, CJ. Why do you have to leave?

The crack in his heart expanded like a huge tree limb iced off in winter.

He glanced at Trevor. Apparently, the sound didn't carry beyond his own head.

"Look," he began. "Like it or not, life is sometimes about loss. People come and go. Sometimes they move on because they can't handle stuff. Sometimes because they need something important in their life."

Trevor grunted.

"I know CJ leaving is a blow, but you only knew her for a little while."

"I like her. She's real. She'd seen things. Done things."

"She's running away." *Damn it.* He hadn't meant to say that.

"From what? You?"

"Lots of stuff. Yeah, me ... I guess." He almost missed their road and had to make a sharp turn, hitting the road wide.

The white pickup heading down the road was going slow enough that he could get back in his own lane, but the driver still gave him a well-deserved salute.

"Then why don't you fix it? Make her stay?"

"I can't make her stay. I'm not the only one she's running from. Things weren't easy for her here. Her parents died, then ... well ..."

"Well what?"

"We were dating in high school." He may as well come out with it. "I met your mother and broke up with CJ. She ... didn't take it well."

"And then you dumped Mom."

"She dumped me, remember?"

"You deserved it."

"Probably," he said. "Probably." He pulled into his parking spot under the pole lamp. The car was still running when Trevor pushed open his door.

"Adults are jerks," he said before shoving the piece of metal home.

There was some truth to that.

Nick followed his son into the house, almost tripping over the size 10 boots Trevor had kicked off in the middle of the mudroom. Nick shoved them to the side then plunked his own size 13s next to them.

From the empty great room, his son kept going.

Not happening.

He stomped down the hallway to Trevor's room.

"Out. Now," he said. "Without the phone."

Trevor threw his phone on the bed, his face distorted by the sullen frown.

Nick walked back to the living area, feeling the angry

presence behind him. "Sit." He pointed to the couch. Once Trevor threw himself down, Nick sat at the other end.

"So," he began, "You feel like everyone's deserting you."

Trevor shrugged.

"Look," he said. "I was your age once. I did harebrained things and got into trouble, but the one thing I never did was talk back to teachers and refuse to do my work. That is not acceptable."

"Whatever."

God, he hated that word.

"From what your mother said," he plowed on, "you were getting into trouble in Seattle, too. Hanging out with the wrong crowd, maybe even involved with gangs or drugs."

"I was taking pictures," Trevor spat out. "I wanted to show everyone what life is really like."

It was like his son and CJ had been cut from the same cloth.

"You're only thirteen. There are boundaries."

"The kids on the street don't have boundaries. They've got nothing."

"And you aren't one of them," Nick said, thanking god for that truth.

"Nobody wanted them and nobody wants me. They made their own family. I can be part of that. I don't need you or Mom or CJ or anyone!"

Pain distorted Trevor's face.

Nick put his hand on his son's knee.

Trevor pulled away.

"I know it can be tough to understand, but we *do* want you. I love you, kid, and so does your mom. That's why she sent you here. She doesn't want you on the streets. She figured you'd be safer here. That's all parents ever want—their kids safe and happy."

"I was safe."

"And happy?"

Trevor shrugged.

Nick looked at his son for a few moments then sought refuge in his view of the Rocky Mountains. Things were starting to green up. As April went by, the animals would shed their unneeded layers. He understood how nature worked, the cycles year after year.

Teenagers? They were the true mystery of the world.

"I can't pretend to know how you feel," he said, turning back to Trevor. "Grandpa and Grandma are still head over heels with each other. Your uncle Henry and his family are doing well. I wish I could have made it work with your mom, but we were two very different people and we were too young to realize it at the time."

Trevor looked out the window.

Great, he was boring the kid.

"Do you like it here?"

That got his son's attention.

"Kinda. I mean. It's okay. Sometimes there's nothing to do except sports ... but it's okay. I don't want to be here forever. I want to go home."

"And home is Seattle."

"I guess."

Nick looked at his hands, trying to figure out where to go with this conversation that would make Trevor feel wanted by both his parents.

"Spring break is in a few weeks. Your mom wants you to come back home for a week. How about you go to Seattle, see your friends, then come back here to finish out the year. I'll drive you back to the city when school's over and we can discuss it then."

"Whatever."

"Can you please drop that word from your vocabulary? I'm trying to help you here."

"What if I don't want your help? I don't want your life—stuck up here with all these trees, never seeing anyone, no girlfriend even. That life sucks!" Trevor stood and stomped back to his room.

Nick pulled in a breath, hoping to ease the ache in his gut. Grabbing a beer, he went out to the porch and stared at view. Being a human sure was complicated compared to other living things. Trevor was right in one way. His existence was lonely. That's why he'd hoped, stupid though it was, that CJ might change her mind and stick around.

He'd never found another woman like her—able to adapt to her surroundings, caring, and smart. Before tragedy struck, she'd been open about her feelings—he'd never had to guess if he'd done something wrong.

Guess there was no going back from this one.

His face softened with sadness and he sank into one of the Adirondack chairs. For the next hour, he simply stared at the setting sun, the birds swooping on their hunt for an evening meal, and the gentle sway of pine tops in the breeze.

# # #

CJ wrapped up the final paperwork and tax planning with Brad Small and was on her way to the Jeep when Trish waved her over to the house. "I'm sorry you're leaving," Trish said.

Today's pies were made with huckleberries Trish had picked and frozen by the pounds during the last summer. The fruit exploded in CJ's mouth, giving a hint of the hot months to come.

"You're going to miss another Montana summer," Trish said.

"What week is it scheduled this year?" CJ smiled. Montana's summers were hot, frenetic, and all too short.

"Ha. Ha."

"What do you think of this?" CJ flipped through the images on her camera and showed Trish the photo she'd captured of the girl being held against her will in a Great Falls hotel.

"Wow," Trish said, putting down her coffee and staring at the picture. "This is great. Horrible, but great. What happened to her?"

"I showed it to the cops and they were able to get her and arrest the man. She's back home on Rocky Boy, but she has to leave the reservation to testify at his trial. I'm also on the witness list. Luckily, it's before I was planning to leave. The cop says she and her parents would like to meet me after the trial."

"Will that be possible?"

"The trial is next week."

Trish cut another sliver of pie for each of them then sat on the stool across from CJ. "You have a gift for this," she said. "Surely, there are enough people taking pictures of people doing the worst they can to each other. Why not stay here? Take pictures of homegrown problems, like trafficking and pollution and the general insanity that goes for society these days?"

"No Pulitzers in that."

"Is that what this is about? A prize?"

"It would prove I meant something." CJ shoveled another piece of pie in her mouth before she said anything else. The crust, which had been buttery and sweet before, tasted like the dust of the desert.

Trish's fork dropped to the counter with a clatter.

"You don't seriously mean that, do you?"

CJ shrugged.

"Wow, I knew your parents messed up your head, but I didn't know it was that much."

Unable to defend herself without spraying huckleberries all over the counter, CJ stayed silent.

Trish picked up her fork.

"No prize is going to feel like you're worth something," she said, using the tines for emphasis. "That's an inside job with a little help from God or whatever you believe in that's bigger than yourself. I thought you were in therapy. Didn't that get covered?"

CJ swallowed the final bit.

"Therapy had a very specific purpose—to get me out of here and back to work."

"But what about the rest of your life? Don't you want to be happy?"

Tempted to slough off the question with a quick retort, CJ opened her mouth, but the concern in Trish's eyes made her shut it again.

Did she even deserve to be happy? Did anyone?

"I don't know, Trish. It's not something I think about. My job keeps me going, knowing I'm making a difference ..." But was she? Really? Did one more war photojournalist make a difference? All the pictures in the world hadn't stopped the Civil War, the stench of the world wars, or the horror of all the wars since.

But her single photograph had saved a girl's life.

"Thanks, Trish," she said with a half-smile. "I guess I needed that." She stood. "And the pie." She walked around the counter. "And thanks for being my friend while I was here. I'll keep in touch."

"Yeah, imagine that," Trish said. "You can tell me about the big bad world and I'll keep you up on the pie business." She pulled

CJ into a long hug. "Think about what I said. You don't have to leave. We've got plenty of room for you here."

"Got it." CJ pulled on her khaki jacket and smiled. "See you."

On her way to the car, she passed one of Trish's kids, who gave her that half-wave Montana parents taught their children to do to be polite.

Leaving home was the pits.

She brushed aside the dampness from her eyes, turned the car, and drove out of the long drive. One more stop before heading back to the ranch.

Chapter Twenty-Two

"So you still haven't found the deed to the mineral rights," Cassandra said after CJ had settled into the attorney's guest chair.

"No."

"That means that you'll still have to pay the taxes, even though you may not have the rights."

"I've got it covered," CJ said. She'd used a chunk of Ben's money to pay the taxes ahead for one year and had the canceled check and receipt in her mother's files, as well as a copy she intended to leave in Jarod's office before she left town.

"Okay, so how can I help you?" the attorney asked.

"I was wondering if you knew a good private detective who could help trace the family line. It seems my great-whatever grandfather had two sons. One stayed here and kept the family farm, and Seth, younger son, went back east. It would make sense that Seth would get the mineral rights, wouldn't it?"

Cassandra's eyes darted to her right then refocused on CJ. "It would seem to."

"I have an old family Bible that lists ancestors on both sides but peters out with a child potentially named Alice. I'd like to hire someone to trace the line and find out for sure about the mineral rights. If we're going to be taxed for them, I sure would like to know if we own them."

"Of course. That makes sense. I might know a few people back in Chicago. How about I contact them and ask them to get in touch with you?"

"How soon do you think that will be?" CJ asked. "I've only got a few more weeks before I leave."

"I'll work on it as soon as I can over the next few days."

It was probably the best she was going to get, but it was an open question she didn't like. Her brothers would be too busy on the ranch to pay it much attention, and she knew what communication to the Middle East was like.

"Thanks. You have all my contact information."

"Yes."

CJ stood and prepared to leave the office. As she did, she caught a glimpse of the photo she'd observed the first time she was in the office. Apparently, Cassandra had put it back up.

"Do you know where that was taken?"

Cassandra glanced toward the photo and shook her head. "It was in a collection of old things my parents had stashed. I like it." She came around from behind the desk. "Very old-fashioned."

"And familiar," CJ said. "I'd swear I took the same photo as a kid."

"Oh? A lot of stuff looks the same to me around here," the attorney said.

"Yeah." Except that the unmistakable shape of Ear Mountain hovered in the far distance of the photo, just like it did from much of her ranchland. Too bad she was running out of time to go exploring.

# # #

The following Wednesday, CJ drove to Great Falls for the trial. Spring had taken firm hold of the land in mid-April, although there was still a chance a snowstorm would come roaring down from Canada.

CJ tossed her khaki coat in the passenger seat along with her purse and the camera she kept by her side again. Hot coffee filled the travel mug she'd gotten from the kitchen. She'd swiped a few of the freshly made oatmeal cookies from the jar. Birdie would frown, but it was one of the last chances she had to enjoy the comforts of home.

Her tickets were booked to New York, where she'd meet with Max and prepare for the next assignment. Jarod was almost back to normal. Things were progressing exactly as they were meant to be.

The mountains in her rearview mirror grew smaller with every mile her car traveled east until they became gray smudges on the horizon. The prairie and big sky rolled off to the other end of the state. What was it that kept people here in spite of the harsh climate and poor economy?

Not for her.

Somehow, she had to convince Nick to let her see Trevor before she left. The bond between her and the teen was stronger than she'd realized—two lost souls finding their way through the art of photography. Pictures showing what they couldn't find the words to say.

And that was exactly why she was going back to the war zone. It seemed like no one took the time to read and analyze anymore. But photos? There was always a reaction to that.

She arrived at the stone structure that housed the U.S. District Court with moments to spare. After locating an officer, she was directed to sit in the audience. A few rows ahead of her, the girl she'd seen sat ramrod straight, her dark, black hair flowing down her back. An older couple surrounded her, leaning slightly toward her as if protecting her against the evil that sat on the other side of the court.

And there he was: the man who'd hunted and chased this young woman—in a totally different persona. Smiles and a fashionable suit. She reached for the camera but stopped. Photography was banned in the courthouse.

But once the trial was over, she could wait on the courthouse steps and snap a photo of his transformation.

The trial began with routine paperwork and motions. The prosecutor's opening statement, delivered by a trim young woman in a dark suit, was measured but still dramatic as she laid out a pattern of fear and abuse. From the sounds of it, this was not the first time this creep had been arrested, but he'd done his time, returned to the street, and repeated the offense.

Maybe they could get him behind bars for a long, long time.

She gave her testimony early in the proceedings, and her photo was entered as evidence. The defense attorney didn't spend much time with her.

After more testimonies from the police who had arrested the trafficker, the young woman she'd helped save, Dyani Mitchell, took the stand. As her story of poor judgment, flirtation with drugs, and abuse went on, CJ's mind flicked back and forth between tales she'd heard from desert women and this young woman's tale. Such different lives, so many things in common.

And there, but for the grace of god, and luck, she might have gone.

As the trial wrapped up for the day, CJ slipped into the hallway, her camera ready.

The man stepped out behind his attorney, and she snapped picture after picture, first of his smiling, affable face, then of the scowl he sent her way before the rest of his defense team blocked her view.

When he disappeared, she left the courthouse to wait on the steps where she had agreed to meet Dyani. The warm spring sun eased some of the dirtiness she had accumulated through the proceeding. The girl endured so much. How would she ever be whole again?

"Miss?" A soft voice brought CJ back to awareness.

"Hi," CJ said with a smile. Although Dyani's eyes were haunted, there was a peace around her that was palpable.

"I want to thank you for what you did."

"It was the right place at the right time."

"Not true," the older woman behind Dyani said. "You were sent in answer to our prayers to bring Dyani home to us." She stepped forward and examined CJ. "And maybe to help you as well."

"Could be." Whatever the woman wanted to believe was fine with her.

"We would bring you to our home," Dyani said, "but they say you're leaving—going away to take pictures of the war. So, I brought these with me." She handed CJ a small tissue paper-wrapped package.

CJ opened it to find a pair of beautifully crafted beaded earrings.

"I made them for you," Dyani said.

"They're wonderful. Thank you." She held open her arms. "May I?"

The girl nodded and CJ enveloped her in a hug. "Be safe," she whispered. When she released her, the bright spots of unshed tears she knew were in her own eyes were mirrored in Dyani's.

The older woman touched CJ's arm. "We, too, have made something for you to thank you for returning our heart to our home. Dyani is our only child now. Without her, our home was broken." Turning to her husband, she took the bundle of fabric he held and gave it to CJ. "It is a star quilt. May it guide you to your own heart and home."

CJ's throat closed up as she took the bundle. "I can't," she squawked.

"You must," the old man said. "It is our way."

The couple nodded to each other and started down the steps. Dyani gave her a brief smile and followed them.

CJ sank to the sun-warmed stone and cradled the gift in her arms.

# # #

Dylan was on the porch talking on his phone when CJ returned home a few hours later, complete with everything everyone had asked her to pick up in the city.

"Let me help you with that," her brother said, trotting down the steps. Like her, he'd shed his coat in the warming spring sun. The freedom to move without layers of down, hats, gloves, and heavy boots was almost intoxicating.

"Kaiden's coming home for a few weeks," Dylan said, picking up the large box of supplies she'd bought at Costco. "Says he wants to see you in the flesh before you take off to parts unknown again."

"Wow, that's unexpected." She'd never been that close to her youngest brother.

"He misses you," Dylan said. "We all do."

"I'm still here."

"You know what I mean." He clomped up the stairs and walked around the porch to the mudroom by the kitchen.

Leaving the Jeep open, she lugged a small box of screws and nails toward the barn. Too bad Dylan hadn't taken that—far heavier than coffee and laundry detergent.

"Jarod," she called as she pushed the door open with her knee. "I've got your stuff."

"Yeah, thanks." He stepped away from the perpetually dysfunctional tractor and took the box. "Anything else I can help you with?"

"Another box of latches and bolts."

"I'll get it." He set the first one down and followed her to the Jeep. Dylan was already there, hoisting a bag of feed on his shoulder. "How'd it go?" he asked, pausing. "I forgot to ask."

"Okay. Jury's out. The cop who nabbed the guy said she'd let me know the outcome."

"Good," Jarod said. "I hope they nail him. Things like that shouldn't happen to girls in our state."

"Things like that shouldn't happen to girls anywhere," she said. "But it does."

"Yeah." Dylan continued on his way to the barn, Jarod in his wake.

It was all so normal.

For the second time that day her throat squeezed shut. She picked up the third Costco box and took it to the mudroom, where Birdie was busy stowing things in the large pantry off the kitchen.

"I'm going to miss you running into town and the city for me," she said. "It won't be the same with you around."

"I hear Kaiden's coming home this weekend."

"Oh? That's new for me. Definitely got to make a chocolate cake. That boy loves his chocolate."

"Yeah."

CJ returned to the Jeep just as her brothers got back.

"We've got the rest," Jarod said.

"Okay." She picked up her camera bag and purse then draped the quilt over her arm.

"What's that?" Dylan said.

"A gift from the girl's parents. They said it's a star quilt." To lead her home.

"Have you looked at it?"

She shook her head. "I will. Inside. Too dusty out here." And she had to look at it alone first.

"You deserve it," Jarod said.

"For what? Taking a picture?"

"Nope. For doing what you've always done—getting other people's stories. Showing the world what they are missing by rushing right by everything."

"We're proud of you, sis," Dylan said. "We may not always show it, but we're darn proud."

The men shouldered the last of the supplies and headed to the barn.

Maybe she'd read her family all wrong.

She closed the doors and headed up the front steps, bypassing Birdie in the kitchen. Once in her room, she laid the quilt out on the bed. From its center of dark yellow, like the sands along the Missouri River, the design delved into the blues of the river and sky, the gray of the mountain, the greens and tans of the grassland, and ended in tips of brick red set in a background of mottled straw.

Sinking on the bed next to it, she stroked the fabric, almost able to sense the intention of the women who made it. A guiding light.

A shadow dipped outside her window and turned, the sun reflecting off the white head of the eagle. Beyond him, the mountains stood sentinel, just as they had when she was a girl.

Maybe it was time to stop running.

# # #

CJ finally found another diary. Unfortunately, it contained only one entry. The rest of the pages were blank.

From Catherine's diary, October 1944:

"I visited Stephen in the hospital in Great Falls. His leg is mangled, but they say he will be able to walk, thank God. He was always so active. It would send him to despair to know he could no longer walk the paths of the ranch.

We didn't talk long—the nurses kicked me out after an hour, but my love is still my love. I told him of my foolishness with George, and he offered to release me to be wherever I needed to go. I told him the only place I needed to be was with him, if he would forgive me.

He held me close. There were things about war, he said, that needed to be forgiven and forgotten for both of us. It was only what happened from now on that mattered."

CJ put the volume down. Forgive and forget. Had she ever been able to do either? Maybe, with Nick, but then they'd created a new problem by allowing a friendship to blossom between them.

Her parents? They did so much damage to the family, but the people they hurt most were each other. And when all was said and done, she'd left her brothers to fend on their own. Maybe she had little choice at the time, but she'd never reconsidered her decision since.

And now there was an opportunity to do just that.

"Kaiden's home!" Birdie's voice sang out through the house.

CJ bolted out of the chair, ran to the kitchen, and enveloped her youngest brother in a bear hug.

"Woof!" he exclaimed. "What's gotten into you?"

"Just glad to see you, little brother."

"Yeah, I can see I'm the little one." Broadly built, Kaiden was the tallest over her brothers, topping six foot. Like the others, he'd been blessed with a broad smile, perfectly straight teeth, and a dreamy set of eyes that had kept the girls swarming his way through high school, Birdie had reported.

"As the only, and oldest, girl, I will always be the boss," she retorted.

"You got to stick around for that to be true," Dylan said, coming into the kitchen and pulling Kaiden close for a few seconds.

"What if I do just that?" she challenged them as Jarod walked into the crowded space.

"What?" Jarod asked. He tapped his ear. "I must be hearing things."

"What are you hearing?" Birdie stood in the door to the dining room. "And what are all you men doing in my kitchen? There's no room for me to work."

"You don't need to work right now. Lunch is barely over and it's not time to start dinner. Have a seat." Dylan turned one of the kitchen chairs around and gestured to it.

Head high, Birdie walked to it and sat.

CJ might be the only and oldest girl, but she was never going to be queen.

She grinned as everyone's eyes turned toward her.

"Max, my bureau chief, has been floating that picture I took as a stock photo for articles on human trafficking. Dyani, the girl in the picture, gave me her permission. She said if it will help other girls, she's all for it. As for the trafficker, he's now a convicted felon and fair game."

"They convicted him?" Kaiden asked.

"Jury was out for only a few hours," CJ said.

286

Kaiden high-fived her. "Way to go!"

CJ leaned against the kitchen table and gazed around her, suddenly unsure. Did they even want her around? Yeah, they said they did, but was that only because they knew she was leaving?

"That's great and all," Kaiden said, "but what does that have to do with you staying here?"

"A man from Helena contacted me. He's starting a magazine, both digital and print, to do with all things Montana. He wants a broad base of readership, and also to shine light on some things the state could do better."

"Like get a handle on the trafficking in the state," Kaiden said.

"It's a huge problem," Dylan added. "Especially on the reservations."

"But he also wants to highlight the good things, like multi-generational families, conservation efforts, that kind of thing," she said. "He's offered me a job to travel and take photos. It would be a lot of time on the road at first, but if the magazine takes off, I'd be on the ground floor."

"Fantastic," Jarod said.

"So-o-o," Dylan began, "are you going to do it?"

The room silenced and four faces turned expectantly at her.

"Some of that depends on you," she said.

"How so?" Jarod asked.

"Well ..." Her fears seemed so groundless.

"Just spit it out," Birdie said.

She looked at the ceiling, hoping the right words were written there.

Nothing.

"After Mom and Dad died," she said, "I ran. I couldn't bear it. I'm sorry. I've always felt guilty for that."

"No need," Jarod said. "You, me, all of us were hurting. You saved yourself." He looked at the floor briefly then back up at her. "I've always known that. Sorry I've been behaving like such a jerk lately. I just hate to see you go away again."

"But I let you down." She stared into his gray eyes, so like her own. "I left you in charge and you were even younger than I was."

"Mom and Dad let us down," he replied. "The rest of us just picked up the pieces as we could. It's done and in the past. You have to let the past sit where it is. No do-overs. Only today and tomorrow are ours to change."

"Sounds downright mystical," Dylan said with a drawl. "What church you been goin' to anyway?"

"Oh, shut up," Jarod said with a grin, and the rest of them laughed along with them.

"Look," Dylan said, "we can pretty much guarantee you'll get in our way, but we want you to stay."

"We need you to stay," Kaiden said. "With you and Cameron gone, this family hasn't been complete. If he's planning on coming home and you stay, we can have some good times, like we used to. Remember when we all went camping in Yellowstone and Jarod pretended to be a bear? Scared the shit out of all of us."

More laughter.

"That was a crazy trip. Cameron fell in the Madison when he caught that big fish, remember?" Dylan said. "It was almost bigger than he was."

Their joy surrounded and enveloped her, fitting her neatly back into the space she'd occupied as a kid, the one she hadn't realized was still empty.

One more slot to fill—Cameron coming home, and then they'd be complete again.

Her phone buzzed in her pocket and she pulled it out to look at it.

"Nick?" she asked when she answered.

"Is Trevor there?"

"No, why?"

"He's missing."

Chapter Twenty-Three

Nick's heart dropped when he heard CJ's answer. He paced the street in front of the school, his eyes focusing this way and that in hopes of spotting Trevor. They'd had another colossal argument last night after Trevor had spoken with his mother. Grace wanted him to head back to Seattle on Friday, a few days before spring break, so he could go to some event with her.

Trevor wanted to go to the dance the school was holding for the younger high school kids on Friday afternoon.

Nick had tried to reason with both of them. Big mistake.

When he'd taken Trevor to school this morning, the boy had reverted to the sullen one-word-answer kid he'd been when Nick had first picked him up from the airport. He counted at least five uses of the word "whatever" in a single mile.

"He's supposed to be here, outside the school, for me to pick him up," he said to CJ. "But he's not. I have no idea where he would be."

"No friends?" Her voice was calm, the direct opposite of the fear coursing through his body.

"Just one that I know of—a girl."

"Have you talked to her?"

"Um, no. I'm not even sure what her name is."

"Some of his teachers might know—I seem to remember they know more than we ever thought they did."

His chuckle relieved some of the steam building inside him.

"I'll go in and check. Good idea. Thanks."

"Nick?"

"What?"

"I'm coming up. We'll find him."

"Yeah."

He hung up the phone as he strode toward the school building. He should have thought to ask.

"Ah, Mr. Sturgis. Just the man I wanted to see." The vice principal planted herself in front of him.

"Okay. But first, I have to ask if you've seen Trevor. He's missing."

"It doesn't surprise me. He caused a big ruckus today during lunch. I've been trying to reach you."

"I was working on a corral. The phone was in the house." He'd forgotten to check for messages because he was late. Why did this woman persist in making him feel like he was sixteen all over again? "We'll deal with his behavior later," he said. "Right now we need to find him. Is there is anyone who may know something about a girl he liked?"

"Not offhand."

"What about ..." Nick searched his mind for the class Trevor had mentioned most often. "His art teacher?"

"I can try." She picked up the phone and got in touch with the teacher.

"She's coming down and bringing a piece of Trevor's artwork with her. She said it may give you an idea of where he might be."

"Thank you. Anything will be helpful."

A short woman in a paint-covered smock arrived within a few minutes—long enough for Nick to feel like he wanted to bolt from the tight confines of the office.

"Hello, Mr. Sturgis," she said. "I'm glad to meet you. Trevor is a talented young man. He's got quite an eye for composition."

"Right now, he's a *missing* young man," Nick said.

"Yes, well, I brought this down." She handed him a landscape that was obviously a study in perspective.

He stared at it for a moment then shook his head. "I don't get it."

She pointed to a figure headed down the road. "That's usually how he portrays himself. I've seen him do it in other pictures." Then she indicated the top of the landscape. "This looks like a city."

He stared at it. Seattle?

"Hi. There was no one at the front desk, so I thought I'd see if you were back here," CJ said as she walked into the small office.

"I'm sorry," Mrs. Hemp said. "This is a private meeting—"

"It's okay," Nick said. "She's here to help." He showed her the drawing. "What do you think? We're trying to figure out which city it is."

"It has to be Great Falls. If it were anywhere else, he would have indicated mountains, wouldn't he? Besides, even if you're thinking like a teenager, getting to a city first makes sense, even if that's not your ultimate destination."

"Makes sense." Nick looked at the art teacher. "Did you notice any girl Trevor hung with? Long, brown hair? Probably quiet."

The teacher nodded. "Brittany Nelson. Nice girl."

"That's true," Mrs. Hemp concurred. "But wait ..." She clicked a few keys on her computer. "I thought so. Her parents split last year and her father moved to Great Falls. The divorce was really hard on her—she idolized her father."

Nick and CJ exchanged glances.

"I'll give her mother a call." Mrs. Hemp looked up at them. "If you could give me a few moments."

They left the office, the art teacher scurrying off to her classroom while CJ and Nick waited in the outer office.

"Poor kid," CJ said.

"Well, he wouldn't be acting out if people would just stick around in his life." Nick glared at her.

"That's unfair. I told you both from the beginning that I was leaving."

"Yeah. I know." Nick propped himself up on a secretary's desk. "But my son is as bad at believing bad news as I am."

"Yeah." She looked down at her hands then brushed her hand through her hair.

He remembered those gestures. They usually happened when she had something to say but wasn't sure if she should.

"What?" he asked.

Mrs. Hemp's door opened.

"The girl's mother was happy to help. Seems she met your son and has a good opinion of him." Her frown indicated she wasn't sure she shared the viewpoint. "Anyway, here's the father's name and phone number. Her daughter told her Trevor didn't say anything to her, but he may be planning to call her later. Does he have his cell phone?"

"I gave it back to him last night."

"Maybe you'll hear from him."

"Maybe."

He and CJ walked to the front of the school. The sun was still high over the horizon as the earth swung on its axis for longer days in the northern hemisphere. It should have been a pleasant Tuesday afternoon to spend with his son, maybe doing something as innocent as playing catch in a nearby park.

Instead ...

"I'm going to have to call Grace," he said.

CJ nodded.

A pickup slid in behind CJ's Jeep. It took him a second to recognize it, but the men getting out gave him a clue—Jarod,

Dylan, and one more who was obviously one of the other brothers.

"Hey, Nick." Jarod held out a hand. "We're here to help."

His spirit eased a little more as he shook with his old friend. The past was finally getting where it needed to be lodged—back when it happened. Maybe he could leave CJ there as well and finally move on with his life.

"Thanks."

"Where should we look?" Dylan asked. "Might be best if we split up. Jarod and Kaiden in the pickup, CJ and I in the Jeep."

"The only clue I have is that he may be headed for the city," Nick said.

"Does he know how to get there?" Jarod asked.

"If he's like his father, he's got a good sense of direction," CJ said, "But who knows. He could even head home." She tossed her keys to Dylan. "Splitting up is good, but I'll go with Nick."

The brothers nodded.

Something had shifted in that family—something Nick hadn't seen since they were kids. It was as if they'd become a cohesive unit again. What had changed?

No time to worry about that now.

"How about you go north, toward the reservation, Jarod," he suggested. "Dylan, maybe retrace the road to my cabin. CJ and I will go east." He gave Dylan directions to the cabin.

"Sounds good."

Doors slammed as they loaded up and headed out.

As soon as they cleared Choteau, he clicked on the phone via Bluetooth and dialed Grace.

"You heard from Trevor?" he asked as soon as she answered.

"Not since last night," she said. "Why?"

"He's missing."

"Missing? What does that mean?"

"It means," he said, trying to keep his tone measured, "when I went to pick him up from school, he wasn't there. He got into trouble."

"Again? I sent him there to get him out of trouble," she complained.

"He was upset about our argument last night."

"He needs to learn to do what he's told. He doesn't need to be at a dance in that one-horse town. He needs to meet people who matter."

Nick swallowed his anger.

"I don't want to rehash this now. We're out looking for him. If he calls, please call me."

"We?"

"The Becks. They're helping."

"As in your old girlfriend?" Grace sneered the last word.

He'd never understood his ex-wife's unbridled animosity toward CJ, but he wasn't going to try now.

"She's in the truck."

"Hi, Grace," CJ said, sugarcoated enough to be just this side of sarcastic.

"Oh, hello. Thanks for helping Nick out with *our* son."

God, the woman couldn't let it rest.

"Talk to you later." He switched off the phone.

He slowed as they traveled southeast on 89, pulling over as the occasional car crept up behind them. Most of the traffic was going the other way.

"Would he have hitched a ride?" she asked.

"God, I hope not. Not in this day and age. You did a good thing for that girl in the city, by the way."

"How did you find out?"

"Small town. Jarod told Mae at the coffee shop about it, and

Mae—"

"Told everyone else in town," she said.

"Pretty much."

CJ's phone rang.

"Dylan," she said.

"He's not here." Dylan's voice crackled over the speakerphone.

"Can you head back into town and look around there?" Nick asked. "Maybe he's wandering down there and we missed him when we left town."

"Sounds like a plan." The phone disconnected.

Silence filled the truck cab as they scanned the road and the prairie around them. Snow lay in patches against the emergent grasses and flowers. In the distance he spotted a few deer, but no human.

How did he reach Trevor? And deal with Grace? Her ideas of the good life had always contradicted the values with which he'd been raised—a hard-work ethic and doing right by your neighbor. It had always boiled down to his father's simple sentence: "Make me proud, son."

Keeping Trevor full time in Montana, with vacation visits to his mother, seemed the only way to install those same values, if it weren't too late. That meant his life was going to have to change. Outfitting gave him the freedom he craved, but it wasn't the right job for his son.

"I'm sorry," CJ said.

"For what?" He'd almost forgotten she was in the truck.

"For wanting to leave."

"You told us. I was the one who read more into the situation than there was."

Again there was the gesture that told him there was more to

say.

"What is it?" he asked. "What aren't you telling me?"

"Later," she said. "Once Trevor is safe."

Cattails clustered next to the road as they passed part of the Freezeout Lake Wildlife Management Area. Beyond them, ducks squawked at their passing and a pair of snow geese skidded to a stop on the open water. The bright flash of a yellow-headed blackbird caught his eye.

So beautiful, so stark, and soon to be too cold and dangerous for his son to be wandering the land. Along with the return of the prey to the plains, predators drifted from the mountains, some more hungry than others.

"Do think he could have gone to the lake? You know, where we went before?"

"It's a chance." The sun was still high enough in the sky for them to take the detour. Thank goodness for Daylight Saving. Besides, the kid couldn't have gotten that far on foot, could he?

Nick pulled off on the dirt road that led to the main lake. While birds clustered through the open water, their numbers paled compared to peak migration.

"Maybe we should walk it," CJ suggested.

"Yeah." He pulled to the side of the road and they got out, the squeak of his door loud in the quiet. In the distance, a green pickup hunkered next to the main body of the lake.

"Maybe they'll know something," she added.

He nodded. All he could do was hope.

They took opposite sides of the dirt road. The swish of birds in the reeds was in direct contrast to the churning in his stomach. What if they never found him?

As they approached the pickup, a man's silhouette took shape. He was leaning against the grill, smoking a cigarette, and staring off to the horizon. Something must have alerted him and he turned to face them.

Ronan Smith.

Ronan gave him a wave and started walking in his direction.

"Howdy, Nick," he said, the voice neither warm nor resentful.

"Heard you were in town," Nick said. The scrape of boots against the rough road told him CJ had moved close to him. "What are you doing out here?"

"Hello, ma'am." Ronan's fingers touched his cap. "Free country, isn't it? I can go where I want, do what I want." Now a steel edge framed the words.

"Look, Ronan, I'm not here to bother you. I'm just looking for my boy. Have you seen a kid, about my height, with straight, brown hair?"

"I haven't forgotten what you did—turn me in to the FWP for trying to make a living. I didn't have much; those traps were all I had between me and the next meal. And you took it away."

"I did what I thought was right."

Flapping madly, a half dozen scaups buzzed passed and landed in the water with loud splashes and outraged quacks.

"Yeah, I know. But sometimes you got to give a guy some slack ... even if that guy is only thirteen."

"You know where he is." Every muscle in Nick's body tensed and he took a step. Was this Ronan's way of getting revenge?

The man's hands went up in a gesture of surrender. "Whoa. Whatever you think of me, I'd never use a kid to get back at you. I've been waiting for him to make a decision. I was at loose ends today ... thought I'd come out and sit here for a while."

Nick waited. The man was going to tell him when he was good and ready and not before.

"Saw the kid. Started up a conversation. Pretty normal kid—

Mom and Dad are assholes and school sucks. Gave him some elk jerky. He was hungry."

Of course, he may have to squeeze the story out of the man.

"Seems he was headed to Great Falls—something about a girl's dad. It's always a girl at that age." Ronan's gaze flicked to CJ and back to Nick. "I mentioned that even though his parents were rotten to the core—and that I could personally vouch for his dad on that account—they might be worried. And it was a long walk to Great Falls. I offered him a lift back to Choteau. He said he needed to think on it."

"Thanks for that," Nick said.

Ronan chuckled. "Funny thing about kids. They can get mad at their parents all they want, but it sure does piss 'em off if someone else does." He pointed to a point jutting into the lake. "He's over there. Been taking pictures for the last half hour. Glad you came along. I was gettin' tired of waiting."

"Thanks," Nick said and held out his hand.

Ronan looked at it for a few seconds then shook it. With a finger tap on the brim of his cap, he stalked off to the truck, started it up, and headed down the road.

The sound must have alerted Trevor that his ride was leaving, because there was a scrambling in the brush and then Trevor emerged. He spotted them and stood stock-still, his camera dangling from his right hand, his backpack from his left.

Without speaking, they walked toward him.

"How'd you find me?" he asked when they reached him.

"Persistence and luck," Nick said then pulled him into a bear hug. "I'm just glad you're safe." His child felt solid in his arms.

After a second, the backpack dropped with a thud and his son wrapped himself around Nick, like he'd done as a child. His body shuddered with silent sobs.

"It's okay, kid," Nick said. "You're safe. That's all that matters."

CJ stepped back and her murmurs caught his ear. Probably calling off her brothers.

"You stay here with him and I'll get the truck," she said to him when he was done.

"Keys are in my right-hand coat pocket," he said.

She slipped her hand in, pulled them out, and was gone.

Nick cradled his son, his gaze half focused on the wildlife around him. It must be so alien to the big city life of Seattle. No wonder Trevor felt out of kilter. The issue should have been dealt with before it resulted in running away. He had a long way to go as a parent.

The truck rumbled up behind them.

"C'mon. Let's go home. We'll get a hot meal and a good night's rest, and discuss it in the morning."

Trevor nodded and Nick released him.

"Got everything?" Nick asked.

"Yeah," Trevor said with a swipe at his eyes.

CJ handed him the keys and they headed back to Choteau in the gathering dark.

# # #

After Nick dropped her off, CJ climbed into the Jeep Dylan had left by the school. She started the engine and waved to Nick as he continued down the road, forcing a smile to cover the emptiness inside.

The time hadn't been right to tell him she was thinking seriously about staying. What would his reaction be? Would he even give her a chance? Or had he already shut his feelings down where she was concerned?

And did it matter anyway?

She put the Jeep in gear and headed back home.

What did she want from Nick? A do-over? Was she ever going to be good at relationships? Gerry had indicated that more therapy would be useful—maybe something she should think about. She and Nick could be friends and if something more developed, so be it. Her first responsibility would be her career, followed by working together with her brothers to get the ranch solidly on its feet.

Yes, that was a plan. Let Nick, Trevor, and Grace straighten out their problems by themselves. They didn't need another person in their lives.

"Everybody safe and sound?" Birdie asked when she walked into the kitchen from the mudroom.

"Yep." CJ sank into the kitchen chair, bone-tired. It had been an extremely long day. "Where is everyone?"

"Dylan went back to his cabin. Kaiden and Jarod are in the den pretending to catch up but really watching some rodeo somewhere."

She chuckled. "Think Jarod can make his dream of training roping horses come true?"

"If you guys start pitching in and give him the time to do it. Are you planning on sticking around for real?"

"I haven't given the magazine an answer, but, yeah, I'm thinking it would be a good idea." She hoisted herself out of the chair, opened the fridge, and stood in front of it. A half-filled bottle of white wine was tucked in a corner. She was too tired to eat.

"Want some?" she asked Birdie as she pulled out the bottle.

"No thanks. Too late in the evening and it interferes with my sleep. One of the delights of getting older," Birdie said.

"I just feel like I'm letting Max down. He found an assignment for me that would wait until I could get out. Not going puts him in a bad spot."

"Is it the kind of picture-taking you really want to do?" Birdie asked.

CJ sipped her wine in the cozy kitchen, the company and light keeping the darkness of the night away. From what Max had told her, the assignment would be similar to the last—different desert, different fighters, same combat issues.

Truthfully, she was sick to death of it.

"No," she said.

"Then that's your answer. Sometimes we need to figure out what we want and stand up for that, no matter what other people may want or think is best for them."

"I always thought when you made a choice, it was either one thing or another. That there was no go-back."

"My pastor is fond of saying, 'God allows U-turns,'" Birdie said. "I'm not sure that a strict do-over is possible, but there's always a time to reconsider and change your path—right up to the moment you die. Of course, there's something to be said for commitment, too, and keeping the promises you make, but you're not married to Max."

"Thank god." CJ laughed and it released something in her chest. Birdie was right. It was time to take a break from running away and see what happened. "Okay. Tomorrow I'll let Max know I'm not coming. And I'll reach out to the guy who offered me a job. I better get serious next week about finishing off Mom's office. I'll need a space to work."

Birdie patted her hand. "I'm glad you're staying, but it's time for me to get some rest now. The boys will want their breakfast in the morning."

CJ smiled as the woman left the kitchen. After pouring the rest of the wine into her glass, she headed for the den for some family time with her brothers.

Chapter Twenty-Four

"I get it," Max said. "I really do."

"But ..." CJ said.

"I have something better."

"Like what?" CJ pushed at one of the boxes in her mother's office, raising another cloud of dust. She really needed to get rid of this stuff. Kaiden would be here for another week and a half, until after Easter. Surely, her three brothers could get this into the attic.

"Our agency is opening a new monthly. The editor wants to take a holistic view of what's happening in the world."

"In other words, soft reporting," she said, trying to keep the scorn from her voice. No way was she going into the hellhole of the women's beat.

"Not really. The idea is to get multiple viewpoints on a different story. A woman's side, yes, but also from different cultural, racial, and religious ideologies."

"Intriguing."

"I figure it's either going to be a colossal success or a resounding flop, but the powers that be are willing to support it. I showed them some of the work you did on your last assignment, the stuff I couldn't sell. They're very interested."

A national magazine. Doing the kind of stories she liked to tell—the impact of world events on ordinary people of every stripe.

But what about all her other plans? The tentative promises she'd made to her brothers?

"Can I have some time to think about it?" she asked.

"I can give you twenty-four hours. They want you there yesterday."

A few minutes later she ended the call.

Crap. What was she supposed to do now?

She dialed the therapist's number and explained that she really needed to see her as soon as possible. Mission completed, she looked around the office, suddenly feeling penned in. Maybe Jarod had some physical labor that needed doing.

"What's up with you?" Jarod asked, looking from up from the yellow legal pad covered with his chicken-scratch handwriting. "You look like you lost your dog or something."

"Something like that. Got anything for me to do?"

Jarod looked around. "Not really. With Kaiden's help, we've pretty much finished up everything that needs doing. Not having to feed the cattle really saves us time."

"What are you doing?" she asked. Maybe she could help him with his website or something. Focus on different problems and questions than the one she faced.

"Brainstorming some ideas I have for the training business."

"Anything I can help with?"

"Yeah," Jarod grinned. "You can leave me alone. I thought I'd appreciate you being around, but now I wonder."

One of the horses neighed in the outside corral.

"I find I do my best thinking on a horse," he said. "Joey needs some exercise. Why don't you take a trail ride or something? It's a beautiful day. Get out of my hair."

"Yes, sir, boss."

It *was* a beautiful day.

After she saddled up Joey, she headed south across the flat section of the ranch. The horse was itching to run, and as soon as she closed the gate behind her, she let him have his head. Soon they were racing down the path the cattle had made, spring mud flying behind them. A few of the cattle looked up and some moved away from the galloping horse, but most ignored them.

The sun warmed her back and the rushing air cooled her face. She let her thoughts flow behind her and concentrated on simple existence—this place, this time, this land.

When she reached the southern border of the land, she turned west, slowing Joey down to steadily climb the hills. Here and there, Indian blanket flowers, with their showy orange and yellow lit the ground. In between, the pinks and purples of plants like larkspur provided a calming field.

As they climbed, her tumble of thoughts returned.

With a national magazine, her shot at a prize like the Pulitzer increased dramatically. She'd be on top of the world with an acknowledgment like that. People would respect her. It's what she'd spent the last years of her life going after—it would be nuts to quit now.

But what would that matter if she couldn't respect herself?

They crested the first rise and the glory of the hills and mountains stretched out before them. About a third of the distance belonged to the ranch. With the smaller herds that Jarod ran, the far reaches were rarely used. They'd been fenced once, but no one was maintaining them. They were too short-staffed.

"C'mon boy, let's do another set or two before we head back."

Joey snorted his approval and they traveled down to where spring runoff wove between the next set of hills. When they reached the creek, she let him slake his thirst. Nearby, a ground squirrel hopped on a rock and, after some consideration, gave them a piece of his mind. A crow swept overhead, adding his opinion to the cacophony. Almost out of sight, a raptor dove down the air currents, talons outstretched for an unsuspecting rodent.

The squirrel ducked under a nearby ledge.

The heat from Joey's body took away whatever chill she had from their mad ride. Sliding off her jacket, she stuffed it under her camera in the saddlebag.

It was magnificently lonely out here. No humans. No conflict. No stress. She'd be nuts to leave it.

"Okay, boy," she said, hoisting herself back on Joey's back. Clicking softly, she urged him up the next rise, followed by one that was slightly higher. At its crest she paused, looking out at the unfamiliar view ... or was it?

She yanked her phone from her pocket and scrolled back to the picture she'd taken in Cassandra's office and compared it to the landscape in front of her. Not quite. Guiding Joey to the right, she kept checking.

"Whoa."

This was it.

Once again she slid off the horse and pulled out her camera. She took a photo from the same angle as the one on her phone then circled around to get the surrounding horizons. Finally, pulling up the compass on her phone, she retrieved the coordinates of where she was standing.

"Why would a Chicago attorney have a photo from our ranch land? An old one at that?" she mused aloud to Joey. She tried to recall the family tree she'd found in the Bible. The ranch had been left to Jacob because her family could trace their lineage back to him, but had the younger brother gotten anything? Where had he gone? While the tree had listed names and dates, there were no locations. Plus the other line petered out with Alice.

Maybe. Maybe the families had lost touch, but that branch still existed.

And ... just maybe ... the younger brother hadn't walked away empty-handed after all.

She climbed on the horse and headed back for the ranch, her mind churning with an entirely new set of thoughts.

# # #

Gerry managed to fit her in on Friday morning right before lunch.

"So what's going on?" the therapist asked.

CJ explained her dilemma.

Gerry smiled. "The universe does have an interesting sense of humor. What is your thinking so far?"

"I should take the opportunity Max is offering. It's what I've worked for my whole life—I'd be a fool not to go."

"Interesting choice of words."

"What do you mean?" CJ asked.

"You said you *should* take Max's offer. What do you *want* to do?"

"I have no idea. That's why I'm here." CJ shifted on the couch.

"You don't have to stay there if you don't want to."

"Huh?"

"Get up and pace if you need to. You don't have to sit there and squirm. It's your choice." Gerry leaned forward. "Just like what job you take is your choice. No one can tell you the right one, not even me."

"Not even a little bit of a hint?"

The therapist laughed and shook her head.

"Remember when I said that you had managed to get past the latest trauma, but there were still things I thought you needed to discuss to be truly healed from the past?"

"Yes. It was the one of the things I was planning before ...

well, before Max's offer came through."

"What else were you thinking of?"

"Helping my brothers a lot more, get the ranch on a solid footing so they can get on with their lives. Of course, the local job would keep me busy—I'd need to travel across the state."

"What about relationships?"

"You mean ... with men?"

"Or women, if that's your bent."

"Uh, no. But I think my time for relationships is over. Friends, yeah, maybe even friends with benefits, but anything long-term? Not happening."

"Life can surprise you."

CJ stood and walked to the window. If life only came with a manual or men came with operating instructions, there might be a shot.

"Could be, but where men and relationships—real relationships—are concerned, I haven't found them trustworthy." She walked back to the couch and sat down.

"I can see that. You don't have a lot of role models in your personal life. Are there any long-term married couples you admire?"

She thought about the parents of kids she'd known when she was growing up. Some were divorced, some had moved away, most she didn't know very well. But ...

"Nick's parents. They always had it together. You could tell they were deeply in love, even though they weren't mushy about it."

"So it can happen."

"Yeah, to other people."

Gerri sighed. "It's going to be a long road, but that doesn't have to be decided right now. How long do you have to get back to Max?"

"Until the end of the day."

"Then we better get to work."

# # #

By the time CJ left the therapist's office, she had a list of pros and cons but was still as unsure as ever. At every stop sign on her way downtown, she changed her mind.

"Why didn't this happen when I was still working?" she railed at the universe when she pulled into a parking space and opened the door.

A young man walking on the sidewalk looked up from his phone, shrugged, and continued on his way.

She trudged up to the Cassandra's office and entered the waiting room. The door to the inner office was closed and voices murmured from the space. The faint aroma of sandalwood was back. CJ took a seat and stared at the list she'd made. If she left, the search for the other branch of the family would die with her. No one else had the time to follow up or look for the mineral rights.

What if someday a stranger showed up one day and claimed ownership of the ground under their feet? The ranch belonged to her family. The whole concept of selling the right to tear up the ground to someone else in perpetuity made no sense.

But that was the law.

Not a lot of it made sense to the average person.

The door opened.

"Hello?" A tall man with broad shoulders and the beginnings of a belly strode out of the office. His clothes weren't the workaday outfits of her neighbors but the regalia out-of-staters imagined

Montanans wore.

"Hi," she said.

Cassandra walked out behind him.

"Oh! Did we have an appointment?"

"No, I just stopped by to see if you'd heard anything."

"Of course. I'll be with you in a second." Cassandra turned to the man. "Nice to see you again, Dave. I'll see what I can find out. Although," she looked at CJ, "this lady may be able to help you. CJ Beck, this is Dave Brockman. He's new to town."

"From California?" CJ guessed.

"How'd you know? Nice to meet you." He held out his hand, and the scent she'd gotten a whiff of earlier wafted over her. She shook his hand without rising from her chair.

"Dave's looking to buy twenty-five, maybe thirty acres for a second home."

CJ tried not to sputter. Most people didn't have that much land for a first home.

"I know you're in a tight spot with the mineral taxes and all. Maybe you'd like to sell off a few acres? Dave is willing to pay top dollar."

"We've got the taxes covered, thanks. It's Beck land. No one is interested in selling any part of it."

"I see," Dave said. "Thanks anyway. See you next week?" he asked Cassandra.

"Sure." The attorney put her hand on the man's arm in a way that suggested more than attorney-client privilege.

Once he was gone, CJ followed Cassandra into the office.

"Have you heard from the PI?" she asked when they were seated.

"Actually, I sent him your information so he can contact you directly. You haven't heard from him?"

311

"No."

"Odd. Let me send him another email."

"Actually, if you could give me his name and contact information, I'll handle it myself. No need to keep you in the middle."

"I thought you were leaving," Cassandra said. "Going back on assignment."

"That's still undecided, but I can get things started before I leave."

Why was the attorney so reluctant to get out of the way? Work must be slow.

Cassandra stared at her for a few seconds, as if making up her mind whether or not she'd oblige. "Sure. Okay. I have the information here somewhere." She clicked a few keys on the keyboard, took out a notepad, and copied down the information.

"Thanks," CJ said, standing and taking the paper.

"Is there anything else I can do for you?" Cassandra rose as well.

"Not at the moment."

CJ forced herself not to look at the picture on the wall as she left the office. What had transpired? Both when Dave Brockman was there and after, she felt there was a subtext to the conversation that she was totally missing.

But she only had one thing to worry about: deciding what she was doing for the next few years.

# # #

"Be here at the end of school," Nick told Trevor when he dropped him off that morning. It had taken him the last two days to negotiate with the school, Grace, and his son to limit the amount of suspension and make it possible for Trevor to attend the dance that had been the source of the problem all along.

Both the school and Grace had tried to convince him Trevor shouldn't be rewarded for running away, but after spending time on the phone with his brother Henry, wise in all things teenage boys, he'd begun to understand the depth of his son's confusion and pain. He had just begun to come to grips with Choteau and its environs, and his mother wanted to rip him away again for her own reasons.

"I will." Trevor paused. "Thanks, Dad. For everything." Then, seeming mortified that he'd revealed too much, he mumbled, "See ya," and loped toward the front door.

Worth the struggle.

As usual, it took hours longer than it should have to complete his work at the county offices. He'd have to head to Great Falls next week to take care of FWP permits for the year. The online option was available, but he always got twisted around in the site and was never sure he was getting the right licenses for the right time period.

Besides, seeing them in person was a great way to catch up on gossip and news about the Bob.

He was heading back up the main drag when he spotted CJ. Guilt flashed through him. She'd leapt to help him a few days ago and he hadn't let her know what was going on, just tried to maintain a friendly distance while he sorted through stuff.

Now she looked like she had the weight of the world on her. Her brow was furrowed and her shoulders slumped. She'd gotten word there was a job waiting for her—just what she wanted. What was the problem?

An SUV pulled out of a spot in front of him and he took it.

"CJ! Wait!" He stopped her right in front of her Jeep.

"Oh, hi," she said, her eyes wide like a doe's that had been startled too close to her fawn. The expression faded and a professional smile hit her lips. "How are things with Trevor? Did the three of you work everything out?"

"Yes. He's at school—even going to the dance."

The smile became more genuine. "I'm glad."

"Say, I was going to stop at Mae's and get a hamburger or something. You want to come? My treat. You can tell me all about the new adventure you've got."

"Uh. Well ..."

"C'mon. It'll do you good. No matter what Birdie's feeding you, you're still too skinny.

She chuckled, but it didn't reach her eyes.

"Sure. I guess."

"Well, that's a positive answer if I ever heard one." He grabbed her hand and started down the road, trying not to think about the warmth of her flesh against his. She didn't pull away, and he grasped it more firmly and grinned at her.

Like old times. Before the world had turned upside down on them.

The coffee shop smelled of noon in small towns all over Montana—burgers and fries.

"Hey, Mae," he called out, feeling like the first time he'd taken CJ out as a teen all those years ago. No accounting for emotions. She was leaving—he should feel nothing but gloom. But somehow, a sliver of hope burst the dark balloon.

"Hey, Nick. CJ. Sit where you can find a spot."

Springtime had sprung people from the insides of their houses, and the small coffee shop was crowded with people he recognized and a few he didn't. A table by one of the two windows in the place beckoned him.

He pulled back the chair for CJ and, after shedding her jacket, she sat.

He picked up the small menus propped behind the ketchup and mustard containers and handed one to CJ. The plastic-covered sheet was essentially the same as it had been when they were kids: four different kinds of burgers or grilled cheese, milkshakes, soda, or coffee. Nothing green marred the menu.

"What'll it be?" Mae stood by them, her order pad at the ready.

Nick glanced at CJ. "Usual?"

She nodded.

"Two cheeseburgers, Cokes," he told Mae.

Mae nodded and launched herself at another table for their order.

They grinned at each other.

"Same old Mae," he said.

"Yes," she said. "With everything going on in the world, it's nice."

"Yeah." He slipped the menus back into their slot and pulled napkins from the dispenser. "So, when do you go? I thought it was soon."

She folded her napkin in half and stared out the window before returning her gaze to him.

"I'm not sure," she said.

"What does that mean?"

Another fold of the napkin. "Just that I'm not sure."

The ease between them slid away, and the rising tension reminded him of another time they'd sat in Mae's—right before he'd told her he was breaking up with her to go out with Grace.

This had been such a bad idea.

"Look," she said. "I just don't want to hurt you again, make

315

you think I'm staying when I'm not."

"I got that message, loud and clear," he said dryly. It was taking every ounce of adulthood he possessed not to throw down a few bills and walk out the door.

Her smile was weak. "Sorry."

"No problem."

Mae placed their Cokes on the table and slipped away again.

He slid the paper off the top of the straw, crinkled it, and tossed it on the table.

"I guess I need to talk to someone," she said.

"I thought you had a therapist," he said.

"She didn't help," CJ said, ridding her straw of its paper before sipping.

"Oh."

She unfolded the napkin to its full size and ironed it with her hand.

"It's going to be shredded before you get to use it," he said, trying to make his tone light.

"What? Oh, yeah." She crumpled it into a ball and put it to the side. Crossing her arms in front of her on the table, she leaned forward.

"I got an offer," she said.

"I know."

"Another offer. Well, really two more."

"I'm impressed."

She shrugged. "Right place, right time. It's all coming from that photo I took in Great Falls."

"Great shot. You probably saved her life."

"Well, maybe. She had the strength to run away in the first place. But that's not the problem." She sipped more Coke. "One of the offers is to stay here, get into a new state magazine that's going to focus on important news stories from the state—features that can make a difference in how people think about things."

"Sounds interesting." His spirit lightened.

"I know. But the kicker is, Max came up with a similar job only at a national level."

"Well, of course, you'll take that. It's what you've been chasing, isn't it?" His hopes dropped again.

"I wish it were that clear-cut to me," she said.

"Have you listed pros and cons?"

She pulled a yellow piece of paper from her purse. "Yep."

"No clearer?"

"Nope."

"What would tip the balance?"

"I wish I knew."

Mae arrived with the burgers, plunked the plates on the table, and dashed back to the kitchen.

"No wonder she stays so skinny," CJ said and picked up her burger.

Food had never tasted so good.

What would get her to stay? He couldn't make promises—he had Trevor to consider. Plus, was that what she really wanted? She'd buried her husband less than a year ago and probably wasn't ready to begin anything new, even if it was rerun of something they'd done before.

Probably a bad idea just for that reason.

"You know how when you're on a road going fast, it's harder to turn?" she asked.

"Uh-huh."

"That's what the last twenty years has felt like. I've been moving faster and faster over time. Every leap of my career had me racing ten miles an hour faster. Ben's death derailed me, but I still feel like it would take no effort to get back to that speed. There's that quote some Greek guy said, 'An unexamined life is not worth living.'"

Where was she going with this?

"How do I really know what I want unless I slow down and take the time to figure out what I'm doing?"

"I don't have an answer to that. Once I moved back to Choteau and Grace took off with Trevor, I almost had too much time on my hands to think."

"Sounds like life happened to you more than you controlled it."

He shrugged. "Grace was a force to be reckoned with. Going along seemed to be a wiser choice than being flattened by a steamroller."

"That bad?" She chuckled.

"Uh-huh."

They had finished their burgers when she finally asked the question he'd been dreading.

"If I stayed, would anything happen between us?"

He rubbed the back of his neck, trying to ease the discomfort.

"Friendship?" he suggested.

"For starters."

He took a deep breath. Being anything but truthful wouldn't help.

"That's all I can guarantee for now," he said. "I have Trevor to consider. And ... well ... if you decide to make another turn, I'd be left here without you."

"I see." She pulled out her wallet.

"My treat," he said.

"No obligations," she replied and tossed down a ten and a few ones.

He left it at that.

Chapter Twenty-Five

She needed to make this decision and there were only a few more hours to make it. Her grandmother had made her choice based on the man she loved and the life she wanted to live. Once she left college, CJ had determined that her life was going to be based on what *she* wanted, and no one else.

Not unlike Grace.

CJ groaned as she stood at the doorway to the office. She could spend the next three hours stewing about the decision she had to make or making some space in the office. Doing something constructive had far more appeal.

She gathered the boxes she'd sorted and toted them to the bottom of the stairs. She'd find a brother to hoist them to the attic. The box with Catherine's diaries sat on the desk. It was bigger than it needed to be, like something else had once been packed in it.

Her phone rang.

"Hi," a male voice said when she answered. "My name is Peter Carlson. You called and left a message on my answering service. I'm a private investigator."

"Oh. Thanks for getting back to me."

"No problem. What can I do for you?"

She explained what little she knew about the Seth Beck side of the family, and how it was important to trace the end of the line to see if they knew anything about the mineral rights.

"I see," he said. "I'm in the middle of a big investigation now and couldn't get started for another month. Would that be acceptable?"

"Yes. Either I or my brother Jarod can handle it."

He told her his fees. Another hit to her inheritance, but it needed to be done.

She stood in the small space she'd cleared and looked around the room at the stacks of boxes still to be reviewed. If only the answer would pop out its head and say, "Here I am!"

She grabbed a smaller box and stacked her grandmother's diaries in them. As she did so, a few slips of paper fell to the bottom.

Quickly unfolding them, she scanned through them before sitting down to read more closely.

"*Stephen passed yesterday,*" the letter began. "*It was a long fight with cancer but a peaceful release finally. The demons of war had gathered close again as he lost the will to fight them. He talked and thrashed when he slept, and I heard things I would give anything to unhear.*

"*My poor, poor husband. And those who experienced what he did.*

"*Although I gave up writing in my journals when I married Stephen, I often wished I'd carried them on. So much has changed in our world, not always for the good. I'm afraid after all my miscarriages, we spoiled our son too much when we finally had him. David isn't a bad man. He's just not as good as I'd hoped. He's married a sweet girl, Jane, but I'm not sure she suits him. His spirit is more adventurous, while she is more of a quiet homebody. They have started having children, so maybe that will settle him down.*

"*It's been good to live on land that's been in the family for generations and to know it will continue on with my child and his children. The land and this family are so interconnected. It's become vital to me, too. I hope my grandchildren can work together to save and protect it.*

"Sometimes restlessness overcomes me. If only I could have experienced two lives—one here in the safety and comfort of my hometown, another in the wider world that George offered. What would have become of that girl? If I had to do it over again, I would still choose Stephen, for he is my best friend, the keeper of my heart, and my strength when I falter. What will I do without him?"

The letter ended there.

Work together to save and protect the land. That's what needed to happen. And CJ had to be part of it.

Picking up the phone, she dialed Max's number. "I'm staying here."

"I'm sorry," he replied, "but I guess I understand. You've been away a long time."

"Yeah."

"If you change your mind—"

"I know where to find you."

By the end of the day, she'd made headway in the office and was starting to see how she could set it up to handle the computer and huge monitor she'd need to edit her photos.

"There's a huge pile of junk in the way of the stairs," Jarod complained as he stood in the doorway.

"I'm glad you noticed. You, Dylan, and Kaiden can store it in the attic."

"Now?"

"It's as good a time as ever."

"If you stay, are you going to continue to be this bossy?" he asked.

"I'm staying," she said, facing him directly. "And probably." She gave him a tentative grin.

"I'm glad, sis," he said. "I really am." He hugged her tight then released her.

"Where do you want these things?" he asked. "I don't mind the heavy lifting, but my decision-making is over for the day."

"C'mon."

Once Dylan and Kaiden appeared, they put the books up. She helped Birdie with supper until they sat down. For once, the conversation was light—Kaiden regaling them with stories from the drilling fields and Jarod and Dylan discussing the dumbness of cows. She even threw in a few stories about camels.

It was good.

The next day, she took a risk and drove up to Nick's. She didn't want to tell him her decision over the phone. She wanted to see the look in his eyes when she told him. Ultimately, she was staying, but it would be nice if there was a chance to explore more than friendship with Nick.

The gravel crunched as she neared the cabin. The sun was bright in the morning sky, deepening the green of the pines and firs that surrounded the space. Off in the distance, the mountains were a smudge of gray on the horizon. Horses nickered as she got out.

"In the corral," Nick's voice sang out.

She walked around the barn to the corral. Nick was saddling his horse.

"Oh, hello," he said, while he pulled on the girth of the saddle. The horse leaned around and rolled his eye at his tormenter.

"Suck it up, Blackie," Nick said, slapping the horse's stomach.

It apparently worked because Nick was able to get a few more inches from the girth.

"A game he likes to play. Annoying, but at least he's consistent. What can I do for you?" He walked to the railing, the black horse trailing behind like an overgrown dog.

"I wanted to let you know I've decided to stay."

His eyes searched hers and then he nodded, a broad smile creasing his face. "I'm glad," he said.

"So am I."

"Want to go for a ride?"

"Now?"

He gestured to the blue sky and mountains around them. "Got anyplace better to be?"

"Nope."

"Well then?"

"Trevor coming?"

"He's with his mother until the day after Easter."

"So just us."

"Yep."

"Let me get my camera."

She started to her car, then stopped and turned back.

"Is this like a date?"

"It's just a ride."

"Oh. Okay." She headed back where she'd been going.

"For now," he added.

She smiled.

# # #

The Easter dinner table groaned with food: ham, asparagus, fresh new potatoes and parsley, hard-boiled eggs, biscuits ... so much that CJ couldn't see the color of her plate. The 1800s dining room, stuffed with sweet and savory aromas, barely fit her, her three brothers, Birdie, and Nick. She'd invited him on the spur of the moment, and he'd accepted instead of going with his parents to his brother's place.

The job was turning out to be exactly what she'd hoped it

would be. Because the magazine was launching, the owner encouraged her input and incorporated her ideas. She wasn't simply reacting to news; she was helping to shape it.

Life was good. She looked at those seated at the table. Life was very good.

"Got things straightened out with your son?" Jared asked Nick as he passed the potatoes.

"For now. With teenagers, it's a moment-by-moment experience."

"Still, you're lucky to have him." A yearning in Jarod's voice caught her attention. There had to be someone for him. She sent a memo to the universe to get on with it.

"Remember some of the scrapes we got into as teens?" Nick said to Jarod.

"I try not to." Jarod grinned. "Good thing our parents never knew half of what we were up to."

"I think they turned a blind eye," Dylan said.

CJ let her brothers' chatter about all their harebrained schemes wash over her. Birdie caught her eye and nodded.

After dinner, they tromped out to the front porch, glasses of wine and beer still in their hands and settled into the Adirondack chairs that lined the front of the house. To the west, the yellows, oranges, and pinks hung over the Rockies. Stretched before them was land. Their land.

"It would be nice if Cameron were here," Jarod said.

Murmurs of assent hummed around them.

"I haven't heard anything since he told us he was going on the mission," Dylan said.

"Sometimes missions take a long time," Nick said.

"I'm sure he's here in spirit," added Birdie.

The housekeeper's comment lightened the tension that had been forming in CJ's shoulders.

Nick placed his hand on hers.

She looked at him and smiled. There were possibilities but no guarantees.

It was good enough for her.

She was finally home.

The End

Did you enjoy this story? Please leave a review on Amazon, Goodreads or another online bookstore.

Why are reviews important to this writer?

- I really want to know what you think. What did you like? Where did I miss the mark?
- Other readers are more willing to take a chance on a new author when there are reviews.
- A good number of reviews help a book get better rankings on Amazon, as well as opportunities to promote the book. More people discover authors you already like.

This author thanks you very much!

Turn the page for an excerpt from Finding Home, available in fall 2019

Finding Home

Chapter 1

The solid sandstone courthouse anchored the center of the roundabout in Choteau, Montana. Isolated Teton County on the Rocky Mountain Front provided a safe haven for her and her daughter. It was exactly why Samantha Deveaux had chosen it.

"Mommy, why are we going here?" Ten-year-old Ava's voice was developing a suspicious whine—a harbinger of the teenage years that were far too close for twenty-eight-year old Samantha.

She pulled into a parking place next to the courthouse. "Hop out," she said as she pushed open the driver's door of her second-hand Toyota Camry.

Operating on her own time schedule, Ava pushed the passenger door halfway open, then became distracted by a bright red lady beetle crawling out from the windshield wiper well. As usual by late morning, her daughter's hair looked like no one had ever run a comb through it, the flyaway brown locks, so like her own, glistening from the hot August sun.

At least here in Choteau, a cool breeze floated in from the mountains now and again, unlike the overheated Yellowstone River valley they'd left a few weeks before.

Patiently, she waited for her daughter to complete her examination. Let the teachers in her new school try to move what could be an immovable object. Samantha had learned long ago to roll with her daughter's timetable whenever possible. Besides, it gave her time to breathe and pretend everything in her life was normal, the total opposite of reality.

Finally they were able to walk up the steps to the courthouse, going one level at a time as Ava played her own internal game with time.

"C'mon, kiddo," Samantha finally said, "we have to get this done so we can visit the new school."

"Okay." Finding her next gear, Ava walked ahead so quickly, Samantha had to rush to keep up with her.

After checking the directory, she found the motor vehicle offices. Good lord, why were all these people here? Didn't they have to work?

With a sigh, she pulled a number from the dispenser and sat down, smoothing her floral skirt and crossing her legs at the ankle the way she'd been taught by her old-fashioned mother. Too bad her mom hadn't given her any useful lessons, like how to get a job that didn't pay minimum wage or stand up for herself.

"I want to look at the license plates," Ava said, standing squarely before her, her blue eyes wide behind glasses with frames of the same hue.

God, she loved her daughter. As much of a challenge as a child on the Asperger's scale could be, Ava had no artifice and a heart of gold.

"Sure, sweetie. Just make sure that's the only place you go."

"Okay."

Samantha smiled and glanced at the numbers on the screens—one for registrations and one for driver's licenses. Too bad changing an address wasn't something she could do online.

Pulling out the high school math curriculum from her oversized bag, she flipped to the spot she'd left off and began to review her notes. The job was only guaranteed for a year and she had to make as good an impression as possible to be invited back.

No pressure.

The freshman curriculum seemed standard enough: quadratic equations, vector analysis, applying mathematics to real life. The trick was to make this come alive for students who were number-challenged. Common core had helped some, hindered some, and left parents baffled. Her time in Billings as a para-teacher with learning-challenged students had given her an intimate understanding of the problem.

That, and dealing with her own daughter. She glanced up.

Ava was staring at the rows of specialty license plates available to Montana drivers, everything from fish to quilting supported some noble cause. Budget constrained Samantha to use whatever the state decided to give her with her registration fee.

Uh-oh. A lanky man with tendrils of raven black hair sneaking out from underneath his Choteau Bulldogs cap was squatting down next to her daughter.

Samantha dropped the curriculum on the chair and dashed over, her heartbeat ramping up.

"Is she bothering you?" she asked, not wanting him to take offense at being told to back off. No need to start a ruckus in the heart of a small town.

A pair of deep gray eyes turned up toward her and the man rose to his full height, a good seven inches above her own five foot three. He yanked the cap from his head.

"No ma'am," he said. "We were simply having a difference of opinion about the best license plate. She likes the ones with cats and dogs, while I'm kind of partial to the one with the horse." He held out his hand, "Jarod Beck," he said.

She shook his hand. Warm. Strong. Caloused.

"Samantha Deveaux. This is my daughter Ava. We just got to

town last week."

"Figured that," he said. "I don't remember seeing you before."

"I'm the new freshman math teacher," she blurted out.

He shook his head. "Not my best subject." Then he grinned.

It was a good smile, the kind that made children and animals feel easy. No wonder Ava had been comfortable enough to start a conversation.

"Number seventy-six!" the clerk called out.

Samantha glanced at the paper stub in her hand.

"That's me," she said and walked to the counter.

"How can I help you?" the clerk asked.

"I need to update my address on the license and registration. Can you do both so I don't have to get back in line?"

"Seems reasonable. Sure. License and registration, please."

She reached down for her purse. It wasn't there.

H E double hockey sticks.

"Looking for this?" Jarod stood next to her holding out her purse and curriculum. "I saw them over there all lonesome and figured they were yours."

"Oh, thanks."

"No problem."

Thank goodness for Montana ethics. Sure there was crime and drugs, just like any other state, but there was also a sense that personal property was just that—personal.

She smiled at him. "Thanks again."

Charged air seemed to surround them for a few moments, then he touched the brim of his cap and walked to the seat she'd vacated.

Whatever had just happened needed to be forgotten. Her only concern needed to be her daughter.

As if to confirm the idea, a put-together blonde strode on her stylish heels to greet Jarod. He stood and gave her a quick kiss on the cheek. They were definitely together, as in dating. He didn't appear to be the kind of man who kissed strangers. There was a reserve about him.

She dug through her purse and came up with the requested documents.

Better be careful, or she'll be making up stories from chance encounters, giving people qualities they didn't have, like she'd done with Ava's father, Cody.

"You must be the new math teacher," the lady behind the counter said.

"Yes, I just took the job a few weeks ago."

The woman behind the counter shook her head. "I'm on the school board, and I tell you, it's harder and harder to find teachers willing to come to these small towns, especially if they're single. Not enough of a dating pool."

"Fortunately, I'm not interested in dating. I'm here to focus on the job and my daughter." That was the image she wanted to project—a dedicated teacher who deserved to be kept on long enough to get tenure.

"Is that your little girl over there?" the clerk pointed to Ava who was still staring at the license plates.

"Yes, she'll be going into fifth grade this year."

"She'll love the elementary school. They have a great principal." The clerk handed back her documents. "You'll receive a new registration in the mail in about a week. The license doesn't change until you renew it."

"Thank you." Samantha smiled at the woman.

The blonde was still with Jarod, smiling, nodding, and touching his wrist. He looked up at Samantha and gave her a smile and a wave as she took Ava's hand to leave. The woman with him gave her a sharp glance, then spoke to Jarod.

Time to get out of here.

"He's a nice man." Ava waved at Jarod as they left the motor vehicle office, and he gave her a big smile and wave.

That earned Samantha another look from the blonde. Who was she?

Samantha would probably find out soon enough. In a place like Choteau, everyone knew everyone.

# # #

The Story Behind the Story

The title for *Home Is Where the Heart Is* came from a song sung by Peter, Paul, and Mary that celebrates different types of love. You can find the lyrics online. I have been a fan of the group my whole life, seeing them multiple times in concert in small venues and large. Mary Travers is sorely missed.

The basic story evolved from my love of that part of the Rocky Mountain Front. For three years in the 1970s, I taught junior high school in the reservation town of Browning and lived the beautiful, but isolated town of East Glacier Park. Every day, the beauty of the front emerged in front of me as I drove west. Like CJ, I once knew the names of all the mountains that formed my home, but that memory is lost in time.

Disappearance of young girls from Native American reservations has been a problem for far too many years now. It was the subject of the compelling movie, *Wind River*. These girls are lost to their families through human trafficking, prostitution, and death. Recently, tribes are publicizing this problem to try to stem the heartbreak they experience.

But *Home Is Where the Heart Is* is a story of hope, celebrating my belief that people, no matter how lost they may become, can find their way home again, whatever that home happens to look like.

I hope you enjoyed the book and will continue on to the next in the series, Jarod's story in *Finding Home*.

If you have questions or comments about *Home Is Where the Heart Is*, I'd love to hear from you: Casey@Stories-about-Love.com.

Other Ways to Connect

Join my newsletter list on Stories About Love (www.Stories-About-Love.com) and get notifications of new releases.

Like my Facebook page (www.facebook.com/Casey.Stories.About.Love/) where I frequently post photos of nature and animals.

To learn about when the next book is released, follow me on Amazon or BookBub.

Other Books by Casey Dawes

California Series

California Sunshine
California Sunset
California Wine

Rocky Mountain Front Series

Home Is Where the Heart Is

Stand Alone Stories

Keep Dancing
Chasing the Tumbleweed
Love on the Wind
Love on Willow Creek

Christmas Titles

A Christmas Hope

About Casey Dawes

Real Life ❦ *Real Problems* ❦ *Real Love*

Casey Dawes has lived a varied life–some by choice, some by circumstance. Her master's degree in theater didn't prepare her for anything practical, so she's been a teacher, stage hand, secretary, database guru, manager in Corporate America, business coach, book shepherd, and writer.

She inherited an itchy foot from her grandfather, traveling to Europe and Australia and many towns and cities across the US while in business. She's lived in towns with a population of 379 and in an apartment complex on 42nd Street and 9th Avenue in Manhattan. She's dragged her belongings from New Jersey ... to Massachusetts, Michigan, Pennsylvania, Virginia, California, and Montana.

She believes in true love and the ability of honest, thoughtful conversations to solve most problems.

Her stories contain characters who have to deal with real life and real problems to find real love.

Made in the USA
Columbia, SC
27 April 2019